*t*P
Texture Press
Norman, Oklahoma
USA

Also by Evald Flisar

Tales of Wandering

My Father's Dreams

Three Loves, One Death

On the Gold Coast

A Journey Too Far

Enchanted Odysseus

The Sorcerer's Apprentice

Tea with the Queen

If I Only Had Time

The Girl Who Would Rather be Elsewhere

That's Where You'll Find Me

Alice in Crazyland

Collected Plays, Vol. 1

Collected Plays, Vol. 2

Words above the Clouds

Evald Flisar

WHO CAN SAY WHERE THE ROAD GOES

Translated from the Slovene by
Timothy Pogacar

*t*P
Texture Press
Norman, Oklahoma
2018

WHO CAN SAY WHERE THE ROAD GOES
Copyright © Evald Flisar 2016

Translation copyright © Timothy Pogacar
Timothy Pogacar has received a grant from the Slovenian Book Agency.

First published in Slovenia as *Dekleta, ki se jih spomnim*
(Ljubljana: Sodobnost International, 2016).

**Published in the United States by
Texture Press, 1108 Westbrooke Terrace
Norman, OK 73072**

Editor
Susan Smith Nash, PhD

Cover design
Arlene Ang

*Published with the financial assistance of Trubar Foundation, Ljubljana,
Slovenia.*

ISBN 978-1-945784-07-1

Printed in the United States of America.

**Texture Press
Norman, OK 73072
USA**
texturepress@beyondutopia.com

Who can say where the road goes?
Where the day flows?
Only time

Eithne Patricia Ní Bhraonáin
(Enya)

Part 1

SUN

An attractive blonde with a broken arm in a dirty cast is sunbathing on a chaise lounge in the small garden of a suburban Ljubljana house. She's listening to Enya on a portable CD-player half hidden in the long grass. As a nurse, she's used to patients' broken arms, not her own. With a useless right arm, she is forced to enjoy doing nothing, of which she has had plenty.

Katarina, twenty-four.

Matej, twenty-two, timid and awkward, presses the doorbell until he realizes it doesn't work. He tries the handle; the door is unlocked. He goes on into the living room and through the open French doors catches sight of a woman in a bikini. He goes into the garden and through the tall grass towards her.

"Hello." Katarina doesn't hear or see him.

He yells over Enya, "I've come about the room!"

Katarina is startled and sits up. "Why are you hollering?"

She looks him over and Matej notices that she's not enthused about his looks. He senses that he has to explain his presence: "I knocked but…"

"What?" Katarina yells, still not hearing him.

"The door," Matej yells back. "It was unlocked."

"The bell doesn't work," Katarina explains.

Matej quickly seizes the opportunity: "I can fix it."

"What?" Katarina yells again. Only now does she remember she can turn off the music; she extends her left hand and does just that.

"I can fix the bell!" Matej yells in the sudden quiet.

"Why are you hollering?" Katarina reprimands him.

"Sorry," Matej says so quietly that Katarina doesn't hear him.

"Are you an electrician?" she asks.

"I'm a student," Matej answers, not without a smidgeon of pride. Maybe it's not pride, maybe it's only satisfaction at knowing that someday, when he graduates and gets a job, he'll be much more than an electrician.

"A student!" exclaims Katarina. "Was it you I talked to on the phone?"

"A good hour ago. I'm Matej."

He extends a hand, but Katarina is holding a magazine in her left hand, so she doesn't respond, and the gesture also seems rather stupid to her, almost forced.

"What are you studying?" she asks as if by the way.

"Architecture. Although I'm thinking of flipping to philosophy."

"Oh, really?" Katarina is genuinely surprised.

"Less stress," Matej explains. "Less lectures."

"You don't like lectures?"

Matej shakes his head. "That's not it. There's no work for architects anymore."

"And all the philosophers are employed?" Katarina asks.

"Almost all," Matej surprises her. "Mostly in government offices."

Katarina chuckles. "Sense of humor, I see."

"What else is left to us?" Matej shrugs.

"True," Katarina agrees. "Not much to me."

She grips the edge of the chaise lounge with her left hand in order to get up. Matej rushes to help her.

Katarina pushes him away. "I'll do it myself." And she thinks: he'd like to touch me. Maybe he's alright. But the thought leaves her cold when she looks him over again.

10

"I suppose you'd like to have a look at the room," she says. "But, as you see... I'm too tired."

"Should I come another time?" Matej asks agreeably.

"Don't be silly," Katarina lays back down. "Go upstairs to the second floor, along the hallway to the end, the last door on the left."

"By myself?" Matej is surprised.

"Didn't I say I can't go with you?"

"Yes, but," Matej is confused, "so that means I can go myself?"

"Weren't the directions clear enough?"

"Yes, but..."

"What?" Katarina sighs, thinking the young man more and more strange.

"I've looked at more than ten rooms," Matej explains. "Everywhere they treated me as if they were afraid I'd steal something."

Katarina lets out a laugh. "You don't exactly look like a thief."

"I don't know how I look," Matej takes the opportunity for a small confession. "I never look in the mirror. I even shave by feel."

"You never look in the mirror?" Katarina is surprised, hardly believing it.

"Never," Matej repeats. "I don't look the way I'd like to, and I don't see the point in looking at something I don't like."

Katarina lets out a barely audible laugh. "I get the feeling you've already abandoned architecture ad switched to philosophy."

"I'm glad you understand why I'm attracted to it."

"I no longer understand anything," says Katarina. "But that's another story. My story. Look, I'd go upstairs with you but..."

"Your arm?" Matej asks.

"Not so much the arm. I'm tired. If I have to repeat what I just said. You obviously don't hear some things." Katarina looks at him. "Do you have any idea what I'm talking about?"

"I sure do," Matej answers quickly. "The world is a great burden."

"For you, too?"

"There are moments when it seems that only for me."

"Well, since we're kindred souls, we'll get along, won't we?" Katarina tries to get rid of him.

"I'd really try."

"Then go and have a look at the room," Katarina almost orders him. "If you like it, it's yours."

Matej goes up the stairs to the second floor. Katarina lays back down on the chaise lounge and reaches to turn on the music. Her cell phone ringing in the grass next to the CD-player stops her. She takes it with her left hand and puts it to her ear.

"Oh, it's you... No, Mom, I didn't use a tone of voice to suggest I'd rather not talk with you. I said it in a tone of voice to suggest that my soul is aching a hundred times more than your head ever hurt at your worst moments...! A soul can't hurt...? The soul survives death and goes to heaven...? Even though you called just to torture me, which has been your favorite pastime for the last twenty years, I'll tell you something... I got a renter... I'm on sick leave, Mom. I need the money...! A student... How does he look...? Like Robert Redford in his peak years... I should watch myself...? Why...? He'll reach up my skirt?"

She notices that Matej is back.

"Good to hear from you, Mom!" She ends the call and tosses the phone into the grass.

"The house is pretty big," says Matej.

"Too big," Katarina agrees.

"But"—Matej looks over at the top of the roof—"it's a great house."

"Until you realize you have to take care of it."

"That's the problem with every house."

"How do you know?"

"My parents," explains Matej. "Theirs is smaller than yours, but there're still expenses…"

"And the room?" Katarina interrupts.

Matej replies slightly haltingly, as if he might not be able to decide, "The room is fine."

"It has everything you need?"

"Oh," says Matej and counts on his fingers, "a day bed, easy chair, desk with a computer, bookshelf, wardrobe, dresser, theater posters on the wall…"

"Will it suit you?"

Matej takes a little time to think. "I'm afraid not."

"Wait…" Katarina replies as if trying to stifle her anger.

"I couldn't afford it," Matej explains.

"I put the rent in the ad." Katarina gets not a little angry.

"Yes, you did." Matej nods.

Katarina looks him over again from head to foot. "You won't be able to?"

"My parents aren't exactly rich. And I'm no longer on really good terms with them. I don't have a scholarship…"

"You like the room but money will be a problem?"

"I'll try so it won't be."

"I'd be very glad if it isn't."

"The thing is," Matej plunges on, "the thing is I didn't expect such a nice room. I don't know if I deserve it."

"Why wouldn't you? But I can't give it to you for free."

"Of course not."

"My husband is an officer," Katarina decides to clear up the situation. "He's been in Afghanistan for some time. I'm alone. And now this arm. I can't drive. The store is far away. I can hardly get dressed. Not to mention taking care of the garden."

"I can imagine," Matej sympathizes with her.

"I need order," she lets him know. "If you're prepared to help me here and there, with necessary things I can't do myself, I'd be satisfied with half the rent."

"Oh," Matej nervously shifts his feet, "that... that would be..."

"Only one thing," Katarina interrupts him. "I wouldn't want to feel that I expect too much from you. If you ever gave me that feeling, the deal would be off. And then you would have to pay the rent in full."

"Never, never," Matej assures her, "would I give you that feeling, ma'am."

"Don't call me 'ma'am.' I'm Katarina. Right?"

Matej nods. "I'm Matej."

"You already told me that. Can you cook?"

"Small things." Despite himself Matej gets on his tiptoes. "If I apply myself, it's quite edible."

"I'm a good cook," Katarina boasts. "My husband says excellent."

A concerned expression appears on Matej's face. "But, as you said, your husband is in... Pakistan."

"Afghanistan. And this arm..."

"It will be a while yet? The cast?"

Katarina shrugs. "It's a compound fracture."

"Does it hurt?"

"I'd rather not talk about it."

"I understand," Matej acquiesces without objection.

"The pain is so..." Katarina stares ahead. "How can I put it? It's a personal thing. Isn't it? Bodily, spiritual, it's all the same."

"I only wanted..." Matej tries to overcome his embarrassment. "If I can help..."

"I have pills for the pain. But you can make my life easier in this house. Which isn't mine, but my husband's. He inherited it from a rich uncle. I myself feel like a renter in it."

"I'll try."

"So the offer suits you."

Matej looks around. "Wonderful garden."

"It's been neglected," Katarina admits.

"I can fix it up." Matej becomes animated.

"You're a gardener, too!"

"If I have to be." Matej tries to tamp down his enthusiasm.

"So?" Katarina looks straight into his eyes.

Matej looks around the garden again. Then he turns to Katarina with his head down, somewhat embarrassed, and asks barely audibly, "When I can move in?"

Several days later, Katarina and Matej are standing in the middle of the living room. Matej is gripping pliers, a hammer, and a screwdriver in his hands. Katarina is slightly amused that she's half a head taller than him. Had her guardian angel sent a spirit to apply his comprehensive handyman skills to fixing things that don't work in the neglected house?

"Laminate," Matej suggests.

"Laminate?" Katarina is surprised. "On the ceiling?"

"Cherry."

"Why cherry?"

"Because it's warm. To go with the greenish color of the walls. And light green with pale yellow wouldn't be bad."

"You can put it up?"

"I don't think so," Matej shakes his head. "But I have a friend who..."

"And painting?"

"Painting?" Matej raises himself slightly on his toes. "That I can do."

"Of course," Katarina admits, "since you study architecture."

"Painting has nothing to do with architecture," Matej corrects her with a hint of surprise. "My grandfather was a house painter. I liked helping him when I was small."

"And what do your parents do?"

"I'd rather not talk about that."

"Fine." Katarina doesn't let herself get upset. "Then what do you suggest?"

Matej shifts his feet to assume the semblance of an authoritative pose. "I'd paint the front door dark green. There's a great oil-based paint, Amazon. One coat does it."

"And the walls?"

"Warm peach. Dulux. Water-based."

"Warm peach?"

"It's softer," Matej assures her.

"And my bedroom?" Katarina looks straight into his eyes.

"For the bedroom I'd suggest..." He's suddenly confused. "I don't know... I'd have to see it first."

"You did."

Matej shakes his head.

"Come on. Curiosity didn't get the better of you? You didn't at least take a peek when you went by?"

"By mistake. I thought I was opening the door to my room. I'm afraid I was out of sorts because of a test."

"The awful mess didn't bother you?"

Matej shrugs. "I didn't notice anything."

"You didn't see how everything is heaped on the floor and bed? Tops, skirts, slacks, and nighties? Panties and bras?"

She emphasizes the last two words to make him feel uncomfortable.

"But after all… It couldn't be otherwise given your broken arm. And in general…"

"In general my bedroom shouldn't concern you. Right?" Katarina's tone sharpens.

The young man visibly reddens. "Like I said, I was out of sorts… and…"

"But all the same I'd be glad if you helped me clean up the mess. Put them into drawers. Each thing where it belongs."

"Right now?" Matej says with surprise.

"When you find the time. We're on colors now. What do you suggest for my bedroom?"

Glad no longer to feel cornered, Matej raises his head and rolls his eyes up. "Moonshadow."

"The shadow of the moon?"

"Something between gray and soft blue. It's very calming."

"Not too much, I hope," Katarina almost winks at him, but controls herself at the last second. "I sleep most of the day as it is."

"The wall by the bed could be terracotta. A Mediterranean color. Encourages dreaming. About the sea, vacation, things like that."

"Those will stay dreams for a long while yet," Katarina jerks the shoulder above the arm in a cast.

"But the arm will heal," Matej assures her.

"It will. The question is whether *I* will."

She herself doesn't know why she said this. Why after all should he care about her inner world.

"I don't understand," Matej confesses.

"And what will you paint your room?" Katarina moves on in order to quickly distance herself from the topic they ought not to share.

"White maybe." Matej cocks his head. "Snow white."

"*Snow* white?"

"Or black," Matej corrects himself. "Totally black."

Katarina is silent a few seconds. Ten, maybe twenty.

"Excuse me if I'm too curious, but... Are you alright? I mean, you don't have any mental problems?"

"I don't know." Matej is almost visibly frightened. "No one has noticed any before now."

"Then you probably don't."

"Sometimes I really do feel something strange is happening to me," Matej admits. "But it doesn't seem to me that..."

"You're not the only one, Matej. There's something strange going on with both of us."

"Not usually," Matej says. "But then there comes a moment... out of the blue... when I'd... when I'd as soon lock myself in a room with black walls."

"There's another room upstairs, as you probably noticed," Katarina tries to redirect the conversation. "A guest room. It was last used five years ago. It just has to be dusted."

"I noticed some mold below the window." Matej nods. "I could wash it off."

"Warm peach? Moonshadow?"

"It depends what kind of guests you're expecting."

"My mom visits every several years. Mostly to tell me what a worthless daughter she has. I almost never see my younger sister. It's a long way from Kočevje to Ljubljana."

"Maybe the Dulux color sunshine," Matej quickly gets his bearings. "It encourages optimism."

"Mom never stays over. So just leave it a guest room. There's probably not a single color that could bring something as exotic as optimism into the house."

"I'd give it a try all the same," Matej says after thinking briefly.

18

"I'm more interested in what you're going to do about the dripping faucet in the bathroom," Katarina reminds him.

"I'm..." He shows her the tools in his hands. "I can't promise. But I'll try." He goes upstairs.

"You're very practical for a philosophy student."

"I'm still in architecture."

"Avoid philosophy. It will only confuse you."

"Isn't the world one big confusion?"

"For you, too?"

"Especially for me."

"It's a good thing I took you under my roof."

"Why?" Matej turns around halfway up the stairs.

"So we can divide the confusion. So there will be less of it."

A twenty-four year old woman finds it hard to resist the temptation to meet with other men during her husband's extended absence, if only to talk about the worries that vex her. So it's no surprise that not long after finding a renter, we find her in a Chinese restaurant with Peter, thirty-two, a lawyer with admittedly average looks, but with attributes that come with professional success, and not completely lacking in sensitivity.

"Peter... that lawsuit," says Katarina and puts down her spoon, which she can use skillfully enough in her left hand so as not to spill soup on the table. "It doesn't seem to me like a good idea."

"Wait." He looks at her. "The thing is just about to go ahead!"

"But how will it look for a wife to sue her husband?"

"He pushed you down the stairs! You have a compound fracture. You could have cracked your skull!"

"And why?" She looks at him. "Because he found out I deceived him with his lawyer! Who's now *my* lawyer."

Peter toys with the rice on his plate. "The fact is he shoved you."

"In a fit of rage," Katarina tries to justify the actions of the absent, hot-blooded man. "My life is already too much of a mess."

And then, to move away from the ticklish subject, she says with satisfaction: "Did I tell you I found a renter? Yesterday he cooked me dinner for the first time."

"No." Peter looks at her with a trace of mistrust.

"Buckwheat. His grandma supposedly makes it."

Peter is silent for a while, looking to his food. "Watch out that the mess of your life doesn't get worse in the end," he warns her.

"I know how to take care of myself." She looks at him defiantly.

Ten days later Peter comes over for dinner. They're sitting at the round table in the dining room. He could hardly wait to meet the young man who supposedly painted almost all the rooms for his lover, fixed the doorbell and faucet, cut the grass in the garden, and thoroughly straightened up the house. Besides that, he cooks all the time! And all because he only has to pay half the rent.

"You managed to get a servant who even pays you?" Peter says with surprise. "You're good."

"You're not jealous, are you?" She looks at him.

"Of him?" Peter smiles when Matej brings the soup and goes back to the kitchen. "Can't you see he's gay?"

"You ought to know," Katarina taunts him.

When Matej brings the pork chops and potatoes, Peter looks him over again. "What do you study?"

"Law," Matej answers with little expression. "I'd like to become a successful lawyer."

Katarina hides a smile. Peter looks at her. He wants to ask whether the young man is joking or possibly telling the truth. They've finished the soup. Katarina has just put down her spoon.

"It's an awkward thing, having to eat with your left hand," Peter observes.

"And I can only scratch with my left hand," Katarina looks at him. "Not to mention the slap I'd like to give certain people."

"I hope I'm not included."

"You never know."

"Actually," says Peter, "slaps can be an exceptionally arousing part of erotic play."

"Why that polite, legal jargon? Why don't you simply say, 'spank me, that turns me on.'"

Before Peter can think of an answer, Matej comes out of the kitchen in a white apron and takes away the soup bowls and spoons, taking the tureen with the remaining soup in his right hand. Katarina and Peter observe him—Katarina kindly and encouragingly, Peter derisively. Matej carries the dishes back to the kitchen.

Peter reaches for the bottle of merlot and pours more wine into two half full glasses. He shakes his head. "I don't know what to say."

"About what?" Katarina looks at him.

"Look, forget it. Pretend I didn't say anything."

"But you didn't. So what should I forget?"

"Is everything alright with you?" Peter asks as if by the way. "I don't mean your arm, I mean otherwise, in general."

"In general, there's always been something wrong with me. Should it be different now, when I'm on sick leave, without a husband and an arm?"

"You still have your husband, and your arm, too."

"It's in a cast. And that's how I feel. As if my life were stuck in a cast. My heart, lungs, brains, everything."

"Don't take it the wrong way, but that sounds a little overstated."

"What?"

"Dramatic," Peter becomes braver.

"I don't know legal jargon."

"Is that a reprimand?"

"I wouldn't dare. You might sue me for slander."

"Sorry, but your renter has a very strange influence on you."

Before Katarina can answer, Matej brings two plates with pork chops, rice, and salad. He puts them in front of Katarina and Peter.

"Thanks, Matej," says Katarina.

Peter sizes him up. "Nice apron," he says. "It's alright to address you informally?"

"No problem," answers Matej with a sigh of forced indifference.

The boy isn't stupid, Katarina thinks.

"This is Peter, my lawyer," she says. "He forgot to introduce himself."

Matej walks away.

"Why are you so uptight?"

"I don't want you to offend my renter. He's painted half the house."

"He paints, fixes bells and faucets, cooks—what kind of renter is that?"

"An ideal one."

"What do you give him?" Peter asks her casually.

"Are you afraid he likes me?"

"Please. I'm afraid he has furtive intent."

"To force himself on me in the middle of the night?"

"To rob you."

"But there's nothing for him to take!"

"There's always something to be found. Your husband's Mercedes out front?"

Katarina takes a deep sigh. "Why are you lawyers all the same? Why is everyone guilty in your eyes until they prove their innocence?"

"No one is innocent," Peter declares emphatically.

"That's what Stalin said. And maybe he was even right. Because I'm not, for sure. You even less."

"And your lieutenant colonel? How do you know he won't kill you next time?"

"We're done, Peter," Katarina declares decisively.

"I'm worried about you."

"Not in the least. You've only been worried since I got a renter."

"By the way, the colors with which he ruined more than half your house, don't they seem to you a little too bright?"

Matej comes out of the kitchen without the apron. "A small problem," he shifts awkwardly. "I'm late for class, and I'd like to ask…"

"Of course, get going, we'll clean up ourselves." She looks at Peter, who averts his eyes.

"It was excellent," Katarina praises him.

"So you're really a student?" Peter asks him. "At a culinary school?"

"Peter…" Katarina warns him.

"And you're really a lawyer?" Matej retorts and walks off.

"Well, you got what you wanted," Katarina doesn't hide her glee.

"You know what," says Peter, "that coward won't make fun of me."

"You're making fun of him!" Katarina raises her voice, unable to help herself. "Since the minute you came you've been looking at him as if you can't understand how I could rent him a room."

"I really can't."

"Because you don't have a soul. Or a heart. Because you only care about money. And prestige. And getting criminals off."

Peter gets up from the table: "Well, then..."

Katarina pulls him back down with her left hand and leans towards him. "Don't be childish on top of everything else. I need a massage. That's why you came over, right?"

"But you have a renter."

"Look..." Katarina moves away. "Just say so if you're no longer interested. And go home to your wife."

Peter gets up. "This is all a little too much, Katarina."

"We had a good time together. Didn't we? How can my renter disorient you like that?"

"I'm quite surprised."

"I was hoping you came because you wanted to give me a massage."

"Did I say I wouldn't?"

They go upstairs to the bedroom for Peter to massage her shoulders. That's how what usually follows starts.

"Is that alright?" Peter asks.

"No. Take off my top."

Peter pulls the top over her head and reveals a net bra through which the tips of her nipples are sticking out. He keeps massaging her shoulders.

"Better?"

"A little more and I'll believe there's a man behind me."

"Harder?"

"A little less on the right. More on the left. The neck muscles. Ah…"

"When will they take the cast off?"

"They don't know."

"Then there's physiotherapy, of course."

"Of course," says Katarina.

"Not bad. It'll be a good several months before you'll be able to slap me again."

"You deserve it right now!"

"Why?" Peter pulls at her right breast. "Did I grab your tits too fast?"

Katarina tries to push him away. "I don't feel at all sexy with this arm."

"But it really arouses me," Peter says, now kneading her left breast.

"I know what arouses you. Power. The feeling that I'm helpless."

"Possibly that, too."

"That's the only thing that excites men. Strength and power."

"The same as women," Peter replies.

"I wasn't aware."

"You seem very happy ever since you assumed power over that student of yours."

"You just don't understand…"

"I'm really curious how he looks at the whole thing."

"He's nice, that's all."

"Maybe he dreams of doing someday what I'm doing right now."

"And what are you doing?"

Peter starts unfastening her bra. "I'm preparing the way for a deeper massage."

He takes off the bra and throws it on the floor.

At that moment the door opens. Matej is standing on the threshold. Katarina automatically covers her bare chest with her left hand. Matej stares at her. Katarina removes her hand and stares curiously at Matej, who tries to conceal his shock.

"I'm very sorry... I forgot the pliers and screwdriver."

He goes back into the hallway and closes the door.

"I can't believe it," Peter raises his voice. "He comes right in without knocking!"

"He forgot the tools, didn't your hear? He fixed my window."

"He could at least knock."

"He couldn't know. The door wasn't locked."

"You couldn't lock it?"

"I have to lock myself in in my own house?"

"Then you'll have to teach him some manners."

"Give me my bra."

"Wait, would you..."

Katarina leans over and picks up the bra. "Fasten it for me."

Peter obeys. "I don't understand why it's necessary..."

"Go, Peter. I don't feel like it."

Peter picks up his jacket from the chair and puts it on.

"Get rid of the kid."

"He's already done a hundred things for me. I told him I need order. He obviously understands my needs more than you do."

"Wonderful order. You renter wandering all over the house."

"Sorry, Peter. I'll call you in a few days. Or maybe not."

Peter opens the door and goes down the stairs. He slams the front door after himself. Katarina covers her face with her left hand.

Suddenly she's aware that Matej is staring through he open door.

"I'm very sorry. Had I known…"

"You couldn't. And just what did you see? A shoulder rub."

"I'm very sorry…"

"Please stop. Bring me a glass of water. I have to take some pills."

"A glass of water," Matej repeats and hurries to the kitchen. Katarina takes off her bra and exposes her breasts. She starts massaging her right shoulder with her left hand. Matej returns from the kitchen with a glass of water. He looks at her and stops. He freezes.

Katarina looks and him, enjoying it. "What is it?"

Matej grabs at his spine with his left hand.

"Something… something in my back."

With his left hand behind him, he slowly slides towards her and offers the glass of water from a distance. Katarina takes it.

"Thanks, Matej. You're very nice. Can you massage my shoulders? They really hurt."

Matej jumps.

"Oh!" He looks at the clock. "My class! Now I'm really going to be late."

He quickly turns and hurries off.

Katarina sits on the edge of the bed half dressed and looks at herself in a wall mirror that reaches the floor. She does this rather often, usually when a feeling of loneliness torments her and she seeks company in her reflection. And then she thinks about herself: about how her attractiveness is actually worthless, although she's prepared to use it, even misuse it. It doesn't help her overcome the suffocating feeling that there is no one in the world who really loves her, not just her body, but her soul as well, the whole of her, with all her flaws. Worse yet, there are moments in front of the mirror when it seems that sailing through time she is gradually loosing parts of herself, her soul and feelings, like a wooden boat shedding the damaged or rotten planks from which it was made, and that it's time to replace the lost planks with new ones from another kind of wood. There's a growing, nagging fear that if this process continues, time will make a completely different person out of her, composed of other, unfamiliar material, which will undermine the image she has of herself and uses as a rudder while sailing through life.

Will she then still be the Katarina she was before?

At the same time she has the feeling that someone not necessarily of this world is accompanying her through life, gathering the lost planks, and reassembling from them her first self, built of memories and thoughts that belonged to the "original" Katarina, while the memories and thoughts of the "new" Katarina, built from other experiences, from a different understanding of those experiences, will become a kind of double, a Katarina number 2. Will they be able to co-exist in the same space and time? Will they have conflicts, war with one another? Will one have to die for the other to live on?

The fear that she is not changing and not remaking herself according to her desires and plans but according to some law, and that tomorrow we can no longer be what we were yesterday, and that some things from the past that we try to cart along into the future are only a burden that slows us down and robs us of our freedom is at times so powerful that it forces her into unpleasant self-interrogation, exploration of unknown areas of her own inner being, which she never liked to do, because each time she would discover something dislikable about herself. When delving into herself, sometimes things go so far that she imagines a more extreme possibility: that her "double" is also loosing damaged and rotten planks, and that someone is gathering them and assembling a third boat named Katarina, and so on into infinity, until there are so many Katarinas that it's impossible to say which one is more real, authentic, and closer to the one that she actually is as a person.

Such thoughts always bring her to the conclusion that her person doesn't exist as a fixed unit, but is only a series of changes while sailing through time, which we call life, a series she experiences as a continuity only because she doesn't notice changes, probably due to the fact that they follow one another too rapidly. And since the lost and damaged planks of her person are ever more decayed and damaged, each time they're assembled into an identical but new Katarina, the journey through time can only be a decline, a chain of transitions from bad to worse, to the bottom, where it seems to her more frequently she will end up in the end.

Three days later, Katarina takes a taxi to her orthopedic check-up. Matej is sitting in the living room with his feet on the table, talking with Brane on the phone.

"So it's a go?" Brane asks.

"That's what I said," Matej assures him.

"Is the room alright?"

"It's a little small. But you can stick some things in mine."

"She won't suspect anything?"

"I hope not," Matej assures himself. "You'll have to be careful."

"Me?" Brane is surprised.

"Both of us."

"Have you laid her yet?"

"You know I haven't."

"You could sometime. For a change. If you'd admit right now that you did, that would really get me excited."

"She's got a guy. Some lawyer. Highly obnoxious."

"Didn't you say you help her get dressed?"

"When did I say that?"

"A while ago."

"Once in a while I fasten or unfasten something," Matej admits. "If she can't do it herself."

"Fasten and unfasten?!" Brane whistles. "I can take on that unpleasant duty."

"Brane, I don't want any trouble," Matej warns him. "I have it good here."

"Don't you want me to have it good?"

"That's not what I said. But I'd rather you don't come here if you're going to clown around."

"You promised."

"And you promise you won't embarrass me the first day."

"Second day is okay?" Brane jokes.

"No, Brane, not the first, second, third, or ever!"

"Have I ever let you down?"

"Maybe not, but it could happen fast here."

"Really? She's that sexy?"

"Let's stop talking about this."

"Then when, tomorrow?"

"I have to ask her."

"What the fuck, you didn't?"

"You're too pushy."

"And if she says no?"

"Leave that to me."

"You have her in your clutches? You're good. What does she look like? Describe her. In detail."

"She looks like a young woman with her right arm in a cast."

"You know..." Brane says.

Matej hears the front door open. "I'll call you," he says, and puts down the phone. He takes his feet off the table, leans back, and pretends he was snoozing. Katarina enters in a pretty bad mood.

"The risotto is ready, I'll just warm it up," says Matej.

"Oh, Matej... I really feel dumb... I should have called you. Peter invited me for Thai. I'm very sorry."

"Well, then... It'll be for tomorrow."

"You go ahead and eat. You must be hungry. Aren't you hungry?"

Matej gets up and goes into the kitchen. Katarina puts down her purse and carefully takes a seat on the couch. Matej comes back with a bottle of wine and two glasses.

"I found this in the garage."

"In the garage?!" Katarina is surprised.

"With the paint cans."

He puts the glasses and bottle on the table. The bottle is already open. Katarina turns it around and looks at the label. "Australian shiraz. That's what my husband drinks. He obviously hid the bottle with the paint and forgot about it."

"Why would he hide it?" Matej asks.

"Because I was always on him about drinking too much."

Matej pours two glasses. "Did he?"

"World's biggest lush," Katarina says in a noticeably poisonous tone. She takes her glass and raises it. "To your health."

Matej takes his glass and likewise raises it. "That your arm heals." He sits on the couch.

"Good wine," Katarina observes.

"What does he do in Afghanistan?" Matej suddenly changes the conversation.

"My husband? He enforces order. He was ignorant of it at home. The house was a shambles, as if we were living in a dump. But there he's trying to bring order to the country!"

"Well, after all…" Matej tries to smooth over her bitterness. "There's quite a few trying."

"Yes, and just the right ones. Drunks, pig heads, violent men. But I don't care. It suits me fine that he's there."

"When does he plan to come back?" Matej asks seemingly casually.

Katarina is silent for a while. "When they replace his unit."

"Will that be soon?"

"I have no idea. When someone decides. Everything having to do with the army is beyond me. But don't worry."

Matej sets his eyes on her arm in a cast. "I know it's not my business, but… is that his doing?"

"We had a little misunderstanding."

"I can't imagine that he'd… that he'd…"

"With men, violence is always just below the surface. Women are cunning, what else can they do? Men get their way by violence. But you're different. At times it seems to me you're not a man at all."

Her eyes meet Matej's. "Sorry, I didn't mean anything by that. I didn't mean…"

"Well, after all…" Matej doesn't know how to react.

"It's actually a compliment," Katarina tries to correct the impression. "I meant that you're unusually understanding, kind, and giving. You have everything that usually belongs to women."

"Really?" Matej replies, noticeably crushed.

"You know why he pushed me down the stairs?" Katarina tries to change the topic and soften the painful moment. "You know why? Because I was listening to just one CD for two years. Enya. The Irish singer. Day and night."

"I like her," Matej observes.

"He did, too. But then he said it's not normal to listen to the same music five hours a day for more than two years. And nothing else. And he asked me to stop, otherwise he'd go crazy."

"And?" Matej asks.

"I couldn't. I said that my soul is in that music. It's called melancholy."

"That's also the name of my soul," Matej almost noticeably cheers up.

"Well, and then he exploded. He pushed me down the stairs. I stopped over there."

She points to the foot of the stairs that go up to the first floor.

"How long will you keep it up?" asks Matej.

"Listening to Enya?" Katarina laughs acidly and empties her glass. "'Till I die, Matej. To the bitter end.'"

"How about my brother?" Matej throws in something completely different.

Katarina is confused. "I don't understand."

"I mentioned him a few days ago," he lies.

"To me? I don't remember anything."

"If he could spend a few nights in the small room. While he has exams."

"I've obviously started forgetting things. But look... of course. No problem. That's what I said. Didn't I? Strange I don't remember."

"He won't be in the way?"

"Your brother? Come on. You do more for me than I expected. I feel, I don't know... that with you in the house, I'm somehow safe here... you know what I think? And I feel almost guilty for charging you half the rent."

"No problem, I can pay that much. Although I don't know how it will go with a scholarship."

"If there's a problem, just say so."

"So it's alright if he comes tomorrow?"

"Already tomorrow?" Katarina seems surprised. "Well... anytime."

She extends her glass to Matej. "Shall we have another? To celebrate your brother's arrival?"

"To mark my gratitude," Matej adds.

Katarina is sitting on the couch in the living room, drinking wine. She hears the doorbell. "Come on in, even if you're the devil!" she hollers.

Peter comes through the living room door with a bouquet of flowers and a bottle of wine.

"Oh..." he stops, surprised.

"How am I supposed to take that?"

"I see you're already hard at work."

"Matej found a real treasure in the cellar. Hidden. That's the way it is if you have a husband who's not worthy to touch your little toe."

"Good to see you," Peter approaches carefully.

"Evidently. Otherwise everyone on the street wouldn't be staring at my cast."

Peter puts the bottle down on the table and sits down on the couch next to Katarina. As to the bouquet, he doesn't really know what to do with it. "That small defect only highlights your beauty," he says.

"Stop it. I haven't been beautiful for a long time."

"Who says?"

"The mirror. Which has no reason to flatter me. Unlike you."

"Unlike me? What would be the reason for me to do that?"

"Judging by the bouquet you don't know what to do with, I'd say you're here to beg for something that was once available to you, and in abundance, but lately the cast has spoiled your fun. Am I mistaken?"

"You know…"

"I understand, after all. You don't get it at home, or you don't like what you get, so you come to bother an invalid."

Peter is nervously silent for a while.

Then he asks cautiously, "How many glasses have you downed?"

"A bottle and a half. Cheers! I see you're also inclined. Toss that bouquet in the garbage and join me."

Peter sets off to the kitchen. "I'll look for a vase. You never know, your renter might like the flowers."

"Well, it was him I just had a bottle of wine with."

"Then all the more."

Peter disappears into the kitchen. Meanwhile, Katarina pours another glass. Peter returns with his own glass.

"Did you find a vase?"

"You don't have one. So I stuck the flowers in the microwave."

"Matej will be glad! He won't have to cook."

"Is he still living up to your expectations?"

Katarina is silent for a few seconds. Then she says abruptly and harshly, "I'll have two from now on."

"You can't be serious," Peter is appalled.

"You never know, maybe he'll be handsome. It's a real suspense to see what kind of guy will come through the door. Doesn't it seem to you?"

Seeing how much she has drunk, Peter obviously doesn't believe her. "Can I suggest something?"

"Be my guest."

Peter takes a sip of wine and gathers his courage. "How much does he pay you? Two, three hundred a month?"

"Two."

"That's quite a bit for a small room if it's only half the rent."

"The price includes board," Katarina explains.

"What?!" Peter almost yells. "Then he's paying too little!"

"Sorry, but don't I have the right to set the rent for a room in my house?"

Peter decides he won't hide the reason he came. "I can give you those two hundred a month."

"To live in my place instead of him?" Katarina is surprised.

"You know very well what I mean. Two hundred euros a month is small change for me."

"For sure," says Katarina. "And I can be all alone in the house."

"Wait..." Peter tries to explain.

"You're at home in the circle of your loving family, and I've got two hundred square meters without being able to open a can. Much less clean up after myself."

"Look..." Peter searches for the right words.

"I submissively wait for you to come over—less often of late—you do me quickly, look in the mirror with satisfaction, and leave."

Peter empties his glass and pours another.

"As long as we're on that..." he begins, but Katarina interrupts him.

"We're not. I'm sorry... Really, Peter, please forgive me. I just don't know what's with me. I'm not myself lately. As if I'm not me."

"Because you don't go anywhere. You've become unsociable. You never were."

"Where am I supposed to go with this arm?"

"With me."

"On a walk in the woods, where no one will see us?"

"To that party. Didn't I mention it to you?"

"I'd rather not."

"You promised."

"Do they need an invalid to make it more fun?"

"Stop exaggerating about your arm. Sure it's awkward, but it doesn't make you a tragic victim."

"I'm a victim even without a broken arm. Not tragic, but comic."

"Do you know how many people are walking around at this minute with their arm in a cast?"

"I'm not interested."

"That's your main problem. The world has stopped being of interest. You don't read the papers, you sold your TV, and you don't even have a computer."

"I don't want trash in the house."

"True, but the world is no different because of that."

Katarina lets out a little laugh. "Would it be different if I read about it every day? Or watched it on TV?"

"You've condemned yourself to house arrest."

Katarina is quiet for a while. Then she sighs deeply and says: "Okay, you got what you want. Who did you say that guy is? A member of parliament?"

"An big wig in the party. Friend of my father."

"And you're his lawyer?"

"I represent some of his businesses."

"Doubtless crooked ones."

"In law, the same thing can be both at the same time."

"Depending on which side you expect to profit from most?"

"I'd rather not talk about that."

"I'll go if you promise me something. That you will cover my mouth before I say something stupid."

"It will do you good to socialize a little."

Katarina gets up from the couch.

"I'm one of those people nothing helps. How is it you haven't noticed? As smart as you are?"

When loneliness wafts her into the depths of meditation, Katarina often asks what plays the greater role in the fate allotted us—events that befall us by the way circumstances coalesce, or bad decisions we thought would benefit us?

She was seriously planning to study medicine after secondary medical school. She was gifted and she would cut a good figure in a white gown with a stethoscope around her neck, with a friendly smile on her face for patients who would look up to her. Being inclined to optimism, the hope that getting there wouldn't be too difficult inspired her and made her believe nothing could stop her.

How quickly that changed when she met her one-time schoolmate, Lieutenant Colonel Osterc! In fact, she didn't like him that much. Not because of his mundane appearance, but because of his limited outlook, intellectual rigidity, taciturnity, and conviction that he could order her around like his soldiers. He simply couldn't imagine that it could be different and that at least in bed he could treat her as an equal, not as an enemy to be vanquished.

But he had a beautiful, comfortable house in a Ljubljana suburb, which he had inherited from an uncle not long before they met, and Katarina had always wanted to live in such a house. She imagined she would live in that kind of a house when she became a doctor. For a child without a father, who had grown up first in the village and then in a one-bedroom apartment in Kočevje with an obnoxious mother and capricious younger sister, the spacious house meant a leap into a dream come true without having to study for it five or six years. It seemed to her that she had attained what she desired all her life, and in the end, a nursing occupation wasn't something she would have to be ashamed of.

Her husband not only agreed with this, but even suggested—almost demanded—that she get a job, since he needed someone to look after the house and earn something on the side. Then things took their course: he left for Afghanistan, and she was left with loneliness. It didn't seem wrong to her to try and ease it by messing around. Should it have bothered her? Would the planks have fallen off the boat on which she sailed through life more slowly?

Matej is sitting at the table in the living room, pouring wine into two glasses. Brane comes downstairs, a towel around him. Well muscled, nicely built, brown-haired, and very attractive.

"Nothing better than a shower with fragrant soap," he says.

Matej looks at him. "You won't be cold?"

"You joking? I'm hot." He unwraps the towel and sits down on the couch next to Matej, completely naked.

"That's not smart," says Matej. "She can come in the door any minute."

"Then she'll see something she's never seen in her life," Brane brags—quite tastelessly in Matej's opinion.

"You promised not to cause problems."

"Right," says Brane and covers up with the towel, "even though she'll be deprived of information that might change her view of men."

"Stop," says Matej. "We'd best celebrate with a glass of good wine."

"You bought it? Especially for me?"

"I found it in the cellar. Hidden behind the boiler."

"She's so stingy that she hides wine from you?"

"At first I thought she was hiding it from her husband," Matej says. "Now it's starting to seem to me that her husband was hiding it from her. Up to now I've found ten bottles in the cellar. There's surely some more somewhere."

"Well, at least we won't be bored," says Brane.

He reaches for a glass and takes a sip. "God, it's good!"

"Cheers," says Matej and raises his glass.

"Cheers, pal."

They drink up.

"It's nice of you to take me in," says Brane. "When is that soldier of hers coming back?"

"Not to soon, I hope."

"Then we're good for at least half a year."

"Wait... I said you'd be here a few days, no more than a week."

"We'll stretch a week into a month," Brane waves confidently.

"You promised not to act stupid."

"I can permit myself a little stupidity, no? Isn't anything allowed here?"

"Depends on what you have in mind."

"You know me. Life is a party or there is no life."

"Things here are complicated. I don't want to risk getting thrown out."

"What about that sporty Benz out front?" asks Brane. "You ever use it?"

"To the grocery store and back."

"Are you crazy? I'd race it all over the country."

"I don't want to take advantage of her hospitality."

"Would I be taking advantage if I turned on the TV?" He looks around. "Where is it?"

"She doesn't have one."

"She doesn't have a TV?!" Brane can't believe it.

"On principle."

"God, the woman isn't normal. Does she seem normal to you?"

"She's unhappy."

"Are you now going to tell me you're fond of her?"

"I am."

"What's happened to you since you came here?"

"Nothing really."

"She's reeducated you," says Brane. "Women know how. Without you even noticing it. Until it's too late."

"Too late for what?" asks Matej.

"What are we supposed to do without a TV?"

"We'll get by just fine."

"Why didn't you warn me that you were offering me a room in the wilderness?"

"You can leave if you don't like it," says Matej after thinking it over a little.

"Ah, go to hell. You know what I'd like to watch right now? Those two comedians. Laurel and Hardy. Remember?"

"Some of their stunts are really dumb.«

"There are good ones, too."

"I like Buster Keaton more."

"Charlie Chaplin. Remember how we used to watch him? All those nights on end? And laughed so much?

41

"You watched him," says Matej. "I was just there."

Brane looks at him defiantly. "Were you bored?"

Matej reaches for his glass. "Let's drink it before she gets back."

A large living room in the spacious house of one of the members of parliament. The party isn't too lively. The music lilting out of the loudspeakers is monotonous. People are sitting, standing, and chatting. There are hors d'oeuvres, glasses, and bottles on the table. A small group, including Peter and Katarina, is listening to the member of parliament.

"But what later came out in the media is another story," says the member. "In this country, investigative reporting is just another name for writing on demand for political godfathers. Let's take Afghanistan…"

"That's right," one of the guests speaks up, a heavy-set fellow with a bushy moustache. "What exactly are we doing there?"

The member looks at him sharply. "If you don't know, I'll find it difficult to explain in five minutes."

Already slightly drunk, Katarina decides to get into the debate. "We're helping the powerful, who are too weak to defeat the very weakest without our help."

Most of the guests turn their heads towards her.

"Who are you, ma'am, to permit yourself statement like that?" the member inquires condescendingly.

"I should have introduced her," Peter intervenes. "Katarina. Her husband is in Afghanistan with our contingent. Lieutenant Colonel Osterc."

"I've heard of Osterc," the member softens his tone. "He's carrying out his duties very well."

"He didn't tell me that," Katarina responds, "although he likes to praise himself."

There's general, polite laughter.

"What happened to your arm?" the member asks. It seems to him least provocative to talk about what is most eye-catching.

"My husband pushed me down the stairs," Katarina says completely calmly.

General laughter, somewhat more sincere than the first, follows her words.

"Well, soldiers are hotheads," the member replies. Like most of the guests, he's convinced her words were in jest.

"All the same," continues the guest with the bushy moustache, "what are Slovene soldiers, of whom there aren't even enough to defend Slovenia, doing in a country that is so far away some people haven't even heard of it?"

"Come on," the people's elected representative bristles slightly. "Where have you been hanging out?"

"I don't understand," the moustache shakes his head.

"I was one of the few Slovenes," says the member, "who traveled to Afghanistan in the early 1970s. When I got home, everyone looked at me like I'd been to the Moon. Now Slovene mothers and wives worry about what's happening to their husbands and sons in places only adventurers once dared to visit. That's how much the world has changed. And we with it, I'd say."

He looks at Katarina. "Do you agree, ma'am?"

Everyone looks over at Katarina.

"I change from day to day," Katarina says without hesitation. "Maybe that's the main feature of the times we live in. Lack of stability."

"You mean in a moral sense?" the member asks after a short pause, unable to hide that he's on shaky ground.

"In all respects," Katarina bewilders him even more.

"You know what…" the member tries to release himself from the awkwardness, "sometimes a small misfortune—a broken arm let's say—can temporarily change a person's perspective."

Katarina doesn't relent. "You didn't understand me. Everything in my life is temporary."

"But not for long," the representative finally finds a way to escape the tortuous feeling that he's at home, in his house, but not equally at home everywhere else. "Just today I heard that our contingent is returning from Afghanistan in a month. A new one will replace it. Isn't that cause for being happy?"

Everyone looks at Katarina.

Her expression is a mix of being stunned and terrified, and she tries her utmost to hide it.

Peter is driving along a wet road towards the northern suburbs. Katarina is sitting next to him. They're silent for a while. Then Peter finally speaks up. "I'm probably only temporary myself."

"You chose that option," Katarina reminds him. "A married man with two children. What do you expect?"

"What I meant was your hero returning."

Katarina is silent. Peter looks at her. Katarina shrugs.

"We'll have to find a solution," Peter suggests.

"You really don't understand?" Katarina gets impatient. "It's not only my arm that's broken. *I* am totally broken."

Peter looks at her, baffled. "How do you mean?"

"I don't know who I am," Katarina's voice breaks. "I don't know what I am. I don't know what I want. I don't know if it makes sense to believe in anything. I'm like the times. Confused and fractured."

"That's how we all are."

"Sometimes it seems someone is following me. Some indistinct, stocky male figure."

"Do you think your husband hired a detective?"

"It's more like a feeling. When I turn around, no one is there."

"You deceive your husband, and the feeling deceives you."

"Maybe someone from the future is following me. That's also possible."

Peter stops at Katarina's house.

"You drank too much," he says. That's all he can think of.

"I don't want to live in a confused and false world. When I was small, I believed it would be different."

"I have to go." Peter looks at his watch.

Katarina gets out. "Of course. Your happy family is waiting. Beautiful wife, two wonderful children, and a large, comfortable house. A successful lawyer. With a few lovers, since I probably wasn't the only one."

"Wasn't?"

"I don't know, Peter. I'm just a nurse. I've always had trouble with grammar."

"Well, then it's…"

"Exactly," says Katarina and heads for the door. "Then it is."

Peter drives off. Katarina starts quietly crying. She unlocks the door and goes into the entryway. She sees Matej at the top of the stairs in his pyjamas.

"Is something wrong?" he asks her. Katarina shakes her head. "It's late, I heard voices, and a door slammed…"

"And you were afraid there might be burglars. That's nice of you."

"Are you alright?"

"I drank too much, ate too much, otherwise never better. And you? Hungry?"

"No, we ate. Eggs. They were in the refrigerator."

"We?" Katarina is surprised.

"My brother is here."

"Oh! Of course. Where is he?"

"Sleeping."

"I'm going right to bed, too. See you tomorrow."

"Do you need help?"

"No, today I'm just going to sleep in my best clothes. I even think I got married in them. Every woman has to fall asleep in her wedding clothes at least once in her life. No? So she remembers what a mistake she made."

Matej shrugs.

"It'll happen to you, too, dear Matej. Thanks for the concern. You know that you're the only one in the world I really like?"

Matej quickly turns and goes to his room. "Good night."

Katarina slowly goes up the stairs to her bedroom. "Good night, Katarina. Good night, arm. Good night, world. Good night, God. Forgive me, but I'd like you a lot more if you hadn't created the world."

When she's going to enter the bedroom, she notices the bathroom door is open. There's sound of water coming out of the shower. She slowly goes to the door and peeks in.

Brane is standing under the shower in the open cabin, back to the door. He's shampooing his hair and whistling. Katarina stands there, running her eyes over his body.

When she sees Brane is about to turn around, she retreats, goes to the bedroom door, and opens it. She goes in, slightly confusedly closes the door, tosses her purse on the easy chair, sits on the edge of the bed, and stares at the wall mirror. For a while she considers herself critically.

She gets up and goes back to the door. She goes slowly along the hallway towards the bathroom. She stops at the door and cautiously peeks around the frame. Brane is now turned towards her, rinsing his hair. Katarina gazes at his nakedness. She can't understand why her heart is suddenly beating more quickly. It's not like her. Had the fractured arm so changed her?

Brane notices her and freezes, his hands resting on his head. He slowly opens his mouth and grins.

"Pardon me," Katarina pronounces the words barely audibly, turns, and hurries to her bedroom.

She goes in and almost slams the door behind her.

She doesn't sleep all night. She's thinking about her life, her fate, young dreams, and about how little of what she expected had come true, how she didn't truly like any man–and there were quite a few. And about how she didn't really care.

Perhaps she will be lucky and it won't remain like this. Perhaps eventually someone will show up to save her from the confines of the monotony in which she is slowly dying.

She dozes off towards morning but is soon awakened by a knock at the door. Rays of sun are coming through the cracks between the curtains.

"Is it you, Matej?" she speaks up.

The door opens wide, and Brane comes in with a breakfast platter. "Good morning," he grins.

"Where's Matej?" Katarina demands.

"He went to a lecture. He told me to…"

"For the first time since he's been living here he went to a lecture?"

"He's a student, isn't it usual to go…"

"Fine. Put the platter on the dresser."

"He told me to put it in your hands," Brane grins again, as if slightly dim-witted.

"I said on the dresser," Katarina repeats. "Thanks for your trouble. You didn't have to."

"Happy to help," Brane replies with an intonation that seems ambiguous to Katarina, although Brane probably knows nothing of ambiguity. Or maybe he does.

"You don't look anything like Matej," she says. "Are you younger or older?"

"We're the same year," says Brane.

"Then you're twins!" Katarina exclaims.

"I mean," Brane quickly recovers, "the same year at school. I took some time off. Matej is two years younger."

"Both in architecture?"

"No," says Brane and finally puts the breakfast platter down on the dresser, "I'm in veterinary science."

"You like animals."

"Not at all," Brane winces. "Some are disgusting. I can't stand goats and sheep, or pigs."

"Then why..."

"You get a job right away," Brane explains.

"There's something to that," Katarina agrees.

Brane shifts his weight, and for the first time since he came into the bedroom he hesitates a little. "If you want, I can help you get dressed. Just say the word."

Katarina stares hard at him. Brane widens his mouth into a grin.

"Why do you grin all the time?"

"Because I'm an optimist."

"About what?"

"About everything."

It doesn't escape Katarina that his eyes are surreptitiously traveling over the contours of her body beneath the blankets.

48

"Don't forget to close the door behind you." She nods at the exit.

Brane stops grinning and turns to go.

"One more thing," adds Katarina. "Can you use the downstairs bathroom?"

"Is the upstairs one yours?" Brane acts stupid.

"Yes."

"Matej didn't tell me," he turns to go.

"One more thing," Katarina stops him again. Brane looks at her. "How long do you plan on staying?"

Brane shrugs. "A week or two."

"I'm not rich enough to feed both of you," Katarina explains in a tone that leaves no doubt.

"I'll pay something," Brane replies almost rudely. "I'll pay."

"You know what you look like? Like you're on drugs."

"And if I am?" Brane looks at her defiantly.

He leaves the room and closes—almost slams—the door.

Several hours later Katarina is sitting in front of the mirror in the bedroom, pensively combing her hair. She's listening to Enya.

Matej comes in and proudly announces, "I succeeded!"

"At what?" Katarina wants to know. She turns off the CD-player with her left hand.

"A leak in the downstairs bathroom. I fixed it."

Katarina, who had expected less boring news, keeps combing her hair. "On top of things, as usual."

"I used wire," Matej explains.

"Hands of gold, really," Katarina answers mechanically, as if answering someone in a parallel, distant life.

"It's nothing," Matej waves.

"That means that from now on you can both use the downstairs bathroom," Katarina tries to deprive him of some of his good humor.

"Both of us?" Matej replies, hurt.

"You and your brother. Is anything wrong?"

"No, no..." Matej hangs his head and sighs deeply, as if trying to calm his emotions.

"Let's put it this way," Katarina eases up, because she's sincerely fond of Matej. "You can keep showering in my bathroom, but let your brother use the downstairs."

Matej hangs his head and turns to the door. "I'll tell him."

"Go ahead," Katarina urges him.

She reaches to turn on the CD-player.

Matej returns. "Can I ask you something?"

Katarina nods.

"My brother and I have to go to grandmother's for a day or two. She's doesn't feel well at all. Mom says it's a small stroke."

"Oh, Matej... I'm very sorry."

And she really is. She's aware she was wrong to have offended him.

"Only for a day or two," Matej explains. "I can cook for several days. You'll only have to heat it up."

"Look..." Katarina looks at him, as if not understanding what the problem is. "Why are you even asking? It's normal that you have to go home."

"I was thinking, could I... could I..." Matej starts to hesitate.

"Could you what?" Katarina asks.

"Since you don't drive because of your arm... and I've already used the car to go to the store... could I borrow it... for a day or two?"

Now Katarina understands Matej's hesitation. She thinks for a while. The decision she has to make won't be easy.

But she feels more and more like she doesn't have a choice.

"If you promise that it's really only for a day or two."

"Two at most," Matej's face brightens. "Exams are coming; there's no time for anything more."

"And you'll drive carefully, right?" Katarina worries.

"As always," Matej shoots back and raises two fingers to signal an oath.

"It's not that it worries me, but the car isn't mine. If my husband finds even one scratch, he'll go nuts."

"I drive to the grocery store twice a week..." Matej explains.

That's true, Katarina admits. "After all, I trust you," she says. "When will you leave?"

"Early evening," Matej replies.

"And where are you from? I never asked you. Maribor?"

"From around Ptuj. I'll cook in advance."

"That would be nice," Katarina smiles gratefully at him.

"Will gypsy goulash be alright?"

"Great!"

Matej leaves. Katarina turns on the Cd-player and returns to combing her hair.

Brane comes up the stairs and stops at the bedroom door. Judging by the sound, someone is showering in the bathroom. No doubt, it's Katarina.

Brane goes into the bedroom and closes the door. He opens the top dresser drawer and looks at Katarina's linens. He takes out some black lace panties and holds them up. He whistles and stuffs them back in. He closes the drawer and sits on the edge of the bed.

The noise in the bathroom stops. Brane waits. Katarina comes in nude, holding a towel in her left hand. She catches sight of Brane and freezes.

She automatically covers her body with the towel. "What are you doing here?"

"I heard someone showering, I didn't know who was in the house, and I came to check."

Katarina can't believe that the young man can pretend like this.

"Whose house is it that you don't know who might be in the shower? And in the bathroom that I told you belongs to me?"

"I didn't expect..."

"Didn't you go home with Matej?"

"He brought me back."

"Why?"

"We had an argument. Sometimes he's impossible."

"You or he?"

"Maybe both of us."

"Get out," Katarina tries to sound as unpleasant as possible. "I'd like to get dressed."

Brane gets up from the edge of the bed and looks at her. "It's probably hard to dress with one hand."

"If you think I'm going to ask you for help, you're mistaken."

Brane takes two steps towards her.

"I don't mean any harm."

Katarina takes a step back. "I'll count to three. One, two..."

Brane reaches for the towel, which Katarina is gripping firmly with her left hand. They look at one another.

"You know what you are?" Brane asks.

"Mad," says Katarina.

"Maybe. Besides that, you're a super sexy piece of meat."

Katarina drops the towel and slaps him.

Brane picks the towel off the floor, wraps it around Katarina's neck, and pulls her to him.

"Girls I remember never resisted so long."

The next day, already close to noon, Katarina comes down the stairs to the living room, wrapped in a silk gown. The sounds of slicing are coming from the kitchen.

"Matej?" she calls.

Matej comes out of the kitchen with a knife in his hand. He's brushing away tears with the side of his hand.

"Why are you crying?"

"I'm slicing onion," he explains.

"Are you sure it's not something else?"

"No, when I slice onions, I always... I always..."

"How's your grandmother?"

"Oh," Matej waves. "She'll live. Although I was really worried. I like her more than anyone in the family."

"What was with you and Brane?"

"Why?" Matej is surprised.

"You apparently had an argument."

"Ah, it was nothing. After a few kilometers, he said he wanted to go back, because he had to study for an exam. And I drove him back and went home myself."

"He told me something else," Katarina decides to dig a little deeper.

"Did he bother you?" Matej replies seriously. "If he bothered you at all, he can leave. I won't put up with his offenses."

"Matej, everything's fine. What are you cooking?"

"Spaghetti Bolognese."

"Perfect. You know what I like to drink with spaghetti? Australian shiraz."

"I'm afraid it's gone."

"Drive to the gas station and get two bottles."

"Right now?" Matej is surprised and looks at the clock.

"That would be best," Katarina gives an encouraging smile.

Matej takes off his apron, puts down the knife, and goes out the door.

Katarina hurries back upstairs. Laughter can be heard, a man and a woman's voices, whispering, and also some clear words in between: "come on, hurry"; "how much time do we have?"; "ten minutes"; and so on.

Matej returns with a bottle of wine he found in the cellar. He tries to make out the noises upstairs, listens for a while, and when he hears the rhythmic creaking of a mattress, he goes into the kitchen and comes back with a towel and corkscrew. He wipes the dust off the bottle with the towel and then starts opening it with the corkscrew. Before he manages to get the corkscrew out, the sound upstairs turn into something that clearly resembles an intense sex act. When Matej pulls out the cork, the bottle slips out of his hands and falls on the floor. Matej falls on his knees and starts sobbing. He watches the wine spreading in all directions. He thinks that the stains would be no different if he were to cut his veins and let the blood out. The sounds upstairs quiet down after the bottle falls. Katarina, wrapped in a gown, comes downstairs.

"Are you back already?" she's surprised.

Matej nods and wipes his eyes with a sleeve. "It fell. It just fell!"

"You'll wipe it up. After all, it's not a carpet, it's laminate. Go on." She goes to the kitchen. "Lately you're always crying. First it's onion, then wine..."

She comes back with a sponge, kneels down, and starts soaking up the spilled wine. Matej pulls the sponge out of her hands. "I'll do it."

He starts cleaning up. "I was going to make spaghetti. Good ones. Bolognese. But now…"

"Forget it. Anyway, Brane says he won't eat."

"Why not?" Matej asks cautiously.

"He says he's tired."

"That's not like him," Matej jokes acidly. "To get tired so fast."

"Maybe he's studying too much."

"It's true that sometimes he overexerts himself, especially if he likes the subject," Matej allows himself another acid comment.

Katarina is not so slow that she wouldn't get it.

"I'm not hungry either," she decides. "But you probably are."

"Not at all after all this," Matej replies.

"Where did you buy the wine that you got back so fast?"

"I brought it from the cellar, where you husband has another ten bottles hidden."

He wipes his eyes again.

"Matej, stop crying. It's only wine. And the bottle isn't even broken."

"It's not? It seems to me I see shards," says Matej.

Peter is sitting on a bench in Tivoli Park late in the afternoon, reading the *Financial Times*. He looks left and right down the path a few times. He looks at his watch.

Katarina approaches over the lawn, from behind and covers his eyes with her left hand.

"I give up," says Peter.

Katarina removes her hand and walks around the bench, stopping in front of Peter. She looks more sad than playful. "Shall we go?"

"Where," Peter is surprised.

"For a walk. Like other people."

Peter folds the newspaper and leaves it one the bench. "I was hoping we'd sit here a while. Hand in hand, like school kids in love."

"Wouldn't that be nice?" Katarina smiles.

"It would be. If you didn't have things to do."

They set off down the path.

"That's what I'd like to talk with you about. About responsibilities."

"Whose to whom?"

"Mine to you."

"I don't understand," Peter shrugs.

Katarina stops and takes Peter by the hand. "Listen to me..."

Peter notices there are tears in her eyes. "Katarina..." he says.

"It seems I'm falling. Sometimes even when I'm in a taxi, I have the urge to grab the wheel with my left hand and turn the car into oncoming traffic. Where does that desire come from?"

"Unfortunately I'm only a lawyer, not a psychologist," Peter shrugs.

"The arm, Peter. The right hand is the main connection to the space that surrounds us. With the world we live in."

"Does that only go for right-handed people, or for lefties, too?"

"I'm not joking, Peter. I wasn't aware of that as long as I had use of the hand. But now... it's as if I'm not in touch with anything. Not even myself. Or my feelings."

"It will pass," Peter comforts her, as if none of this really interests him.

"Maybe, but then it will be too late," Katarina says with a doomed sigh.

"You've always had your life on a leash!"

"Peter, help me," Katarina digs in with the fingers of her left hand, hurting him.

"How?" Peter tries to free himself from her nails.

"I don't know," Katarina breaks into crying. "You tell me. Find a solution. Help me. I'm sinking. Deep. I'm getting lost. Don't men exist to help lost women?"

"On the contrary," says Peter. "As a nurse, it's your duty to help wounded men."

"Thanks, Peter."

"Would you like to return to firm ground? At least for an hour, maybe two?"

Katarina moves away from him slightly. "And what does that mean?"

Peter looks at his watch. "Are you up for an early dinner?"

Katarina can't hide her sarcasm. "Genius, Peter. That will solve all my problems."

It's just gotten dark. Peter's Audi stops in front of the house. Katarina gets out and looks at an upstairs window.

"Someone is in my room!"

Peter lowers the window. "You forgot to turn out the light."

"I left in the afternoon, and I don't turn lights on in the afternoon."

"One of the boys?"

"They're not home. They went to some party."

"Maybe they're back."

"How, if the car is gone?"

Peter looks and sees that the parking space in front of the garage is empty.

"Wait," he says, "you loaned them the car?"

"You have some objection?" Katarina looks at him challengingly.

"Well, then you forgot to turn off the light." The matter is closed for Peter. He turns the wheel to leave.

"Come with me," Katarina begs. "Maybe it's robbers. Please."

"Oh," says Peter and gets out of the car.

Katarina unlocks the door and goes in. Peter follows, closing the door behind him just in case. Katarina goes to the foot of the stairs with Peter following. Katarina goes up quietly.

She stops at the turn, from where she can see that her bedroom door is open. A light shines out into the hallway.

Peter stops behind Katarina. Voices are coming from the bedroom.

"Do you think she'll be mad?" Katarina recognizes Brane's voice.

"We have to tell her," says Matej.

"That's up to you," Brane replies.

"It's not my fault," Matej gets excited. "You were driving!"

"You know what will make her feel better? If we invite her in. In the middle. Between us."

"Are you nuts?" Matej is horrified.

"I think she'll jump at it."

There's a short silence, then Matej says, "You know very well that I wouldn't be able to touch her."

"Come on. You've had a woman. You had one last year. And at least one more for sure."

"Katarina is something else. She's... a kind of substitute mom."

"At twenty-four?"

"Well that's how I look at her. She's good to me, and I respect her. And I'm fond of her."

"Then you'll watch," Brane suggests. "She's great at banging. She enjoys it like crazy."

"I don't like it that you two are doing that," says Matej.

"That's what you wanted," Brane confronts him. "You said that way we'd stay here longer."

"I know, but..."

"The fact is," says Brane, "that we won't find such amenities anywhere else. It's better than five stars. We've landed with our asses in the butter!"

"If you tell her what we have between us," Matej threatens, "I'll kill you. I swear!"

"That we're not brothers but just good buddies?" Brane tweaks him.

Peter can't help himself and coughs.

"I heard something!" Matej is worried.

"Maybe I farted," Brane says.

"No, really!" Matej insists.

"You left the key in the door. Don't tell me you didn't!"

"Yes," says Matej, "but... she can come in through the garage."

"She'd call first."

"Let's go to our rooms," Matej suggests.

"No. It's nice here, in her bed. I can imagine her sitting there in the corner watching you choke on my cock."

"You're a pervert," Matej hurls at him.

"Totally," Brane agrees. "The world being the way it is, is it worth being anything else?"

"I'll go check," says Matej.

The bedroom door opens a little more. The patch of light falling into the hallway widens. Matej thrusts his head past the doorframe. He sees Peter and Katarina.

Katarina and Matej stare at each other.

"I told you no one is there," Brane's voice can be heard from the bedroom. "Look how you've got me up. A little more and it'll reach the ceiling. Take advantage of it before it droops again."

Matej's head disappears.

Katarina slowly turns and follows Peter back to the hall and from there to the living room. She throws herself on the couch and starts sobbing wildly. Peter stands and looks at her.

"What are you going to do?" he asks with a legal chill.

Katarina keeps sobbing.

"I'm leaving," Peter decides.

"No," Katarina begs through her tears. "No. Don't leave me alone."

"If you decide to sue, call me," says Peter and leaves.

Katarina hears the entryway door open and slam.

Silence.

Katarina gets up into a sitting position, disheveled and teary. She leans on the edge of the couch.

"Matej!" she hollers hoarsely, at the top of her voice. "Come here!"

She tries to find a handkerchief in her purse. With no luck. Then she makes a fist and angrily hits the purse. She wipes away the tears with her sleeve.

Matej comes slowly down the stairs and looks at Katarina. He immediately averts his eyes.

"Where's the car?" Katarina demands. It doesn't escape her that Matej gives a big sigh.

"We had a little accident," he admits.

"Who was driving?"

"Ah...," Matej stammers, "I was."

"That's not true. Brane was driving."

"It doesn't matter," Matej shrugs, crushed.

"Was anyone hurt?"

"No," Matej shakes his head. "We hit the shoulder and the wheel turned on its own. And we smashed into a tree by the road."

"Into a tree by the road," Katarina says.

"Yes, into a tree by the road," Matej repeats, as if it were something ordinary.

"In other words, it was totaled."

"I don't think so. At least not 100%."

"Did you call the police?" Katarina wants to know.

"We didn't dare," Matej admits.

"You just left the car and walked home. To my bedroom!"

Matej doesn't know what to say, so he just shrugs and stares at the floor.

"You have half an hour to get out of this house," Katarina orders without a hint of gentleness that could indicate she might change her mind.

"I'm very sorry for everything," Matej emits humbly.

Katarina looks at her watch. "Twenty-nine minutes."

Matej retreats and goes up the stairs, his head hanging.

Katarina sits, staring into emptiness.

A half-hour later headlights shine through the window. She waits for steps on the stairs and the sound of the front door, which one of the renters slams harder than necessary. Doubtless Brane.

Only then does she step to the window. The taxi has already turned around in the yard. Matej gets in on the right side, Brane slams the trunk and gets in on the left. The taxi drives off.

Katarina lets out a sigh.

At the same time she has a shot of pain in her heart of the kind she's never felt. She slowly and tortuously goes up the stairs and throws open her bedroom door.

She tries to change the sheets with her left hand. She can't. She collapses on the bed and starts sobbing. After a while she stops crying and sits on the edge of the half-made bed. She stretches out her left arm and turns on the music.

Enya. *"Who can say where the road goes…"*

She sits on the edge of the bed and stares at her reflection in the mirror.

Katarina goes into the kitchen. There's a mountain of dirty dishes. Trash is spilling from the container. Katarina tries to cut a piece of a white bun. She can't manage. She hurls the knife to the floor and tries to break off a piece. She isn't able to do that either. She grabs the bun and bites off a piece.

She goes back to the living room and reaches for her cell phone. "Peter, why don't you call…? I'm by myself for five days already… Well, three… At least an eternity… No, the car's here, out front, I don't know why they brought it here. I'll call a mechanic… No, Peter, I'm not going to file suit… Against whom…? Come over some time… I need to talk… Who should I ask? A psychiatrist?"

She hangs up. "I won't forget this, Mr. Lawyer."

She looks for another number in her contacts. She calls.

"Mom? How are you…? Me…? How am I supposed to be with a broken arm…? Will you come over some time? Jani is in Afghanistan, as you know, I'm alone… But someone can give you a ride! I'll ask Uncle Milan… Now it's your back all of a sudden. When did it start hurting, a second ago? Mom, how can I take care of you when I can't take care of myself?!"

She hangs up fuming, searches her contacts, and calls another number.

"Hi, Manca. It's been a while... Where...? In Australia!?"

She hangs up. She puts the cell phone aside and stares into emptiness. Should she call one of her coworkers? What would they think? She's never been close to anyone. Should she call the doctor who liked her?

Should she call Peter again?

No. Her husband in Afghanistan? Too complicated, through all those lines, verifications, and doubts that maybe she's not his wife.

Call God?

It seems to her she probably would if she had his number.

Katarina comes back from the store. She comes in with a shopping bag in her left hand and closes the door with a kick. She stops in her steps.

Brane is sitting on the couch, smiling smugly.

"How did you get into the house?"

"I unlocked the door," Brane laughs.

"How?"

"Matej had a copy of the key made."

Katarina puts the shopping bag on the floor. "I'll call the police."

"Wait, let me explain," Brane gets up from the couch.

"Save the explanation for the cops." She pulls her cell phone out of her pocket.

"Go in the kitchen," says Brane. "Go on. Peek in the kitchen."

Katarina hesitates. Then she nonetheless decides and goes towards the kitchen. She peeks in. It takes her breath away.

"Everything is cleaned up!"

"Turn around and look in the dining room," Brane calls to her.

Katarina looks at the set table. "You made Thai?!"

"Carry out," Brane boasts.

"Since when do you have money?"

"I borrowed some from a nice girlfriend."

"Really."

"No, I actually rob ATMs," he laughs loudly. He seems to Katarina different from before, less pushy, nicer, even imploring.

"If you think I'm going to forgive the awful things you did on account of carry-out food..."

"Not on account of that, for sure."

"Then for what?"

"Go to the bedroom and I'll show you."

"What did you put there? Not a bouquet of flowers, I hope!"

"Go have a look."

An hour later we find Katarina and Brane in bed, hot, sweaty, and pleasantly tired.

"Well?" says Brane. "Forgiven? Or do you need another round?"

"I'm not in the habit of sleeping with fags," Katarina says.

"Matej is a fag."

"And you're not?"

"No. I like to experiment, that's all. You know. Life is short, then you die."

"Life is short, so it's good to make something of it," Katarina corrects him.

"And what did you make of yours?"

"Nothing," Katarina replies after thinking about it. "Luckily I'm so numb that not even that hurts anymore."

"Then pleasure is all that matters."

"I don't know," she doubts. "Are you sure?"

"What else? Struggling for prestige? In a world that resembles a rotten tomato in the final phase of decomposition?"

"They teach you that in veterinary school?"

"They taught me that people are animals, too."

"You for sure," Katarina says and tickles his ribs with her left hand. "A real monster."

"And you're a rhino. Look how the arm in a cast sticks up!"

"It seems to me that excites you."

"I knew the first time I saw you."

"What?"

"That you yearn for someone with whom you could sink into the depths. To the bottom. With the animals."

"I'm sinking. But I don't know where."

"Into total debauchery," Brane explains.

"Maybe. Only I don't know what I'll get for that."

"You'll escape this world. Into ours. An imaginary one."

"Is it nicer that the real one?"

"The main thing is that it hurts less. Aren't you tired of the pain you carry inside?"

Brane reaches for his jeans lying on the floor. He finds two pills in a pocket. He puts one on his tongue and offers the other to Katarina.

"Aspirin?"

"Ecstasy," Brane explains.

"I won't die?"

"It will kill you gently. Open your mouth and stick out your tongue."

Katarina opens her mouth. Brane puts the ecstasy on her tongue. Katarina swallows it. Brane swallows his.

"And now?"

"Now we go on a trip."

"Far?"

"Not at all. To heaven."

"Is heaven close?"

"For those of us who know the way."

"I hope hell isn't a stop on the way."

"Don't worry. I'm on good terms with the devil."

"I believe it," says Katarina.

"Are you ready?" Brane asks her.

Katarina cautiously wraps herself around him and leans on his shoulder with her left arm. "Can I be on top?"

"I you're not too fast," he says. "I like it when you go up and down slowly. With feeling."

"We need accompaniment," Katarina says and turns on Enya.

"Who can say why your heart cries when your love lies..."

The living room is a mess. Everything is lying about. Brane is sitting on the couch doing a crossword puzzle. Katarina comes in from the kitchen.

"I have to go to the store," she says.

"The Hindu goddess of death, four letters," Brane asks.

"I have no idea."

"Come on. You're a nurse and you don't know that?"

"A nurse?" Katarina laughs. "Maybe I really was. A thousand years ago. Now I look more like the wrecked car out front."

"Place an ad," Brane says. "Sell it."

"I'm waiting for the mechanic. Who you supposedly called. Because you know him."

"He probably has a lot of work."

Katarina looks around the room. "This house has become a pigsty."

66

"I noticed," says Brane, engrossed in the crossword.

"You want to clean up? Carry out the garbage? Wash the dishes?"

"I don't have a gift for those sorts of things."

"I know you don't. But I don't want to live with garbage and filth."

"Why don't you hire a maid? I know a girl who would be happy to earn some money."

"Are you going to pay her?"

"Doesn't he send you money? Your guy in Afghanistan?"

"Excuse me, but you're permitting yourself a little too much," Katarina sharpens her tone a little.

"But you like that about me, no?" Brane looks at her triumphantly.

"Less and less, Brane. Less and less. And it might come to…"

Brane lurches up. "I'll call the mechanic again."

"Why?"

"I'm bored. I'd like to go for a ride, visit friends."

"When did the busses stop running?"

"*And* girlfriends," Brane emphasizes. He realizes too late that he's made a mistake.

"Here's what we'll agree on," Katarina says. "You'll wash the dishes, clean the kitchen, take out the garbage, vacuum the living room, and cut the grass in the garden. If I'm satisfied with your work, we'll have lunch at the Mexican restaurant."

"And if you're not?"

"You can pack up and leave," Katarina says icily.

Brane sits down and again becomes engrossed in the crossword. "The Hindu goddess of death, four letters."

"Go to the kitchen and get to work!" Katarina screams.

Brane puts aside his ballpoint, slowly gets up, and goes upstairs, his head bowed. Katarina goes to the foot of the stairs and yells: "I'm not joking, Brane!"

"I'm not your servant," flies back down.

"And I'm not a woman who should have to pay for sex!"

"Would you rather men pay you?"

"I can't believe it," Katarina says to herself hopelessly. She pounds her head with her left fist.

Brane comes down the stairs with a traveling bag in his hand. He stops in front of Katarina at the foot of the stairs.

"Get out of the way," he says.

"You're not going anywhere."

"I'm going to a woman who's satisfied with my body and doesn't expect cleaning service besides."

"Then go," Katarina moves. "Deceiver!"

"I'm not married," Brane smiles sweetly. "You are. So who's deceiving?"

Katarina puts out her left hand. "The keys!"

"What keys?" Brane pretends.

"Right. I'll call the police."

Brane reaches in his pocket, pulls out the keys, and throws them at Katarina's feet. "Call them. Maybe they'll wash your dishes."

He goes out and slams the door. Katarina stares at the closed door. She fights off tears. Then she explodes into an animal cry.

The Hindu goddess of death. Four letters. Katarina bends over the crossword that Brane left on the table. In order to occupy herself, she tries to guess the missing letter in K LI. She tries o, e, i, a, and u, but nothing sounds right. She tries some consonants; they sound even less probable.

There's not a book in the house to help her, just some women's magazines, romances, and reference books for nurses – no encyclopedia or even computer on which to google the "Hindu goddess of death." She learned to live without resources that might broaden her perspective.

She herself doesn't know how it came to this. There simply wasn't room in her mom's small apartment in Kočevje, and when she moved into her husband's house, there was a computer, but it crashed not long after he left for Afghanistan. She didn't know who to call to fix it, and finally decided she didn't need it.

Not long after that the TV broke. Peter took it to the scrap metal recycling at her request. She was afraid of becoming addicted to the Spanish soap operas her coworkers watched and talked about all the time. She was afraid of sitting in front of the screen, with life passing her by. She wanted life.

How could she find the name of the Hindu goddess of death? She goes to Matej's room, but what few books he had he took with him when he left. He had very few for a student. Was he actually a student? Did he study at all? She never checked; she simply believed him.

First she decides to ask Peter; he should know, but she quickly changes her mind. He hasn't called her for a long time, so why should she call him. And why for heaven's sake is she interested in the name of the Hindu goddess of death. What use is it to her? But the thought won't leave her head, and it soon grows into a need. Somewhere deep in her subconscious the question pecks like a persistent bird that won't quit until it gets an answer.

She calls a taxi and goes to the Bežigrad library, waits for a free computer, asks one of the librarians to google "Hindu goddess of death," and then reads.

Kali. Four letters.

It seems to her that she knew it was Kali all along, not Ku-li, Koli, Keli, or Kili. And that she actually wanted to know *what* the goddess of death is, what it represents, and what it does. Is the goddess responsible for all the dying and dead she has to deal with when working in the hospital? Will she be responsible for her end? She could never completely erase the awareness that her turn will come, too, in surroundings where everything smells of sickness and death. With time it became part of the fabric of her soul. She could temporarily mute it only with sex, which gradually became the single effective escape from the thought of her own end.

And now she's reading. About Kali, the goddess of death. About her two forms: the one with four arms, the other with ten. About her two colors: black and blue. About her eyes, which blaze in drunken anger; about her disheveled hair, which sticks out in all directions; about her talons, which jut out of her mouth. She is often naked, and if not, her skirt is woven of severed human arms, and she has a necklace of skulls around her neck. She is covered with snakes. She stands with her left foot on the stomach of the prostrate god Shiva, her companion, who laid down in front of her for her to step on him and realize that she has gone too far in her battle with demons, gone mad, and become cruel. She defeated all the demons but one, whose every drop of blood that fell to the ground turned into his double, and the more wounds she inflicted on him and the more blood he lost, the more cloned demons there were on the field of battle. The more success she had in the battle, the greater the danger she would lose it.

When Katarina returns by taxi to the empty house, a vague realization creeps into her mind that Kali is to some extent present in every woman, and more in her than in most. The prostrate Shiva, with Kali's leg on his chest, is a man who represents all the men in her life with whom she's had relations, and all the ones with whom she might have them in future, because she can't imagine staying with a man who pushed her down the stairs in a fit of jealousy. She's staying with him temporarily, only for the convenience of his house. She realizes this for the first time.

Will she ever meet a man she won't hate and fear at once? And who will keep loving her after he learns of her dark side? With whom the relationship won't be emotionally vapid, superficial, just a temporary substitute for what she really desires? An all-round man who won't only be her equal but who will best her in all regards? So superior that she won't dare step on his chest? Who won't lay down before her in her rage at the demons in her soul in order to quench her rage?

And if she has feelings for which she can't find reasons, perhaps there's not even a reason to cling to life. Is she clinging to it just to overcome the demons causing her pain? She suspects that somewhere in the near or distant future punishment awaits her for her sins. The broken arm is far from punishment enough for everything she did and might do to the men who might incautiously enter her circle of rage. The Kali in her will make sure that the punishment is no less than they deserve. The goddess of death, four letters. Fuck you, Brane!

Katarina is lying on the couch in the living room, listening to Enya. She's still thinking about Kali. She turns down the music, reaches for her cell phone, and enters a number. She waits.

"Come on, Peter, answer."

She waits. A long time.

71

She moves the phone from her ear. "Right. I, too, can be a pig."

She pulls the phone book from under the coffee table, opens it, turns the pages with a finger on her left hand, stops, enters a number in her cell phone, and puts it to her ear.

"Good evening. I'd like to speak with Peter."

"And who's calling?" a suave female voice asks on the other end.

"Katarina."

"In regards to what?"

"He's representing me in a lawsuit against my husband, who pushed me down the stairs."

Silence falls on the other end. Then the female voice says: "This is a private number. Call him at the office."

"He doesn't answer. I urgently need advice. Tell him to call me."

"At what number?"

"He has it. Or tell him to stop by. He has done that quite a few times. But now it seems he has chosen a new game. Being faithful."

She hangs up and laughs maliciously. She gets up and goes to the kitchen.

That's just when the doorbell rings. Katarina returns to the living room and looks at the clock. "That fast?"

She takes two steps towards the entryway and yells: "Peter, the door isn't locked!"

A moment later the door opens. Matej is standing on the threshold.

Katarina can't believe it. "You?!"

"Just for a minute!" Matej folds his hands. "Please."

"We have nothing to say to each other," Katarina is ready to close the door.

"I'd like to take care of the rent!" Matej insists.

"You don't owe me anything."

"For the last month. Half the rent. Please."

"Right," Katarina changes her mind. "Come in. I'd like to ask you something."

Matej enters and sits down on the edge of the easy chair. Katarina looks at him.

"I've been here twice, but you weren't home," the unexpected guest hurries to say. "It's been eating at me the whole time. And I'd like to apologize. I know it wasn't right, but... you know... When we give in to our feelings we do things we wouldn't in a normal state... It's not nice for me to cast the blame on Brane, but the fact is he's been using me all this time... And you... I was blind, and you were, too... I didn't know there was anything between you... Had I known, I would have... Broken off with him, really!"

"Why didn't you tell me you're gay?"

"I didn't dare. And maybe I'm not at all. Only half."

"I'm a grown up. I'd understand."

"My parents. It would kill them if they found out."

"Me, Matej. Why didn't you tell me?"

Matej shifts agitatedly. He folds and unfolds his hands. "I'd like to work off what I owe you. And what Brane owes you. Give me the chance."

Katarina takes two steps across the room, turns, and asks as if incidentally: "Do you ever see him?"

"I have no idea where he might be. I'm not at all interested. But I'd like to be honest with you."

"Can I trust you with something very important? Something intimate?"

Matej swallows and nods.

"Do you know I always loved only my husband? Who never returned my love? Not because he might not have loved me, but perhaps because he didn't know how."

Matej is silent. It seems he doesn't know what to say. This is beyond his experience. He finally says: "Step by step, that's the answer."

"What do you mean?"

"Each of us passes himself on the right. That's the problem."

"You've transferred to philosophy!"

"No. I quit school. I work as a waiter in a gay bar."

"Well, at least you're among your own," Katarina relaxes. "Where are you living?"

"Here a while, there a while."

"That's awkward."

"I'm to blame. If I hadn't brought Brane…"

"You could still be living with me," Katarina finishes.

"Maybe that's true."

"In short, you're not interested in women."

"More as friends."

"Then come up to the bedroom and massage your friend's shoulders like you used to."

"You don't mean…" Matej is surprised.

"Matej, there's no shortage of men who would like to empty themselves in me. But as far as friends go, you're the only one I have right now."

"You mean… that everything can be like it was again?"

"Until my husband gets back."

"And then?"

"Then you can't help me any more, Matej. Then only God can help me."

Late in the evening, Matej is sitting in the living room, which has been straightened up, leafing through a magazine. The doorbell rings. Matej looks at the clock and goes to open the door.

Brane is standing on the doorstep with a travel bag in his hand.

"No," says Matej and tries to close the door. Brane reaches out and holds it.

"Who's in charge here, you or her?"

"You've made enough trouble."

"I'd like to talk with her."

"You can't, because she's asleep."

"Wake her up."

"You're not going to set up camp in this house again."

Katarina's voice comes down the stairs. "Matej! Who are you talking to?"

"Well?" Brane roughly shoves Matej aside. "Go clean the kitchen. And make me a good sandwich."

He goes upstairs.

A good week later Brane is lying in the living room, stretched out on the couch, with a joint in his hand. Katarina is standing by the window, staring at the garden. It's raining.

There's again a terrible mess in the living room: newspapers and magazines on the floor, a laundry basket behind the couch, some laundry on the radiators, plates with half-eaten snacks on the coffee table, glasses with the remains of wine, cups with the remains of coffee, and two ashtrays full of butts.

Katarina is wearing a wrinkled gray running suit, her hair is dirty and uncombed, and her eyes are tired.

Her cell phone rings on the coffee table. Katarina doesn't move.

Brane reaches out, picks up the cell phone, and takes the call. "This is Mrs. Katarina Osterc's residence. Who? Never heard." He offers Katarina the phone.

Katarina turns around slowly, takes the phone, and with an effort brings it to her ear. "Yes?"

Brane gets up and goes to the kitchen.

"Oh, it's you, Peter."

"I've already called three times. Why don't you call back?" Peter gets excited on the other end.

"I called, too. Not three times but a hundred. Did you ever call back?"

"Look, Katarina. Don't call me on the home phone again. Okay?"

"*You* call me on the home phone. What's the difference?"

"The difference is I'm married!"

"And I'm not?"

"I have a family, for God's sake. We've been over this already once. Why have you become mean?"

Katarina laughs out loud. "Maybe I really am. It's something new for me."

"If you need something, call my cell phone."

"Maybe I'll even call you at home sometime. I like your wife's voice."

Katarina hangs up and tosses the phone on the coffee table.

Brane comes from the kitchen with a bottle of beer and sprawls back on the couch. "When is the last time you were in the kitchen?"

"Why?"

"It's a pigsty, the worst I've seen. What's that renter of yours doing?"

"Which one?"

"The one upstairs, Matej."

"I don't know. He's jealous, maybe he wants revenge."

"I invited him to our bed. But he doesn't want to. He's a total fag."

"Maybe I should have invited him."

"Go on."

"Not now. When he came. When things were still somewhat..."

"What?"

"Ah, it doesn't matter. All the same it's too late now."

"But you can't say I don't see to you feeling good. I organized something for you today."

"Let me guess," says Katarina. "A performance at the Puppet Theater."

"A young couple is coming over."

"For what?"

"Young and sexy. She has tits that will knock you out, and he has a dick that will scare you."

"Really? And what will we do?"

"Don't worry, I have the scenario worked out."

"And the couple is coming here? To this pigsty?"

"They live in a pigsty themselves. An even worse one. She sells herself; he finds the customers."

"I can hardly wait. Four pigs together, what could be more exciting?"

"I'm joking," says Brane. "I have something else in mind."

"Too bad."

"We need money. The mechanic said the engine is ruined and a repair would cost fifteen thousand euros."

"Small change. I'll check my pockets."

"I'm serious. You know what sells best nowadays?"

"Drugs? The ones you turned me into a zombie with?"

"Pornography."

"Then I don't know what you're waiting for. Call Matej, bring me a camera, and I'll film you sucking each other. And we can buy two Mercedes!"

"I was thinking Matej could film us."

"You and me? A drugged up low life and a nurse with a broken arm who has lost the ground beneath her feet? The patients I took care of at work are mostly poor, but I'm sure at least one could get enough money together for the DVD and sell it to the gossip columns. They could feature a new twist on health care."

"But no one would recognize you," Brane says impatiently, as if explaining something she should know. "You'll be wearing a mask."

"A masked hooker with a broken arm plays out scenes from Kamasutra."

"What a hit! People are so sated that only something bizarre excites them."

"And that's me?"

"Your arm."

"My arm. Of course. My arm. The sexiest part of my person. Or, more precisely, my non-person."

"What do you have to lose, considering that no one would recognize you?"

"I don't know. An ounce of self-respect? But there's none of it left as it is, so you're right. I wouldn't lose anything."

They're silent for a while.

Then Brane says: "I ordered Matej to get the camera ready."

"What an organizer!"

"Someone has to be."

"Brane, I don't go for such games."

"I'll convince you."

Katarina covers her face with her left hand and is quiet for a while.

Then she decides.

"You have exactly half an hour to get out of this house."

"Why?" Brane is surprised. "Because every time you chase me off, you take me back again. You can't get by without me. You're lonely as hell, why don't you admit it?"

"Go!" Katarina points to the door with her left hand.

"And who is going to get you the drugs you can't do without any more? You're getting them from me for free; others will charge you. Heroin is expensive. In a year or two you won't have a house."

Katarina sits down on the couch and starts sobbing.

"My husband will come back! He'll save me!"

"For sure. So you'll have your left arm in a cast, too. Along with your head."

"But," Katarina wipes away the tears with the edge of her hand, "none of that can be true!"

"Why not?"

"Because things like that don't happen in the normal world."

"What do you know about the normal world? You don't watch TV, read the papers, and you don't even have a computer. You wanted to escape the world, but it's come after you."

"There's nothing but dead bodies on TV! On all the channels! And if the real ones aren't enough, there are thousands of fictional ones!"

"Who am I that you're holding that against me?"

"Go! I ask you."

Brane looks at the clock. "It'll be time for another dose of heroin."

"No!" She shows him the marks on her left arm. "I'm stuck all over."

"If you don't take it, in three hours you'll be in hell."

Powerful sobs start to shake Katarina.

Brane sits down next to her on the couch and puts a hand on her shoulder. Her head flops onto his shoulder. Her left hand presses his hand in spasms.

"Stay," she sobs in his ear. "Please."

Brane tenderly caresses her hair.

"Just obey me, and nothing bad will happen."

The living room couch is turned to the window, into which the sun is shining. Brane is lying on the couch, his head resting on the left and his bare feet sticking over the right side. Katarina is crouching over him, rhythmically raising and lowering herself. She is gripping the back of the couch with her left hand. She's naked, with only a black mask over her head, which resembles a likeness of death— white eyes, nose, and mouth.

Matej is kneeling on the floor by the window, filming.

"Go on and move a little left, you're blocking the light," Brane orders him.

Matej moves to the left on his knees and keeps filming.

The living room door opens quietly, and Lieutenant Colonel Osterc, in his uniform and a traveling bag in his hand, steps in. He stops and watches. No one notices him.

"Come on, Katarina," Brane encourages her. "Put a little passion into what you're doing."

"But I'm trying," Katarina replies breathlessly.

"You usually don't have to... Come on, who's going to watch this...? Breathe and moan like you're enjoying it... You're enjoying it, after all, so why not show it?"

Katarina starts groaning and moaning, but it's only put on, because the sounds border on crying.

Osterc puts his traveling bag down, opens it, pulls out a pistol, and takes three steps towards the couch. First he shoots Matej, who falls back by the window. The camera slides out of his hands.

Brane gets up on his elbows and lifts his head over the couch, staring at Osterc.

The next instant a bullet hits him in the chest.

"What... what's going on?" screams Katarina, who sees nothing.

She tries to tear the mask from her face with her left hand.

Oster shoots her in the stomach at close range. Katarina falls off the couch. Her head, still in the mask, lies on Matej's body. She's not dead, but groaning in pain.

Osterc shoves the pistol into his left jacket pocket, pulls a cell phone from his right pocket, and enters a number.

"Police...? You'll find three bodies in the house at Betnavska 136... Who am I...? I'm back from places where there are a thousand more bodies."

He hangs up and looks at Katarina, who is still groaning. She moves and tries once again to take off the mask. This time she manages.

She stares at Osterc.

"Jani!?" she murmurs with great effort.

"What is it, dear?" her husband asks kindly, in a casual tone.

"I need help..." Katarina groans.

"You know how many people I watched die slowly, without being able to help them? Anyway, you're a nurse, and I'm only a soldier. That's what you told me once."

"Jani, please!" Katarina writhes in agony.

"Those two will help you," Osterc looks at the two male bodies. Matej is still barely noticeably twitching.

Osterc turns and goes to his traveling bag on the floor near the door. He sees the CD-player on the coffee table. He approaches.

"Still the same thing?" he asks himself. He turns on the music.

"Who can say why your heart sighs when your love flies?"

Osterc laughs bitterly, picks up his bag, goes out, and closes the door behind him.

At that moment, a cloud covers the sun, and the rays that were shining in the window give way to a menacing darkness. Katarina groans in great pain and listens to her favorite singer.

Osterc stops in the yard and looks at the wreck of his Mercedes for a while. His face conveys no feeling.

Then he turns and marches down the street.

Part 2

RAIN

The rented studio flat in an east London suburb gives the impression of belonging to someone trying to live modestly, probably not out of a conviction that extravagance is a fault, but because they can't afford anything more comfortable.

Although they'd like to.

There are many such studios in London, and many people who would rather live in houses or in spacious apartments on the bank of the Thames, but their lives turned out differently, and they have to be satisfied with a place near the bottom of the social ladder. Not at the very bottom, but close to it. It hurts, but that's the way things are, the way the world is. Life has a way of taking this or that turn, sometimes in an unexpectedly wrong direction.

That's what Matej is thinking, the collar on his white shirt turned up, rifling through the dresser and nervously looking for something. He quietly curses and slams the dresser shut.

"Katarina, I can't find a tie!"

He looks in the open bathroom door, where Katarina is standing in front of the mirror and putting make up on before going to work.

"You don't need one."

"Don't tell me what I need." He starts rifling through the dresser again.

Katarina comes out of the bathroom. "I haven't seen you with a tie since we met."

"I wore one at the wedding."

"Four years ago."

Matej looks around the room. "Where could it have disappeared?"

"You're not going to an audience with the queen, after all."

"You don't know my parents."

"No, because you haven't introduced them."

"You're going to keep bringing that up even when they're here?"

"They're not here, but in Brighton."

"You know what... I'm not going."

He sits down on the edge of the bed, squeezes his hands between his knees, and stares glumly in front of him. Katarina looks at him, then sits down and puts an arm around his shoulders.

"What is it, my little renter? You're not nervous?"

"Stop calling me a renter. We're both renters now, have been that for four years."

"Will you have something to eat before you go?"

"My stomach isn't right."

"Matej, look at me." She seizes him by the chin and the top of his head and almost forces his face towards her. "I know you haven't seen each other for five years. I know it won't be easy. But they're here, and you have to go through with it."

"My brother and sister are here. Mom and dad and more like their luggage."

"Do you at all realize how happy I am finally to meet them?"

"And if you don't like them?"

"Of course I will. They're your parents."

"Maybe you have a mistaken view of them."

"I have no view."

Matej gets up and moves to the window. "Maybe you will, after you meet them, look at me differently, too."

"Is that what's worrying you?"

"Yes."

86

Katarina gets up, goes over to him, and hugs him from behind, putting her head on his shoulder. "Listen, my little renter. I know you're a tender soul, and maybe too sensitive. But that's what I like in you. Your relatives have nothing to do with that."

"Really?"

"Really. But I'd still like to meet them."

"You will."

"Sometimes I get the impression you'd rather I didn't."

"We were never especially close."

"That doesn't change anything."

"Maybe they'll be disappointed. In us."

"That will be their problem."

Matej turns to her. "But you will... whatever happens... understand me?"

"Haven't I always?"

"I've never had such a great abyss gaping in front of me."

"Abyss? We both almost died. We survived. What other abyss can gape in front of you?"

"I don't know any more what I am."

"My husband. Isn't that enough?"

"Maybe not for you."

"I understand you," says Katarina. "That's how I felt when I had my arm in a cast. But now I have to go to work, dear."

She kisses him on the forehead, like a child, grabs her purse, and leaves.

Matej starts rifling through the mess in the dresser again, hoping to find a tie.

Someone rings.

Matej goes to the door and opens it. In front of him is the middle-aged neighbor lady with a list in her hand.

"A white shirt!" she exclaims. "What's happening?"

"Mrs. Winter," Matej suddenly remembers, "might you have a tie?"

"I haven't ever seen you dressed so nicely, since... to be honest, ever."

"Somewhere in a dresser?" Matej continues. "It seems to me impossible that your husband didn't wear ties."

"He had only one," says Mrs. Winter regretfully. "A black one. For funerals."

"Can you loan it to me for a day or two?"

Feigned shock appears on Mrs. Winter's face. "Did someone you know die?"

"No, no," Matej calms her. "I'm going to Brighton. My parents are coming to visit."

"Ohhh!"

"And my brother and sister," Matej adds. "I haven't seen them for quite a few years."

"That's unusual." Mrs. Winter is surprised. "After all, Slovakia isn't that far."

"Slovenia, Mrs. Winter, Slovenia," Matej reminds her kindly.

"Of course, of course," Mrs. Winter excuses herself, "I haven't had time to study the map of Europe that you gave me. That means you're both going?"

"Katarina is at work. She'll meet them tomorrow, when they come to London."

"Where are you going to put them?" Mrs. Winter is frightened.

"In a hotel, of course," says Matej. "What about... the tie, Mrs. Winter?"

"I'll look," says the lady and goes to the apartment across the hall. Matej follows her. Mrs. Winter searches boxes and drawers with her right hand, still holding the shopping list in her left.

"Will you even recognize them after all these years?"

"When I look at my mom, I always think of the English queen," says Matej.

Mrs. Winter is surprised. "A royal bearing?"

"No, the queen wears the same kind of peasant kerchief as my mom. The queen only wears it on rainy days, my mom all the time."

"Has Katarina ever met them?" Mrs. Winter asks.

"No," Matej admits.

"Then she must be very excited," says Mrs. Winter. "The first meeting with your husband's relatives, especially his parents, is something special for every woman. I know from personal experience."

She finally finds the tie in one of the stuffed drawers.

"I knew it was here. My brains are alright; it's the eyes that are a problem."

Matej pulls the tie out of her hands. "Thank you, Mrs. Winter. I promise I'll take care of it."

He hurries to leave. A sad, even plaintive voice stops him.

"That means I won't have greens today?" Mrs. Winter stretches out her hand with the list. Matej takes the list.

"I'll ask Katarina to bring the things on the way home."

"I know the store isn't far," his neighbor insincerely excuses herself, "but my legs, you know..."

"No worries," Matej replies and closes the door behind him. "Has there ever been a time I didn't bring you greens from the market?

"Not until now," says his neighbor with a barely noticeable hint of warning.

Katarina and her coworker, Mary, are sitting on wooden chairs at a narrow table in the staff room of the gerontology department of Hammersmith Hospital. They're talking about the patients in their care.

Katarina's cell phone rings. She pulls it out of her gown pocket and checks who's calling.

She takes the call.

"I can't hear you! Are you on the train? The connection is bad, I can't hear you!"

She ends the call and shoves the phone back in her pocket.

"Your husband?" Mary asks.

Katarina nods.

"Why Brighton? Why don't they come to London?"

"He says that before introducing his wife to them and them to her, he'd like to spend a day or two alone with them. After all, they haven't seen each other for five years."

"Isn't that unusual? You said it's less than two hours to Ljubljana by plane."

"I'm trying to understand him. He didn't talk a lot about his parents even when he was renting from me in Ljubljana. He told me more about his grandmother, whom he really liked. Only in London did he confide that they're very important people and would never accept his sexual orientation."

"Nowadays that's normal."

"He says it would harm their reputation."

"But the fact that he didn't get a degree and works as a grocer's assistant at the market also hurts their reputation."

"They don't know about that."

"But if they come to London, they'll find out."

"And that's why he didn't want them to come. *They* insisted on seeing him. And meeting his wife."

"His wife?!"

"In his letters to his mom, he always referred to me as his wife. Sorry I didn't tell you. We're married."

"You won't be offended if I say something?"

"Mary, you know very well that I should be dead. I let you know all the other details only because I *had* to trust someone with them."

"I don't understand how you can live with someone who's gay."

"Because you didn't go through what we went through. When we met in London by accident, that meant we had to live together. For the first time in our lives we felt human. The experience changed us both, and bound us together."

"And now he's looking for partners in gay bars, and you are abstaining."

"Not entirely," Katarina admits.

"Blind dates? Ads?"

"That, too."

"But you never tried...?"

"Once. Neither of us liked it. We felt it could harm our truly friendly relationship, so we stopped."

"What about the other one, the third one, who was to blame for the whole thing. Did he survive?"

"I don't know," says Katarina. "I hope not. He was shot twice in the chest, Matej and I in the stomach."

"But you liked him?"

"In bed. Only in bed. Otherwise, it seems to me, I almost despised him. And I hated his influence on me."

"You cooperated."

"The Hindu goddess of death from a crossword started living in me. Kali, four letters. I obeyed her, I wanted to please her."

"What are you talking about?"

"Forget it, Mary. I won't hide from you that I'm partly guilty for what happened. But I'm different now. Completely. Now I'm a normal, respectable person. Maybe too respectable, but that doesn't bother me."

"Are you convinced of that?"

"Convinced' is too strong a word. I'm trying to be different."

"And if the third one, who's to blame for everything—I keep forgetting his name—suddenly appeared in London, alive, what would you do?"

"I'd avoid him."

"I don't believe it."

"Mary, after all that happened the last thing I want is to go back to my old life. The one I have now is good enough for me. Matej and I are joined by the scars of the healed wounds on our stomachs. Believe it or not, that's more than a good enough reason to stay together. I've never been as close to anyone."

"Bless you," says Mary. "I'm thinking of leaving my husband."

"Do it, if that's the way you feel. It's not us who live life. Life lives us."

"You sound like you read a lot," Mary says.

"I never have. But since I've been in London, I often stop at the library. Matej, too. Actually, we read the same books. And then we talk about them."

"What kind of books?"

"On health, psychology, some on psychiatry."

"Unusual choices."

"Matej has problems. He admitted to me that he's had them since childhood. Panic attacks. Depression. Fears."

"On top of everything else."

"I have to reconcile myself to it. That's the whole secret of wisdom, about which thousands of books have been written. Accept life as it is."

They hear a whistle. One of the lights on the wall starts to flicker.

"Mrs. Diarrhea again," says Mary. "She's ringing every two hours today. Want me to go?"

"No," says Katarina and gets up. "It's unpleasant, but it's a part of my repentance."

Hotel Brighton isn't one of the best. Matej couldn't afford one of those, but it's in a good location, by the road that runs along the shore, with a bar that doubles as a breakfast room, and from which you can see the ocean through a bay window. There are five round tables with wicker chairs in the room, nothing special, but at first glance it seems good enough to Matej's guests. Except his father, who enters first, leaning on a cane. His mother follows him, a peasant wife with a kerchief on her head and a big black plastic bag made in times long past.

"Go on, sit down," she reminds her husband, "so you don't fall."

"Are you afraid I'm going to fall on you?" her elderly husband shoots back. "You're not so young any more that I'd be glad about that."

"Can I ask you something?" his wife says in a tone indicating she's put the question to him at least a hundred times.

"Have I ever refused you anything?" her husband asks defiantly.

"Can you watch your tongue with other people around?"

Matej's father sinks into one of the chairs with difficulty and looks around the room.

"Quite a hotel!"

"It'll be fine," Matej's mother says and sits down at the next table.

"It seems to me I saw a mouse under the bed in the room," her husband tries to scare her.

"More likely a rat," Mother says calmly. "Considering how well you see."

She opens her purse, takes out a pair of glasses, and offers them to Father.

"What's that?" Father asks and glares at her.

"Your eyes," she informs him.

"I don't need glasses to see that our dear son has stuck us in a doghouse."

Mother shoves the glasses back in her purse. "How many hotels have you been in, that you're able to compare?"

"I thought we were going to England, and where did we end up? In Albania."

"Be quiet," Mother says.

"I'll be quiet when I'm gone. That will be soon, you'll be glad to know. I don't doubt you will be."

He reaches into his pants, pulls out a pocket watch, and studies it.

Matej's sister and older brother come in. "Father, you've already looked at your watch ten times," Sister says.

"It keeps showing the same time."

"That's it! What sense is there looking at a watch that's stopped?"

"Why does everything have to make sense?"

"You're right, Father," Matej's older brother puts in, "our presence in this hotel also makes less and less sense. Because it's starting to seem that your youngest doesn't have the slightest intention of coming."

"He'll come," Mother affirms decisively.

"Well, if you say so, Mom," the older brother shrugs. "I'd like to have a little something to drink while we're waiting."

"As always," Sister rebukes him.

The older brother bristles slightly. "Is that an innocent comment, a reproach, or a prohibition?"

Mother shuts her eyes and puts her hands to her ears. "Not here! Not now!"

The older brother goes towards the exit, since the bar is in the hallway near the reception desk. "Does anyone want anything?"

"A double whiskey," Father raises two fingers.

"Father, you'll collapse under the table!" Matej's sister warns him.

"When I collapse, it will be into the grave. Never under a table."

"You never drink at home."

"How do you know what I drink at home? How often do you visit?"

"So, a double whiskey," the older brother concludes. "Anything else?"

"Kool-Aid," his mother recalls.

"I doubt they have anything that exotic in a Brighton hotel."

"Then a glass of water."

"Son," Father says, "I said a *triple* whiskey, didn't I?"

"Jesus Christ," Sister complains.

"I'll just bring a bottle," the older brother decides and goes to the bar.

"Look at that!" Sister says and looks out the window. "A Rolls Royce had come to a stop in front of the hotel."

"That will be Matej!" Mother gets excited.

"Sure thing," says Sister. "He probably even has a chauffer. In uniform," she ends with a sarcastic laugh.

"And why not," says Father, "didn't he write all the time how well he's doing?"

"He never mentioned a Rolls Royce," Sister points out. "Only that he's living in a big house."

"With a garden," Mother adds proudly. "In the very center of London. There's not many houses with gardens there."

Sister laughs. "How often are you in London, Mom?"

"Leave her alone." Father raises his voice a little.

"He wrote only to me all those years," Mother boasts. "In one of his letters, he listed the plants growing in his garden. Rhododendrons. Azaleas. Japanese maples."

To which Father adds: "He was quiet about the Rolls Royce out of respect for his older sister. So that jealousy wouldn't cause her untimely end."

"It won't, Father, because an English gentleman just stepped out of the Rolls Royce."

"Matej' is now an English gentleman," Mother steps in to defend him.

"But that one out there is a genuine gentleman," Sister spoils her happiness.

Mother leans over to Father.

"Are you alright?"

"Why?"

"You've completely crawled into your shell."

"Where else should I crawl? I've never crawled up people's asses, and even if I was in the habit, it's no longer worth it."

"Father," Sister reprimands him, "does every other word have to be 'ass'?"

"You pronounced it without any trouble. Your tongue didn't twist, and lightning didn't strike you."

"Sometimes I really wish it would."

"Nowhere in the dictionary does it say that some words are forbidden. Unless I'm blind. But I'm not blind, I have glasses. I had no idea that a behind is called ass. I learned it in some crossword."

"Father, you can say the word a hundred times a day at home if it's fun, but here we're in a hotel."

"I didn't know the English say the word, too. I assumed they used some noble word."

"Cut it out." Mother puts a hand on his elbow.

"I cut it out years ago."

Sister gets up. "I've had enough. I'm going to the room. Call me when Matej gets here."

At that moment Matej and his older brother come through the door. Matej halts and hesitates. His older brother hurries ahead.

"He was standing at the bar as if ashamed of his relatives."

"I didn't know you were here," Matej justifies himself.

His mother gets halfway up and sinks back. "Oh...! My baby boy!"

Tears start running down her wrinkled cheeks. Matej takes a step towards her. "Mom... Don't cry!"

"I haven't seen you for so long!"

"The main thing is you arrived safely, that you're alive and well. The main thing is that we're seeing each other now."

"Who's that?" Father asks.

"Oh, here he goes again." Sister shakes her head.

"Don't you see?" Mother gets angry.

"Your youngest, Father," says older brother. "Come on, let's help him up."

He takes his father around the waist, his sister jumps up on the other side, and they stand him up. Father wavers slightly, then gets his balance and stands straight.

"My youngest son?"

"Don't you remember, we came to visit him," Sister scolds him.

"I remember everything, I don't forget anything."

Matej is uncomfortable. "Father... how are you?"

"I'm fine, and how are you?"

"Why are you acting dumb?" Mother howls at him through tears.

"Your son, Father," says Brother. "Your youngest and dearest son. He left for England years ago to get rich."

"That's not my son," Father shakes his head firmly. "He was smaller than me, but this one's bigger."

"Holy Mary!" wails Sister.

"You've shrunk," Brother says to Father. "That's normal at your age."

"Katarina didn't come?" Matej's mother glances at him.

"She's at work, Mom. She'll come tomorrow."

"Wait a minute"—Brother becomes visibly impatient—"I thought we were going to London."

"Me, too," Sister adds.

"Of course we're going," says Mother, "who says we're not?"

"I've shrunk?" Father is surprised. "How didn't I notice?"

Matej shifts nervously. "As I wrote in my last letter... it would be nice to spend the first day by the sea... after all, it's the middle of summer..."

"Ha!" Brother snorts. "I'm sorry I didn't bring gloves!"

"That's the way it is in England."

"The weather isn't his fault," Mother defends him.

"Although lately we have also had quite a few hot spells," Matej recalls, as if not knowing what to say.

"You probably know that we fly back in three days," Brother reminds him.

"Why can't we go to London today?" Sister wants to know.

"Tomorrow after breakfast," Matej answers firmly. "I suggest we have a drink, and then you'll go and unpack."

"We already did," says Mother.

"The light above the nightstand in my room doesn't work," Sister complains.

"I'll tell them at the reception desk," Matej calms her. "Everything alright, apart from that?"

"To be honest," says Sister, "I expected a little more from an English hotel."

"Everything's fine, Matej," Mother intervenes. "All we need is a bed and bathroom."

"Except my bathroom is terribly dirty," Sister continues. "Not to mention the towels, which have a strange smell."

"I'm sorry," Matej says dejectedly. "I can go ask if they have another room."

"Forget it." Brother puts a hand on his shoulder. "No room will satisfy her."

Father suddenly comes to life. "Who's not satisfied with me?"

"We're all satisfied with you, Father," says older brother, "don't worry."

"Well, I'm not satisfied with you," Father says cuttingly, "it's the same thing."

"I said he shouldn't fly." Mother shakes her head. "The pressure above the clouds is very low."

"Father..." Matej takes a step towards him.

"Why are you calling me 'father' if I've never seen you?"

"Pull yourself together," Mother whispers into Father's ear, "how can it be you suddenly don't remember?"

"What are you saying? I remember very well that I was supposed to get a triple whiskey. Did I already drink it?"

"I'll bring it, Father," Brother sighs patiently. "What do you want, Matej?"

"Nothing actually..." Matej replies timidly.

"After all these years you're not going to have a glass with your family?"

"Leave him alone," Mother says, "don't you see he's crying?"

Matej sniffles and wipes away a tear with the knuckle of his forefinger.

"Yes, of course I will… A dark beer… I'll go."

"The first round is on me," older brother decides and goes to the bar.

"Look, Father," visibly shaken Sister says. "You've made your dearest son cry."

"No, no…" Matej quenches yet another tear. "We haven't seen each other for a long time."

"Matej has always been very sensitive." Mother takes him gently by the sleeve. "And you not sensitive enough." She looks at Sister.

"That's good to know. At least I won't have to cook for you two anymore."

"Can't we at least not argue today?" Matej pleads. "Please."

"It's not an argument, son. When our family argues, dishes and kitchen chairs fly through the air. Have you forgotten?"

"Well, at least he recognized him," Sister sighs.

Mother crosses herself. "God be praised."

"Matej, come here." Father gestures with a finger. Matej approaches and stands in front of him. "Help your old man up."

Matej takes his father around the waist and tries to pull him up. Sister jumps up to help. Father pushes her away.

"It's a matter for me and my son." He supports himself on the back of the chair and finally stands up on wavering legs.

"Now give me a hug, son."

They hug each other and calm down.

Behind them, Mother starts wiping away her tears. The scene has moved her. Father finally releases himself from the embrace but leaves his hands on Matej's shoulders.

"You alright son, no? Your health and such?"

"How are you, Father?" Matej returns the question.

"Me? I think something's wrong with me. I feel too good for my years."

"That's great news," Matej is relieved.

"And you," Father suddenly remembers, "you still have your ups and downs?"

"Sometimes, Father, sometimes," Matej replies as if he'd rather not talk about it.

"Oh," his mother exclaims is if she just remembered. "The gifts!"

"Of course." Father remembers, too. "Come here, son, and sit down."

"You sit down, Father. Can I help you?"

With Matej's help, he sinks back into the chair. "I can't get it up, so I don't get up anymore."

"Father, please..." Sister threatens him.

"And now a person can't even tell the truth?" Father protests.

"Look what we brought for you, Matej," Mother says. In her hand she's holding a lump in wrapping paper. With two hands she raises it to Matej. Matej takes the gift and unwraps it.

"Oh, Mom... Smoked ham!"

"You always liked it best," Father says. "Besides pork tail."

"We would have brought that, too," says Mother, "but the butcher didn't have any."

"Well, this alone is..." Matej mumbles. He doesn't know what to do with the leg; it would be awkward to wrap it back up in the paper.

"Did you smell it?" Father wants to know.

"Yes, Father."

"If that's what hell smells like, I'll be happy!"

"Hell smells of burnt flesh," Sister corrects him, "not smoked."

"We don't know much about Katarina..." Mother unsuccessfully strives to keep a reproof out of her words. "So we brought her a box of candies."

She hands the box of candies to Matej as she did the ham.

"It's full of chocolate candies."

Matej puts the ham on the table to take the box.

"Katarina adores chocolates."

"What?" Father leans over.

Mother raises her voice. "She adores chocolates!"

"Why are you shrieking, I'm not deaf."

"I don't want you to miss anything," Mother says. "It's a special moment."

"Really special." Father frowns. "We brought him things he can get here, at the shop around the corner. Except for the ham. You can only get a ham like that at home."

Sister pulls three boxed shirts out of the big gift bag by her chair.

"You can get shirts here, too, but I brought them for you all the same. I'm sorry I didn't have time to wrap them."

She offers them to Matej. Matej puts the candies on the table and takes the shirts. "It really wasn't necessary..."

"If the collar is too tight," Sister says, "I can take them back and send new ones."

"I think they're just right," Matej replies.

"If they don't fit, say so," Mother says. "Your brother-in-law gets them for free at work."

Sister tries with all her might not to explode. "They're not free at all! He works there, he spends a third of his life at the factory!"

"He's paid for his work, but the shirts he gets for free."

"Not for free, at a discount." Sister gets slightly hysterical. "Sometime you're really evil."

"The shirts are beautiful," Matej tries to smooth it over. "I don't know if I have anything this nice in the dresser."

"Look at him," Mother says tenderly. "Still the same. Agreeable and polite."

"Of course, he's a chip off the old block."

Sister's laugh sounds like a dog's bark. "Of everything I've heard today, that's by far the best!"

Older brother returns with a tray. He pushes the gifts away and sets the glasses on the table.

"Finally I hear some good humor. Here, Father, is the triple whiskey, like you said."

He offers Father a glass.

"But I don't drink whiskey, son. You know that."

"Father…" Brother catches his breath.

"Only home-made schnapps."

Older brother doesn't know what to do with the glass.

"God Almighty!"

"Well, so be it if it's so important to you," Father relents and takes the glass.

Older brother raises his, which is full to the brim. "Cheers, for our little one, the only one in the family who managed to escape our sorrowful existence."

They all reach for their glasses, except for Sister. "Nothing for me?"

"You didn't order anything." Brother looks at her. "I asked you."

"When? Am I deaf all of a sudden?"

Matej puts down his beer and gets up. "What will you have?"

"I'm not thirsty any more," Sister replies curtly.

"Cheers, son." Father raises his whiskey. "Welcome to the family circle. It hasn't changed, as you can see."

"Cheers, brother," says Brother.

Mother raises her glass of water and says: "I don't remember how many years I've dreamt of this moment."

"Well, I'm clearly not part of the family, so you won't miss me," says Sister.

She gets up, grabs her purse, and marches out the door to the reception area with her head held high. Matej puts down his beer to hurry after her.

"Let her go, she'll come back." Brother stops him. "You know what grade school teachers are like."

Matej can't hide his discomfort. "I don't want anyone to be unhappy."

"She's not unhappy," says Father. "She's just mean."

"I see gifts have already been bestowed upon you," says Brother. "Since I know you already have everything, I didn't take the trouble to enhance your wardrobe. But I did bring you something special."

He pulls a small date book out of his left jacket pocket and offers it to Matej. Matej takes it, opens and quickly leafs through it, slightly confused.

"Interesting little calendar."

"True, half the year has already passed," Brother admits, "but I didn't bring it for you to mark meetings in it."

"We also got one like that," Mother boasts. "He gets them for free at the newspaper where he works."

"Thanks, Mom," older brother replies acidly, "for even more help that wasn't really needed. Unfortunately, I can't compete with smoked hams; that's not my field."

"I didn't mean anything bad," Mother tries to explain.

"As long as we're on it," Brother quickly tries to take revenge, "isn't that the box of candies I brought you from Austria not long ago?"

Mother is about to cry; she reaches for a handkerchief. "Your father and I aren't as wealthy as you. We're both on a pension."

"Look," Matej interrupts, " I didn't expect any gifts."

"Where's that cold coming from?" Father looks around. "Isn't there any heat?"

"It's summer, Father," Brother reminds him.

"It hails in the summer." Father nods. "And hail is usually icy. And it knocks down a lot of things."

After a small pause, Brother continues, "Let me finish. I brought the date book so you would have something of mine. Because I'm proud of it. I won't hide that. It's human to be proud of your accomplishments. You know yourself. The letters you sent to Mom made her glow with pride."

"Well…" Matej is confused.

"And she glowed with pride in her son. That's right. Where would we be if we couldn't hold our heads high?"

"I've always been proud of you, too," says Mother through tears.

"Thanks, Mom, the last time I heard that—let me think— was twenty years ago? But I don't hold it against you, for heaven's sake. I'd just like to tell my younger brother without interruptions why I brought him what is at first glance an unexceptional gift."

"As I said…" Matej tries to smooth over the bad feelings.

"Look at the last page."

Matej opens the date book at the back. "Ah… quotations."

"From my columns, articles, and reports."

"Congratulations!" Matej tries to cheer him.

"Last year's date book contained quotations from world renowned figures. But this year management decided on a selection of pearls from the articles of its best journalist. A quarter million copies!"

"Unbelievable," Matej is surprised.

"Well, that's what I wanted you to have," Brother concludes.

"Thanks," replies Matej, who doesn't know what else to say.

"So you won't think that we've been sitting on our hands on the other side of the Alps, while you were enriching yourself here in England." He jerks his head towards the window.

"What is it?" Mother is visibly frightened.

"You won't believe it. It's raining!"

"That's nothing unusual for England." Matej shrugs.

Sister comes from the bar with a glass of wine.

"Cheers to you all."

She raises her glass and takes a sip. She looks at the date book in Matej's hands. "I see you've gotten the collected thoughts of your older brother."

"It's a big thing, for sure..." Matej passes the book from hand to hand.

"Now you'll finally understand everything," Sister takes another swallow.

Matej poses as if he wants to explain something. "I'm quite embarrassed, because I left my presents in London. Katarina and I decided to give them to you just before you leave."

"We don't need anything." Mother tenderly pats his shoulder.

"I'd like to buy myself one of those tall hats, a top hat," Father puts in.

"A top hat!" Sister laughs. "What will you do with it?"

"I'd like to scare neighbors."

"I don't think people wear them anymore," Matej says.

"I don't care," Father insists. "I always imagined Englishmen in top hats."

"We haven't seen any Englishmen yet," older brother reminds him. "Only foreigners work at the hotel. Even the bartender is Croatian. They opened the doors, and look what they got."

"Are you hungry, Father?" Sister asks and lets it be known that she's the one who is hungry.

"Do you mean to invite me to lunch?" Father looks at her with surprise. "That doesn't happen very often."

"No, no," Matej jumps in, "I intended to invite you. There's an Indian restaurant two hundred meters down the coast, and I thought…"

"Aren't there any others?" Sister frowns.

"I mean, I thought that we could… try something different ," Matej's tone suggests he wants to justify himself.

"Two hundred meters?" Sister objects. "It's pouring outside."

"Do any of us even have an umbrella?" Brother asks.

Mother unhappily waves a hand. "It was too big, it didn't fit in the suitcase."

"A little rain won't hurt anyone," Father says.

Matej gets up. "I'll ask at the reception desk."

"Why?" Brother stops him. "You'll pull the car up to the door, we'll cram in, you'll pull up to the restaurant door, and that's that."

Matej hesitates a little and then admits: "I came by train."

"You came by train?" older brother asks with disbelief after a long pause.

"It's faster. The roads are… Sometimes you sit in traffic for hours on end."

"And your wife?" Sister asks. "Is she coming by train, too?"

"No, she'll come by car, of course."

"Despite the traffic?" Sister gets a little testy.

"She'll come late in the evening."

"But you said she's coming in the morning," Sister remembers. "We were supposed to go to London in the morning. How do these two things go together?"

"I can call and tell her not to come," Matej makes an effort to hide his discomfort.

"Fine," Brother claps his hands, "weren't we talking about how to get to the Indian restaurant?"

"I'd as soon skip that experience," Sister decides. "Unless I can get a steak."

Older brother responds with a short laugh. "You want them to serve you a piece of the sacred cow?"

"Mom, do you want to burn your throat with hot curry?" Sister tries to find an ally.

"Not everything is hot," Matej explains. "Some things are..."

"I'll wait here," Sister decides, "they have sandwiches at the bar."

"Are they good?" Father wonders. "Because if they're good... Know what, son, I don't eat much for lunch. I rather eat my fill in the evening and then go to bed."

"I'd rather have a sandwich, too," Mother says.

"I thought that... since at home you probably don't... but anyway, we can go to an Indian restaurant tomorrow."

"You mean in London?" asks Brother.

"The Indian restaurants in London are very good."

"Because the English don't know how to cook," Brother recalls. "Without immigrants they'd be eating only potatoes."

"So then?" Sister asks impatiently. "Sandwiches?"

Older brother waves a hand. "Go order them. I have complete faith in you."

"Can *I* go?" Matej offers.

"You can go with me," Sister invites him. "I didn't change enough money."

"Charge it to the room," says older brother. "We're putting everything on the room. Didn't you tell us to put everything on the room?" He looks at Matej.

"Yes, of course." Matej nods and maintains a calm expression.

Sister goes off to the bar.

"Too bad you didn't bring Katarina," Mother says after a short silence. "I was so looking forward."

"Mother, her name is Catherine," older brother corrects her. "If she's English, she's not Katarina but Catherine."

"She's probably very beautiful." Mother looks at Matej.

"I hope not," Father says. "A beautiful woman only causes her husband trouble. I avoided that."

Mother's shoulders heave but she says nothing.

Older brother breaks the tension. "Why is it you never sent us a picture?"

"I didn't think you'd be interested," Matej tries to dodge the topic.

"I beg you," says older brother. "It would take you less than a minute to attach a photo to a message."

"Mom doesn't have internet," says Matej.

"But others do, for heaven's sake. Did you ever write us? Not once. We don't even have your e-mail address. Not to mention your phone number."

"He wrote me," Mother says emphatically.

"Handwritten letters he mailed by ordinary post, as if we were living in the nineteenth century. To think about it, I really don't understand. And he could have dropped a photo of his wife in a letter. At least for his mother."

"He doesn't want to boast," Mother defends him. "He never did."

"He didn't mind wasting words describing the house he supposedly lives in."

"A house is something else," Mother insists.

"How did you meet her, your wife?" older brother asks. "Can you at least confide that?"

"At the doctor's office," Matej replies.

"Two patients whose desire for good health ended at the altar. Romantic."

"I was the patient. She came to call me in."

"A nurse!" his older brother exclaims. "Mom, did you know your daughter-in-law is a nurse?"

"Actually she's a doctor," Matej corrects him.

"And why did you have to hide that from us?"

"An occupation is just that," Matej shrugs, "each of us does something."

"That's right," Father agrees, "but having a doctor in the family is something else."

"She could, for example, cure us of various family sicknesses," older brother says harshly. "But she'd have to be a psychiatrist, which she probably isn't."

"She works in a medical center as a general practitioner."

"The main thing is she cured you. Did you have something serious?"

"Ordinary flu," Matej says.

"Well, even a virus brings luck sometimes," Brother offers one of his witticisms. "Are you happy? You don't look it."

"What about you?" Matej hurls back fairly sharply, quite unlike him. "Happy?"

"We're talking about you, we came to visit you."

"Leave the boy alone," Father orders Brother.

"I'm only asking."

"Stop it. You're all after him. He can't even breathe."

Mother leans over to him and puts a hand on his shoulder. "Calm down."

Older brother heads for the door. "If I can't talk with my own brother…"

At that moment Sister and a waiter come through the door with two sandwich platters.

"Make room," Sister orders.

Mother and Brother pick things off the table and move them to the next one. Sister and the waiter unload the platters. Sister puts her purse on the floor by a chair.

"Would you like something more to drink?" the waiter asks in Croatian.

Older brother glances at the glasses. "We're fine for now."

The waiter leaves.

"What language is he talking?" his father asks, surprised.

"Croatian," says Brother. "We're in Split, that's the Adriatic out there. We're having *čevapčiči* for dinner."

"Before he was talking English with me," Father insists.

"He clearly took you for an Englishman," Brother gives a short laugh.

"Are you making fun of me?" Father looks at him sharply.

"No, Father, of the waiter."

"Why him? He has to earn a living somehow."

"You're right, Father, I won't make fun of waiters anymore. Alright?"

Mother offers Father a sandwich. "Here, eat."

The others reach for sandwiches, too, and start eating. They look at each other to see who will be the first to comment.

"I've never had a sandwich with cucumbers," Mother speaks up.

"When the British Empire was at the height of its power, they ate these kind of sandwiches at afternoon parties," says Matej.

"Not surprising the empire collapsed," observes Sister.

"Let's not make fun of Brits," says Brother, "after all, now we have one in the family. Did you finish studying anything since you hung it all up at home?"

"Of course." Matej nods.

"Oxford? Cambridge?"

"The London School of Economics."

"Are you joking?" older brother shows surprise with a thrust of his head. "And all that in five years!"

"Then you're an economist," Sister says. "Just like my husband!"

"No offence, Sis, but the London School of Economics is far from the institution where your husband got his diploma. And you finished," he turns to Matej, "you graduated?"

"Of course," Matej replies.

"With a degree like that, the doors of the highest positions in business must be wide open to you. Have you passed through any of them?"

"Whatever turns up," Matej shrugs modestly. "At the moment I work for a large international company. Public opinion research."

"Gallup?" asks his older brother.

"Something like that."

"As a director?"

"Program director."

"You hear that, Mom?" Brother exclaims. "Your youngest son is a director! Who would have thought!"

"He was very bright even in high school," Mother boasts.

"That's right," Sister puts in. "Every year he passed at least three do-over exams. And he repeated only one grade."

Her words clearly hurt her mother a great deal. "He wasn't feeling well then. He was sick."

"How much do you earn?" Sister wants to know. "For comparison's sake."

Matej shakes his head. "In England, that's considered an impolite question."

"Five times more than your husband, I'd say," Brother answers. "The only problem is that he disappointed Father."

"What are you saying?" Father looks at him.

Older brother doesn't stop. "Father always wanted one of us to share his occupation."

"Since when is selling vegetables an occupation?" Sister laughs.

"We've always been greengrocers," says Brother. "Father, grandfather, great-grandfather. We sold vitamins and good health."

"I liked meat best ever since I was small," Father looks at him confrontationally. He pulls a paper package out of his left jacket pocket and starts to unwrap it.

"Oh, not salami again, Father!" Sister is appalled. "Not here!"

"It's not like I stole it," says Father and takes a big piece of fatty homemade salami out of the paper.

"Someone can come in at any minute!"

"Give him his pleasure," says Mother. "You know he never goes anywhere without homemade salami."

"It's always good to have a reserve." Father nods.

"To tell the truth, I'm really sorry I don't have one, too," says Brother and swallows the last piece of sandwich.

"I can order another round," Matej gets up.

"Forget the sandwiches, son," says Father. "Try this."

He cuts off a piece of salami with a pocket knife and offers it to Matej.

"Thanks, I'd rather not, Father."

"That's why you're so pale. Because you don't eat salami."

Father puts a piece in his mouth and chews.

"Father," says Sister, "you've lost your senses in old age."

"On the contrary," Father assumes a wise pose and keeps talking while he's chewing. "Old age is a time of renewal. New ideas come to mind. You know you'll soon die, so you don't care if you make a fool of yourself. You see more when you're old."

"Your vision improves?" his daughter is surprised.

"What?" Father leans towards her.

"Or your hearing?"

Father decides to ignore her. "Son, can I tell you something?" He puts the salami and knife on the table and pulls out his pocket watch.

"Take a look at this. It's always stopping. A month or so ago your mother dragged me to the doctor. And what happens? I pull out my watch in the waiting room to check how long we've been there. Of course, it stopped. I look at the wall clock in the waiting room. I see it shows 11:30. And my watch is showing 11:30, too! Even though it stopped."

"Interesting coincidence," Matej nods politely.

"But a week later the same thing happens. Not at 11:30 but at 11:45. And a third time a week later, at 11:55. Three times in two weeks, son, I reached for my watch exactly twelve hours after it had stopped."

"I try to convince him," says Mother, "to get rid of the watch. But he doesn't want to listen."

"Matej will buy you a new one," Brother says. "An English one."

"Well, nowadays watches are the same all over," says Matej as if he's not excited about the idea.

"Listen, son." Father leans towards Matej. "Your mother thinks that when it happens a fourth time, the watch will show exactly 12:00. And that, she says, will be my final hour."

"I didn't say that," Mother firmly declares.

"You did."

"All I said was that such signs can also mean something bad."

"Why? Doesn't a man's final hour come sooner or later? Why should I be an exception? I lived honorably and have the right to die."

"Oh, stop, please." Mother reaches for her handkerchief.

"I know you'll be bored without me..." Father tries to continue, and he would have, had Sister not interrupted.

"Father, doesn't it seem to you that you said what you wanted?"

"No," Father stubbornly persists.

"You told us you have a worthless watch, so can we change the topic?"

"I'm talking with my youngest son, if you didn't notice," Father raises his voice a little.

"For that very reason," Brother interjects. "I doubt he's interested in a retired fruit and vegetable vendor's metaphysical ponderings."

Father turns to Matej. "Am I boring you, son?"

"Not at all, Father," Matej remains polite throughout.

Mother unobtrusively wipes her tears. "I almost fell asleep."

"It's time for a short rest, Mom," Sister says. "We got up early. And this rich lunch besides..."

"You wanted the sandwiches," Brother rebukes her.

"Come on, Mom, let me help you," Sister says.

Mother pushes her away and gets up. "I'll do it myself."

"Father, are you going to rest?" Brother asks.

"You go ahead," says Father. "I'd like to be alone with my son."

Everyone starts moving towards the door to the reception area.

"Don't keep boring him with that watch," Sister says.

"Allow *me* to decide how to bore him." Father looks at her.

"Let's go," says Brother.

Mother stops by Matej, reaches out a hand, and caresses his face. "My little boy."

They leave, first Brother, then Mother, then Sister.

A short silence. Then Father turns to Matej. "Son?"

"Father?"

"Would you be so kind as to help your father to his feet?"

"Of course, Father."

He jumps up and helps his father out of the chair. Father sways a little, then straightens up.

"If I sit too long, I loose my sense of balance. You don't have that problem?"

"Not yet."

"Now let's go over there to the window. I'd like to ask you something."

He slowly shuffles to the window. Matej accompanies him. Father stumbles. Matej catches him.

"Now you see what happens to a person who lives too long," says Father with a hint of bitterness.

"You're holding up well, Father. Very well."

They stop in front of the window. "What's that out there? A desert or a big cloud?"

"Where, Father?"

"Out there. Don't you see the big shadow spreading all over?"

"You mean the sea?"

"Is that what the sea looks like?" Father is surprised.

"You must have seen the sea at least once in your life, Father!"

"I don't recall having seen it. Where's the water?"

"All of that is water."

"I thought the sea would be more watery. Like a big lake. It's strange how much a person mistakenly imagines."

"Almost everything, Father." Matej nods. "Almost everything."

Father reaches into his pocket and asks secretively: "Would you like a piece of salami now that we're alone?"

"Not really, Father."

"You've become too much of a gentleman," says Father and shoves the package with salami back into his pocket.

"No, not all…"

"That's right," Father interrupts him. "There's nothing wrong with going abroad, becoming a gentleman." He looks sharply at Matej. "You've come to my funeral, no?"

"I don't understand." Matej is visibly confused.

"You are wearing a black tie."

"Father, I had an important meeting…"

"Black ties are for funerals."

"I grabbed the first one I put my hands on when I opened the dresser!"

"All the same."

"Father…"

"It's nice at least someone dressed up for my funeral. Because the others…"

He waves a hand.

"Father, don't take offence, but I want to ask you something. The bitterness, rudeness, those constant little quarrels among you. I don't remember it being that way when I was at home."

"But you weren't at home. You went to Ljubljana right after high school and didn't visit even at Christmas. As if you weren't one of us."

"Father, I was in school."

"You found time for grandma."

"How is grandma?"

"Ask Mom. She's the only one who is in touch with her."

"I doesn't seem right that you're always quarreling."

Father is clearly surprised and takes some time to answer.

"There's a lot of tension in every family. It has to be diffused. We do it by offending one another. How about you?"

"Me?"

"How do you get rid of tension?"

Matej searches for a suitable answer. "I don't even know if there is any."

"Then one day it will tear you to pieces. You know that, don't you?"

"Maybe that's true," Matej admits.

"I was the same when I was your age."

"That's hard to believe," says Matej.

"Calm on the outside but like a storm inside. And then one day it broke. So as not to kill someone or grab a rope, I went to the forest and cursed the trees for two hours. Good thing firs don't have ears. I go cold when I remember what all I threw at their bark and needles. But I calmed down. When I came out of the forest, I was a different person."

"Really?" Matej asks almost hopefully.

"For ten years I went to the forest to curse the trees," Father goes on. "Then it didn't work anymore. And I started cursing customers. I had a sharp remark to go with every head of cabbage or lettuce, every bunch of carrots, and every apple or pear."

"And... it worked?" Matej asks.

"It did, for me. Not for the customers. When I noticed their numbers dwindling I became polite again. And I started cursing your mother. And she me. I won't tell you what all the air we breathed heard. And you mother has talent: she could return a double dose of what she got!"

"I didn't notice that when I was still at home."

"We did it secretly. You were children. Especially you. Your older brother was already on his own. But your sister—she soon joined the cursing. But she took it seriously. Your sister doesn't have any imagination."

"Well…," Matej objects but doesn't know how to continue.

"It's this way, son. At least let me explain." He bends over to Matej and almost whispers in his ear: "Your mother and father love each other."

"I'm very happy to hear that," Matej gives a sigh of relief.

"But we also loved each other when it seemed we couldn't stand each other. Your sister often asked when we would part. It didn't even occur to us."

"It always seemed to me," says Matej, "that… you didn't hate each other but in fact… couldn't stand each other."

"We can't stand each other now. What about you?"

"Me?" asks Matej, who doesn't know exactly what Father has in mind.

"How is it with your friendship?"

"You mean… do I have many friends?"

"No, son. I'm interested in whether you've realized you're not alone."

Now Matej understands even less.

"That there are two inside you. The one who hopes, and the one who's disappointed when his hopes don't come true."

"Doesn't all that happen to me?"

"No," says Father, "it happens to two people."

"What do you mean?"

"The two people we carry inside. One flies above the clouds, and the other is buried in the ground up to his neck. Isn't that you? You were once. We had to help you get better. Did you forget?"

Matej bows his head. "No, Father."

"It's very important that the two you have inside are on good terms."

"Maybe that's true."

"As long as they're friends, everything is fine. The one who is disappointed when things go wrong can prevent the other one, who hopes, from hoping too much. And he prevents the first one from being distraught if something goes wrong. And so they steer things more or less successfully."

"More or less." Matej nods.

"So, my son, take care of that friendship."

"Thanks, Father. For the advice."

"I hope it's not too late." Father looks sharply at Matej.

"I don't think so."

"Are you sure?"

"Don't worry, Father."

"Your mother couldn't sleep for five years. She was afraid you would do something to yourself. She shuddered every time the phone rang."

"She shouldn't have been afraid."

"No?"

"Of course not, and you should have told her so."

Father looks at him. "Would you like to tell me something, son? Everything will remain between us."

"Will it?" Matej finally asks.

"Who did you trust more when you were small? Your mother or me?"

"You, I think," says Matej, not to disappoint him.

"Was I worthy of your trust?" Father wants to know.

Matej takes a breath. "The thing is... things aren't exactly as they appear."

"That was clear to me the minute you came in the door."

"Things are very complicated."

"Problems with you wife."

"No, Katarina is a blessing I don't even deserve."

"Did you confide to her what you'd like to confide to me?"

"No, Father. And that's part of the problem. That I can't confide it to her."

"Why not?"

For a moment, Matej steps closer to the window and presses his forehead to the glass. "I'm afraid you won't be proud of me, Father."

"Would you like me to be proud of you?"

Matej removes his forehead from the glass. "I want you to think all the best about me. But when I tell you what I think I have to, that will no longer be possible."

"You never know."

"Shall we sit down?" Matej motions to the closest table with chairs.

"I'd rather stand and look at the fog out there, which you say is the sea."

"Right. I'll start from when I left for England..."

At that moment Brother comes through the door with a glass of wine in his hand. "Ah, you're here. I was starting to think you went swimming."

"What do you want?" Father looks at him severely.

"A few words with my younger brother. If I may. If Father permits. After all these years of not having seen him."

Father bows his head and slowly sets off for the exit. "I'll go rest for a while."

Matej tries to detain him. "Father…"

"There will still be time, son."

"Can I see you to your room?"

"No need. It's on the ground floor, room seven. Through the reception area and past the bar. Twenty-five steps. I counted them on the way here."

He goes out the door surprisingly nimbly.

Matej and his older brother remain alone. A moment of barely perceptible awkwardness hangs over them.

"Did I interrupt something important?"

"Only a conversation with Father after five years," Matej replies.

"Excuse me, the five years of silence between you isn't my fault."

"Surely not," Matej admits.

"Or the five years of silence between us. You had my address, you knew where I work, and you had my telephone number and e-mail address…"

"Yes, dear brother, all that is true. Anything else?"

"Look," his older brother walks around him. "Have you ever thought of coming back to Slovenia?"

"Why?"

"Excuse me if I'm brutally frank, but you're not happy here."

"Oh, come on," Matej turns his back on him. "Happiness, come on. That's the kind of thing they talk about in romances for women."

"There is something you lack. Not so much self-confidence, it seems to me, but more, I'd say, self-respect."

"Really?" Matej whirls back towards him. "And you?"

"What do you mean by that?"

"Do you remember the day twenty years ago? I was a little boy, living with our parents in the village. You came on one of your rare visits, a gentleman from the city."

"And?" Brother demands.

"When you were saying good-bye, you gave me a hundred tolars."

"That was a lot of money back then."

"Later I found out that you gave the neighbor's boy two hundred tolars."

"He was two years older than you."

"But I was your brother."

"Listen," Brother takes a breath after a pause. "You're insulting me."

"Now, of course, I understand why you did that."

"Then you understand more than I do."

"Your image was safe with me. A hundred tolars seemed to you enough to ensure that. With the neighbor, you had to *create* the image of a generous gentleman from the city. The initial investment had to be bigger."

"What the hell are you talking about? Some tolars? After twenty years? Are you normal? You're not, because you never were. I came here to talk with you like an intelligent, grown-up person about an important matter..."

"That requires two."

"But you don't even listen to me!"

"Why are you so aggressive?"

"I'm only defending myself. I came here to talk with you about an important matter, but you..."

"Maybe this isn't the best time."

Mother comes through the door. Older brother catches sight of her. "Maybe not."

"Mom," Matej turns to her. "Why aren't you resting?"

"There will be time to rest during the long night ahead."

"You used to tell me that when I was ten years old."

"Well, then you know how close it is."

Older brother empties his glass. "I'm going to borrow an umbrella."

"Where are you going?" Mother is surprised.

"Across the street, to the sea. I could use some fresh air," he says pointedly.

Mother sinks into the closest chair. Matej sits down cautiously. Mother is looking at him.

"What's wrong, son?"

"Nothing really."

"You're not happy, are you?"

"Why does everyone…" Matej gets excited but immediately calms down. "Of course I am."

"You don't even believe it yourself."

"The main thing is that that you're here and we're seeing each other."

"You're unhappy because you don't have a child?" Mother asks.

Matej laughs darkly. "Absolutely not."

"You don't plan on having any?"

"Women have children, Mom."

"Give me your hand."

Matej slowly unclenches his hand. His mother takes it and softly presses it. "Are you still my little boy?"

Matej removes his hand. "I don't know, Mom. Am I?"

"Your brother and sister wouldn't care if your father and I died today. Right here, in this hotel. They would even be happy. They could unload the funeral expenses on you."

"Mom, what are you saying?"

Mother wipes away the tears with the side of her hand.

"You have no idea…"

"Don't cry, please."

"That's what your sister tells me all the time. 'You have no right to complain,' she tells me three times a day. You're warm, I bring you food, you're not bored, you can watch TV, and when you're tired of it, you can nap."

"But Mom... in a way she's right."

"When your brother comes to visit, which is twice a year, he never stays more than a few minutes. And he looks at us as if we're stealing the most precious minutes of his life."

"He's obviously very busy."

"Just one thought has comforted me all these years. That you would come back and take care of us. As you often promised in your letters."

"Mom, I have a wife."

"She's welcome, too."

"And what would she do there?"

"To begin with, she could have a child. While I still have enough strength to help her."

"Mom, Katarina is an independent woman who thinks for herself."

His mother leans over to Matej and without warning whispers in his ear: "They'd like to have the house."

Matej doesn't understand. "What do you mean by that?"

"They'd like to sell it and split the money. And they'd stick your father and me in an old age home."

"You must be mistaken."

"Or in your sister's attic. Where we couldn't move. Because your father couldn't make it down the steps, and I would fear running into the Bigmouth your sister calls a husband."

"Mom... they're married, they have children, how could they..."

"I'll never admit he's her husband. She deserves something better, although she's never been good to me."

"And what does Father say?"

"Your father doesn't know. And don't you tell him!"

"Mom, maybe my sister really can't show her feelings, but in the end she would always want what's best for you two."

"Oh, Matej..." His mother reaches out and caresses him. "It's as if life hasn't touched you."

Matej laughs bitterly. "Has it ever!"

"Why are you so secretive? You said more in your letters."

"It's easier in letters."

"Trust me. What's bothering you?"

"My brother and sister have already hurt you enough."

"Problems with Katarina, right? That's why she didn't come."

"There are no problems with her."

"Give me your hand, my son."

Matej stretches out his hand again, and his mother presses it.

Matej removes his hand. "No one can help me."

"Is it that again? What you were treated for?"

"Something like that. But worse."

His mother crosses herself. "You're not serious."

"I'm losing a friend, Mom."

"Is he sick?"

"Incurable."

"My poor son. I'm so sorry."

"I am, too, Mom. I am, too."

"Do you still pray sometimes?"

"Not very often."

"How fast time passes! It seems only yesterday I was teaching you the Our Father and Hail Mary."

"Sometimes it's even too late for prayers."

"Never, my son. Not even on your death bed."

"You have to have faith for that. But I lost it. Along with other baggage that got too heavy."

126

"Once you have it, you never lose faith. It just fades. Prayer awakens it."

"I'm afraid that's a fairytale, Mom."

"Who beat such stupid things into your head? Katarina? I thought so."

"Mom…"

"Pray with me. Don't be ashamed."

"I ask you…"

Mother gets up from her chair slowly. "We'll kneel down and pray."

"Someone can come in at any moment."

"So can death. Will you be ashamed then, too?"

"Oh, Mom…"

"Let's, we'll pray quickly, as long as we're alone." She kneels by the chair. "Come here."

"Only for your sake, Mom." Matej takes a breath and kneels down next to her with obvious resistance.

"For your sake, my son," his mother corrects him. "For your friend who's dying."

She starts to pray. "Our Father, who art in heaven…"

Matej repeats after her: "Our Father, who art in heaven…"

"Thy kingdom come…"

Matej suddenly starts to laugh. Mother looks at him, stunned. His laughter changes to moaning and then to crying. Matej covers his face with his hands, bends over almost to the floor, and shakes with sobs.

Sister and Brother come in. They stop and look at the scene in bewilderment.

His mother notices them. She puts a hand on Matej's back.

Matej gets up and stops crying. He wipes his eyes with his jacket sleeve. He goes to the window and stares out. A tortured silence. Mother gets up and sits down again.

"Are you alright, Mom?" Sister asks.

"I am. Matej is the one who isn't. His best friend is dying."

Sister lets out a sigh. "That's the reason..."

"I'm sorry, brother," Brother says. "I didn't know."

That minute Father comes in and slowly, leaning on a cane, wavers towards the chair he was sitting in before. He sinks into it.

"So," he says decisively. "And now I'm not moving from here until we go to that damned London."

"Please don't make trouble," Mother tries to calm him.

"Bedbugs bit me. I'm itching all over. I want to meet my son's wife. I want to see where and how he lives. Isn't that why we came? Then I want to go home, to my own bed."

"You're not the only one, Father," Sister says.

"Let's vote on it." Brother moves to the middle of the bar. "I suggest we pay the bill, call a taxi, go to the train station, and leave for London. Who's for it?"

He raises his hand. So does Sister. They look at Father.

"I said what I think."

Older brother looks at Mother.

"Matej will decide when we go," Mother says.

Matej turns around. "I can't get her on the phone!" His voice still has the sound of crying. "I'm calling and calling, but she doesn't answer! She obviously has an urgent case. I'm going to London right now, and I'll come back tomorrow with a car."

"Why, if we can go to London together?" Brother shakes his head as if he no longer understands any of it.

"But not on the train," Matej insists. "It would be to stressful for Father and Mother. Katarina and I will drive you to London. Tomorrow morning."

He heads for the exit.

"What kind of car does she have?" Brother hollers after him. "A mini-van? There are six of us."

"Mom, tell him that's nonsense," Sister says.

Mother remains calm. "He knows what he's doing."

Then she leaves. There's a short silence.

"One more night with the bedbugs, Father," Sister adds.

"Something isn't right," says Brother. "Something's not right about this."

The bar is empty. Katarina enters and looks around the room. She walks to the window. She opens her purse, takes out a pack of cigarettes, and lights one. She smokes, staring out the window.

Older brother comes in. He approaches her slowly. Katarina turns and looks at him, then stares out the window again.

"Not a nice day," Brother says with a noticeable foreign accent.

"No," Katarina answers, "quite a horrible day."

"In my country we would say *posran dan*."

"Very *posran*," Katarina agrees.

"Do you speak Slovene?" Brother replies, stunned.

"Don't you think that's normal for a Slovene?" Katarina blows smoke at him.

"It didn't seem possible that someone else from Slovenia could be here."

"I live in England," says Katarina.

"And what brings you to this famous hotel?" Brother asks.

"I have to meet someone."

"Business, personal?" Brother gets just a little pushy.

"What about you?" Katarina returns the question.

"Oh, we came to visit a relative in London. But, God knows why, we are sitting around in Brighton."

"And the weather besides," Katarina adds.

"Have you been in England long?"

"Maybe too long," Katarina deflects the question.

"And what do you do, if I may ask?"

"Nothing special."

"Interesting occupation. First I've heard of it."

"Nothing special is the occupation," Katarina corrects him, "of a lot of people. In particular of the half million of those who came to England with other dreams."

"The fateful attraction of the West." Brother nods. "The greatest folly of all time."

"You think so?" Katarina looks at him.

"Of course. Everything is ideal on the TV screen, but when you get here, you find yourself in a line for a hot lunch."

"Without a doubt that happens. But I'm talking about the ones who nonetheless accomplished something but didn't fulfill their dreams."

"Although that false shimmer didn't hook many Slovenes," Brother gives his opinion. "I think you can count those on the fingers of two hands."

"I'm one of those fingers," Katarina says. "And my husband is another."

"And my brother a third," Brother adds.

"Really?" Katarina suddenly shows interest. "You have a brother in England?"

"Younger one. He didn't visit us for five years. Which is, to put it mildly, very unusual. So we decided to visit him instead."

"Does he work in this hotel?"

"No way!" The question seems to irk Brother. "He wanted us to stay by the sea the first day, and then we were supposed to go to London together. His wife lives there. What does your husband do?"

"He sells fruits and vegetables in a poor part of London."

"What a coincidence! That's what my brother should be doing. At least that was our father's desire. Because all his life he, too, sold fruits and vegetables."

"And what... does... your brother do?" Katarina asks cautiously.

"Director of an international corporation. He graduated from the London School of Economics."

"You're probably proud of him," Katarina says with a grain of bitterness. "The whole family."

"Mother for certain. Father, too, although he doesn't show it. What's wrong is that my brother is not at all proud of himself."

"Too modest?"

"Embittered. A cloud of depression has accompanied him his entire life. He always wanted more than he was capable of achieving."

"What did he want to achieve?"

"Fame. Prominence. He wanted people to notice and respect him. He wanted to be someone special, not one of many. That's why he sees himself as a failure. He lives in a large house in the center of London, his wife is a doctor, and he secretly thinks about parting with the world which has so wronged him."

"Did he say that?" Katarina asks.

"He didn't say it, but you can see it in his eyes."

"I wanted to be a doctor, too." Katarina admits.

"And?"

"I managed to finish nursing school. I work as a nursing aide in the gerontology department."

"There's nothing wrong with that," says Brother. "You're doing socially useful work."

"Are you kidding?"

"Why? We can't all be doctors. At least you bring some beauty, freshness, and happiness into old people's lives."

"You speak well," Katarina praises him with a hint of irony. "You obviously fulfilled your dreams."

"Far from it." Brother waves a hand.

"I think you're at least a university professor."

"Do I act so boring?"

"Self-assured." Katarina looks him over from head to toe. "As if no one can harm you in any way."

"That might be right," Brother says, flattered. "In fact, I'm something that doesn't rank high on the social ladder. A journalist."

"There are also stars among journalists."

"Well, maybe I'm one of them." Brother seizes the opportunity. "But let's drop that."

"My husband's older brother is a university professor," says Katarina. She tries to give the impression that she's proud of that. "He teaches nuclear physics."

"Congratulations. What's his name? Maybe I even know him."

"Let's leave names aside," says Katarina. "In general, everyone in my husband's family is an important person. His father was a diplomat. An ambassador in Berlin, Madrid, and Cairo. He's retired now. His mother was a translator from Greek and Latin, and she speaks thirteen languages. Not to mention his sister, who married an Australian and is now flying a war plane in the Australian air force."

Older brother can't help but be surprised. "And a young man from such a family is selling fruits and vegetables?"

"Now you know why he feels that he's wasted his life."

"But, don't be offended," Brother says, "in view of everything you told me, he really did waste his life. I can't imagine how he managed that."

"Neither can he."

"Tell me more," Brother tries to encourage her.

"I don't want to bore you."

"No, really, I feel as if I have a chance here to get some great material to analyze a problem that highlights an essential failing of contemporary society."

Katarina shrugs. "I don't know what society has to do with it."

"Much more than you think."

"Most of all I'm afraid of losing my husband."

"Are you afraid he'll leave you?"

"I'm afraid he'll do something."

"Why?"

"He can't reconcile himself to the fact that he slipped up so bad in life. He's so unhappy that he's immobilized from bitterness. He goes to a psychiatrist, takes some pills, but to no effect."

"I can imagine how you feel." Brother nods.

"'Mr. Nobody,'" he calls himself.

"But the reasons, where are the reasons?"

"He expected too much."

"From himself or from the world?"

"From both. Just like your brother, as you said before. My husband also wanted that the world would respect and admire him."

"What did he want to become?"

"Anything, as long as he could feel himself the equal of his parents. And brother. And sister. Not the same, but something more. To rise above them. Only then would he be happy."

"Don't they like him?"

"I'm sure they did. Before he left home. Although he never talked with me about them. Now he doesn't want me to meet them. He's ashamed."

"But," says Brother, "he must have had something concrete in mind, you can't find fame on the sidewalk like a lost coin."

"He was too impatient. Every time something new would grab his interest."

"The role of a misunderstood genius is very attractive."

"The may be true," Katarina nods. "But my husband suffers. He's had depression his entire life."

"I'm not surprised," Brother says. "We live in a system that in the interests of its own survival promotes the illusion that all is possible. That achieving prominence, riches, and status is no more difficult that changing the TV channel."

"I don't think society ruined my husband," says Katarina. "His parents did. He's competing with them, he wants to win against them."

"Had he not set that as his goal, he would have won a long time ago."

"I'd like to meet them. They have the answer. They have the solution."

"You're not in contact?" Older brother is surprised.

"My husband would do anything to prevent me from ever meeting them. I think he's just as ashamed of me as of his failures."

"Go visit them. After all, he doesn't have to know."

"In the end, I won't have a choice." She reaches for her purse and heads for the door.

"Are you in a hurry? We could have a drink."

"I don't drink."

"Come on."

"I overdid it in my time. Now I'm doing penance. I've given up all those pleasures."

"I hope not absolutely everything."

"Everything, so to speak."

"And what does your husband have to say about that?"

"He's glad. He prefers boys."

"Come on. And despite that you stay with him?"

"There are relations that go deeper than sex. They're called friendship."

"Oh," says Brother. "I didn't know."

"I'm going now. My husband is coming from London. I have to wait for him at the train station."

"Well, then we'll surely see each other again."

"Almost certainly," Katarina answers.

Father, Mother, and Sister come in. They stop in surprise. Katarina studies them. They study her.

"The lady is Slovene, too," Brother explains.

"Well there's no one else in this hotel," says Father. "Croatians and Slovenes."

"I think the owner is from our part of the world as well," Katarina explains.

The waiter brings a platter with four cups of instant coffee and puts it on the table.

"Please," he says and goes off.

"Who ordered this?" his older brother asks.

"I did," says Sister.

"You know I don't drink coffee. Will you join us?" He looks at Katarina.

"Sorry, I'm in a hurry."

"If we don't happen to see each other, I'd like to give you a little something in remembrance of our meeting." Older brother pulls a little calendar out of his pocket. "I know that half the year is already past, but on the last pages you have a selection of the best quotations from my newspaper pieces. Maybe you'll find some of them entertaining."

Katarina takes the calendar and shoves it in her purse. "Thanks."

"And maybe one will be of use, you never know," Brother adds.

Katarina laughs politely and leaves. The family members confusedly stare after her for a while.

"She looks nice," Father notes.

Mother opens her purse, gets out Father's glasses, and offers them to him. "Here, so you will see better."

"Look at her, even at that age she's jealous," Father jokes.

Mother puts the glasses back in her purse without a word.

"Father, the coffee is dripping on your beard," says Sister.

"What?" Father leans towards her and bends an ear.

"Leave him alone," says Mother, "you can see he doesn't have any teeth."

"I'd like to go home," Father announces and leans back.

"You're not the only one, Father," Sister agrees.

"But those fried eggs were good." Father chomps. "The sausages, too. And the bacon, that was the best."

"English breakfast," says Brother. "The one thing they do well."

"Everything was too fatty," Sister disagrees.

"Where did Matej go?" Mother wants to know.

"He went to London for his wife," older brother remembers. "Didn't he say they would come with the first train?"

"By car," Sister says emphatically. "They'll come by car, he said."

Mother looks for her handkerchief. "I'm so afraid."

"Of what, Mom?" Brother asks.

"Didn't you see how sad he is? I couldn't sleep all night."

"I didn't either," says Brother. "I've slept in some lousy hotels, but here they've raised discomfort to the level of an art."

"I think he's terribly unhappy," Mother continues.

"I don't remember him being any different," says Brother. "Clammed up, seemingly calm, not wanting you to come too close. I often thought he might be gay."

"Don't say stupid things," Mother scolds him. "You never liked him."

"And you were in love with him. That's fateful for a child, especially for a boy, because later he can't become independent."

Sister turns to Father. "Why are you so pensive?"

"I'm thinking," Father says, "why you can't simply dream up a child. Because then I would have dreamt up different ones."

"It's good," Brother replies acidly, "that children can't dream up their parents. Because then both of you might not exist."

"Come on, control yourself a little, what's wrong with you?" Sister attacks him.

"All my life I've been hearing I have to be different." Brother gets excited. "Not only from my parents, but from their children, too. Nobody says what I'm supposed to be like, just not like I am."

"Apologize to Father," Sister insists.

"Sorry, Father, that my presence in the world shames you."

"That's not what I meant," says Father, visibly hurt.

"You've caused Mom to cry." Sister looks sharply at Brother.

Mother blows her nose and wipes the tears. "I'm worried about Matej. You two will be okay. But he was always living on the edge."

"The seemingly weak are the strongest," Brother says.

"What do you mean?" Sister demands.

"You can break up the soil if you step on it, but not mud. Soft and slimy as it is, it submissively encircles your shoes."

"How can you talk about your brother like that?!"

Suddenly Matej comes through the door.

Mother crosses herself and demands almost accusingly: "Where were you?"

Matej comes closer, takes a long box wrapped in paper from a plastic bag and offers it to Father. "For you, Father."

"For me?"

"A gift," Matej explains.

"He bought you a new watch," Sister guesses.

"But I have a watch," Father objects.

"A watch that works," says Matej.

"Is it a pocket watch?" Father wants to know.

"A wristwatch," says Matej. "There are hardly any pocket watches anymore."

"I never wore a wristwatch. I have arthritic fingers. I would need half a day to wind it."

"Take it," Mother almost commands him. "It's not right to turn down a gift."

"I'm not turning down a gift, it's just that I don't want a wristwatch."

Matej handles the box. "Take it just the same, Father. Maybe you'll change your mind."

"I'm not going to start looking at a watch again to see if I'm late. Then I'll always be in a hurry."

Matej offers the watch to Mother. "Will you take it?"

Mother takes the watch and puts it in her purse. She can no longer hide her anger and leans towards Father.

"You could have taken it to make your son happy. You haven't seen him for five years! But no, your stubbornness is more important than his feelings."

"Give me the watch." Father reaches out.

"Oh, for heaven's sake." Brother gets excited. "We're not in kindergarten! Remember, after all, why we've come."

"That's right, when are we leaving?"

Everyone looks at Matej. Matej hesitates.

"Katarina is coming after lunch."

"Well, that's what I expected," Brother says.

"She can't get out of the emergency room any earlier. We could go for a walk. To the pier. So Father can see the ocean."

"He'll freeze in this weather," Sister objects.

"It stopped raining a while ago," says Matej.

"But it's really cold outside," Mother agrees. "I opened the window to air the room. I closed it right away."

"That's why the English are so cold," says Sister. "Because of the weather."

"They're cold?" Matej is surprised.

"Reserved. In the family and with each other. I read it somewhere. They can't stand each other, parents hate their children, and children despise their parents and each other."

There are a few moments of tortured silence.

"In general, the weather is pleasant and warm," Matej finally speaks up.

Older brother moves to the middle of the bar. It's obvious he's preparing something to make an impression. "I'd like to say something. What we're experiencing on account of our youngest, our parents' favorite, whom we've come to visit after five years, not on *his* but on our initiative, only so that his parents, who have always exalted him to the heavens, can finally see the woman with whom he's made a family nest, what we're experiencing thanks to the graduate of the best school of economics in the world who is standing here and trying his utmost to pretend he doesn't know what this is all about, is, to put it mildly, the greatest disgrace for a family that deserves at least the Slovene if not the world prize for the number of disgraces…"

"Can you please stop?" Mother interrupts him.

"No, because I'm boiling over!"

"If I had a pistol right now, I would shoot all of you," says Father.

"Don't you see what's happening?" Brother continues. "We'll never meet his wife. She's probably so ugly he's ashamed of her. If she's not ugly, she's dumb. And if she's not dumb, he doesn't want to introduce her to us, because he's ashamed of *us*."

"Of you," says Father. "He doesn't have to be ashamed of others."

"I'll call her again," Matej gets up. "Maybe she can cancel urgent appointments and come two hours earlier."

He goes out the door to the bar, his head hanging.

There's a short silence. Mother wipes away tears. She sniffles a few times.

"Can't you control yourself?" Sister hisses into brother's ear. "You won't accomplish anything with that sarcasm of yours."

"Accomplish what?" asks Mother, whose hearing is obviously better than Sister assumed.

A moment of silence.

"What's to accomplish is for Matej to be happy about our visit," Sister finally says.

Mother replies: " If I were him, I could hardly wait for us to leave."

"His wish will be fulfilled no later than the day after tomorrow, when this memorable trip will be over," says Brother. "From Gatwick to Brighton, from Brighton to Gatwick and back home. All the while stuck in a hotel that the English ought to be ashamed of. Does someone have a camera so we can document this dive for the family album?"

Mother gets up and grabs her purse. "I'm going to my room to crawl under the blanket. I like it best there."

Several moments of silence follow her departure.

"You're not going, Father?" Sister asks. "With Mom to the room?"

"No, because I'm watching the clock on the wall."

Sister gets up and reaches for her purse. "I'm going to walk around the town a little. To see what kind of stores there are. Are you going with me?" she winks at older brother.

"It's not like you're going to get lost."

"We should talk about a few things," she lowers her voice a little.

"But that's what we're doing. We know what we're doing."

"We'll need to find an opportunity."

"I'll find it sooner if we're not all together all the time," says Brother.

Sister leaves. Older brother hesitates for a moment. Then he heads to the exit.

"And where are you going?" asks Father.

"To my room, Father. Have to make some notes. Or would you rather I stay with you?"

"God forbid," Father sends him off.

Older brother leaves. Father sits and stares at the clock on the wall.

The waiter comes in with a platter and starts to pick up the cups. Father looks at him.

"You want a drink?" the waiter asks.

"*Trinken? Ja, ich woll etwas trinken. Viski.*" He holds up three fingers. "*Dreimal.*"

"Whiskey?" the waiter is surprised.

"Don't you understand?" Father asks in Slovene.

"Naturally I understand," the waiter answers.

"Why didn't you stay in Dalmatia? At least it's warm there."

The waiter leaves without a word. Father once again stares at the wall clock. He pulls out his pocket watch and compares the times.

Matej enters and comes up to him. "Are you alright, Father?"

"I'm watching the wall clock," Father replies, as if wanting to convey something important to him.

"It's almost twelve," says Matej.

"In two minutes. I took mine, the one that doesn't work, out of my pocket three minutes ago. It was dead, of course, but it showed the same time as the one on the wall. And then, you won't believe it, it started working! Look."

He holds the watch out to Matej. "This one will also show twelve in two minutes."

He puts away the pocket watch and starts getting up from his chair. Matej hurries to help him.

"I'm going to the room."

"Are you tired?"

"Best of luck, son. I'm glad that I saw you after these long years."

"Father..."

"The only thing I regret is that you're not selling fruits and vegetables."

"Would you believe me if I told you that that's really what I do?"

"No."

"But it's true. I'm a greengrocer's assistant."

"You don't have to lie to make a sentimental old man happy." Father pats him on the shoulder. "You've become an English gentleman, and I'm reconciled to that. There are worse things in the world."

"Can I walk you to your room?"

Father shakes his head. "A man has to set off on his final journey alone."

He slowly limps off.

Matej takes out his cell phone and enters a number. "Katarina, where are you…? I was in London. You weren't at home… Did you have a night shift…? No, you don't have to come to Brighton, we're just leaving for London… Yes, I went to London so we could come back together, but there's no sense for you to come now, since we'll be gone… The train, yes, we'll take the train…"

Older brother and Sister come in.

"I'll call you back." Matej ends the call and puts the phone in his pocket.

"Time for a family council?" older brother asks.

"Right now?" Matej looks at the clock.

"Right now," Sister says and sits down. Older brother stands in front of Matej.

"Listen. I'm not going to say that it wouldn't be nice to have you at home again. Most of all because of our parents, who would be unbelievably happy. But the fact is you don't have a reason to return. Beautiful wife, good job, comfortable house, and social status some might envy… Is that how it is?"

"Maybe," says Matej after a short pause.

"Doesn't it seem to you that you ought to formulate your uncertain feelings in this regard into some sort of opinion, especially for the sake of Father and Mom?"

"My opinion is that Father and Mother deserve a little more understanding."

"And how much understanding have you shown them these past five years?" Brother leans towards him. "Or before, when you were supposedly studying in Ljubljana and didn't even visit them at Christmas?"

"Or send them a picture of your wife." Sister jabs at him.

To which Brother adds: "We would never have dragged Mom onto a plane if she didn't want to meet her so badly. And now you're hiding her?"

"I'm not hiding her at all..."

"Let's leave this aside," says Sister. "There are more important things."

"You're right," Brother agrees.

"I'm ready to take care of them," says Sister. "But they won't listen to me at all until you assure them that you don't intend to come home."

"They don't want to go to an old age home," Brother raises his voice. "They don't want to move in with me. They don't want to move in with our sister. Brother dear, Father and Mom can barely walk! Even at ninety, grandma is more mobile!"

"I'm not blind," Matej replies.

"Listen, Sister takes over. "You'll never come back. You're not interested in the house. You can't move it here, and you can't do anything with it there."

"It's different with us, we live there," Brother adds.

"If we sell the house now, we can still get some money out of it," Sister explains.

"It's not a matter of *us* getting anything," Brother tries to correct her.

Matej interrupts him. "They said they're not leaving the house."

Sister and older brother exchange glances.

"To whom?" asks older brother. "To you?"

"That house is their home," says Matej. "They'd like to die there."

"Listen," says Sister after a short pause. "If you talk with Mom behind our backs, explain to her we're trying to help."

"That's not what Mom thinks," says Matej.

Sister turns to Brother. "Will you tell him?"

"Listen, brother. I'll take off the gloves. Okay? The last five years these two old people have been kept in great suspense. For reasons that are known, I hope, at least to you, you increased their hope until they started believing that your return would be something like Jesus' rising from the dead. But the whole time you didn't have the least intention of returning! Now, when they've finally gathered their remaining savings *and* remaining strength to come and visit you, since it's easier for the mountain to go to Mohammed than Mohammed to the mountain, right, now you've shut them up in a musty, moldy room in a miserable hotel in a provincial English town like two dogs in a kennel!"

Matej bows his head. "Is that why you've come?"

"That's it," Brother decides to stop beating about the bush. "We need a declaration from you that you relinquish responsibility for Father and Mom to your older brother and sister, as they deem fit."

"And you two will get the house," says Matej.

"The house will be sold. Half the proceeds will go for their care in an old age home, and we can divide the other half."

"Why don't you take care of them at home, at your place?" asks Matej.

"Should I take an early retirement?" Brother almost roars.

"You could hire a private caregiver," Matej suggests.

"Send us one from England. Ask your wife, maybe she'll feel like taking on the care of two senile people."

"Don't talk like that," Sister reproaches him.

"A private caregiver! For God's sake..."

"It's not about the house, Matej," Sister tries to calm things down. "It's about..."

Older brother pulls a folded piece of paper out of his pocket. "The declaration is ready. Just sign and date it."

He holds the paper out to Matej. "You'll get a reward."

There are several moments of silence.

Then Matej takes the paper, folds it without looking at what is on it, and shoves it in his pocket. "A declaration is something I have to read in peace."

"Listen," Brother wants to take it up again.

"Let him read it." Sister stops him. "Let him read it."

"Right," Brother relents.

"We're going for a short walk along this wonderful rainy coast," Sister suggests.

"And when we come back, we expect an answer," says Brother.

He heads for the exit. He turns around in the doorway.

"Actually, no. For me, this conversation is over. Shove the declaration under my door. If I don't find it there, we're packing and leaving. Do we have an understanding? Brother?"

They leave. Matej stands there. He takes out the paper, unfolds it, and reads it. He folds it again and puts it back in his pocket.

He goes to the window and stares out.

Rain. He had always seen it as a blessing. Even when it's not pouring, but just drizzling, cloaking the world and concealing the sharp edges of everyday life, which is ever the same. And the rain awakens a pain that is impossible to suppress, because it fills every corner inside and surges through him like an alternative blood flow. Like an awareness that he made too many mistakes in life to be able to hope for success, even modest, or happiness, which is clearly available only to the chosen and to fools.

The bad feeling he had when he thought of how he wasn't able to confide his sexual orientation to his parents, brother, sister or the few friends he had kept sucking from him the will to study, to exert himself, or do what is necessary so that life would not pass him by in the other lane. Would he have been freer had he had more will and energy, if he had stopped pretending he was something he was not? Perhaps, but he never got up enough courage, and now it was too late; now he would just make a fool of himself.

Was that the only reason that several times during puberty he had to be treated in a psychiatric institution? Or was it due to the realization—maybe to an even greater degree—that life was not an uncle who brings gifts but a series of heavy stones that he had to roll off the road by force or cunning if he wanted to get ahead? And that there would be no end to it? And the chasm between desires and reality would always be too great, and because of that he would experience life as a wrong and a failure?

If only he had died then, when he was shot! Although in that case his parents would have found out about all the circumstances of his death, and what an embarrassment that would have been! He would have remained in their memory as a creep with no right to respect.

And now? Would they be proud of him if they found out what he had done now?

The waiter comes in. "Would you like something to drink?" he asks.

"What do you suggest?"

"Whatever."

Matej thinks. "Not really," he finally decides.

The waiter turns to go.

"Can I ask you something?"

The waiter stops.

"If we stay two more nights, what would the total be? I mean for the rooms and breakfast."

"Just a minute..." says the waiter. "Three times three singles, one double..." He closes his eyes and figures in Croatian. "Five hundred forty pounds."

"That much?!" Matej says with surprise. "Is there a... possible discount?"

"Unfortunately not in season."

Matej looks out the window. "Nice season."

"You have another bill here... just a minute..."

"One hundred eight-five pounds," he continues in Croatian.

"For what?" Matej can't believe it.

"Drinks. At the bar."

"I don't understand."

"The party asked me to put everything they drink on the room bill."

Without realizing it, Matej starts speaking Croatian. "One hundred eighty-five pounds?"

"Exactly. If you stay two more nights... should I tell them they have to pay cash?"

"No, no," says Matej. "Absolutely not. What are they drinking?"

"Not the same thing twice. They started on the upper left end of the bar and gradually made their way to the lower right hand."

"Do they drink together or by themselves?"

"In general by themselves. The old gentleman drinks more than the young one and handles it better."

"I'll pay with a credit card before I leave," Matej turns back to the window.

"No problem," says the waiter and turns to go.

"Do you have something to write with?" Matej stops him. "A ballpoint or something?"

The waiter hands him his pen and leaves. Matej sits down at a table, takes out the declaration, and reads it once again. He hesitates for a while, then signs it, folds it back up on the same creases, and carefully puts it in his jacket pocket.

He takes out his cell phone and enters a number.

"Katarina, I'm sorry, something has come up... No, you're right... Just come... If you come here, they won't have to go to London... I know, I know, but that would be too much stress for Father... And for Mom... You're leaving right away...? In two hours then... I'll be waiting at the station."

The conversation over, he puts the cell phone in his pocket. He goes back to the window. He stares out.

Then he goes to the exit.

The bar is empty. The waiter is picking up and wiping the tables. Katarina and Matej come in. The waiter looks at them, surprised.

"You're back?"

"Where are my relatives?" Matej asks.

"They left," says the waiter.

"You mean to see Brighton?" Matej asks.

"No, they emptied their rooms and left. They took a taxi. A van. A half hour ago."

"That can't be! We said we were staying until Sunday."

The waiter shrugs.

"Where did they go?"

"I don't know," the waiter shrugs again. "The airport?"

Matej is totally confused. "But…"

Katarina takes his hand. "Matej…"

"Can you bring me the bill?" Matej asks the waiter.

"The bill is paid."

"How is that?"

"The old gentleman paid. For the rooms and for the drinks. He left me a tip. Your father?"

"Matej, let's go," says Katarina.

"Did he pay for my room, too?"

"Yes."

"But… that's impossible. They just left?"

The waiter shrugs a third time.

"They didn't want to wait for me? To say good-bye?"

"The old lady wanted to, but the young gentleman convinced her that you had gone to London for good."

"But all of my things are in the room!" Matej protests.

"I know."

"Why didn't you tell them?" Matej gets slightly aggressive.

"Matej…" Katarina tries to calm him.

"I can't get involved in the affairs of people I don't know," the waiter replies coolly.

"Matej," Katarina tries again. "It's not his fault. Let's go."

Matej decides to resist. "Bring me a triple whiskey," he orders the waiter.

The waiter leaves. Matej collapses in the nearest chair, leans back, and stares at the ceiling. Katarina sits down next to him and tries to take his hand.

Matej withdraws it.

"Matej…" Katarina begins again patiently.

"It's your fault," he reproaches her. "If I wouldn't have been waiting for you at the station for two hours…"

Katarina moves away. "Then what? Your relatives wouldn't have left without saying good-bye?"

"I would have returned earlier, and they would have still been here," Matej fights back tears.

"And then what?" asks Katarina. "You would have fulfilled their desire and taken them to London?"

The waiter brings the whiskey and sets it in front of Matej. He leaves. Matej raises the glass and takes a sip. He holds the glass in his hand.

"Actually... I had no such intention."

"I know," says Katarina. "You're ashamed of the studio we live in, you're ashamed of me..."

"No, not of you."

"Are you sure?"

"You have many more reasons to be ashamed of me."

"If I didn't love you in a certain way, I would. I would like to help you, I feel I owe it."

"After all this?" Matej is surprised.

"After all this you need help more than ever."

"Because I did everything for you not to meet them?"

A few tortuous moments of silence.

Then Katarina says: "Matej, I met your parents."

"What?" Matej looks at her after a short pause.

"And your brother," Katarina adds. "And your sister."

"What are you talking about?"

"I got to Brighton late in the evening. I didn't know you were on your way to London. I took a room. This morning after breakfast I spoke with your brother. When you went to the station to wait for my train, I met your sister, father, and mom. I took them around the town. We had coffee on the pier. We had a nice talk."

Matej is visibly shocked. "But you told me to wait at the station!"

"I lied. But that's not as bad as how you lied to me. You've been lying to me since you rented a room from me in Ljubljana."

Matej swallows and stares at the ceiling.

"I had to, Matej, I had to meet your parents."

"But I would have introduced them to you!"

"Really?" Katarina doesn't believe him.

"Didn't I call you, didn't I ask you to come? But you didn't even say a word to hint that you were already here!"

"Sorry. It wouldn't work otherwise."

"And did you tell Father I sell fruits and vegetables?"

"I didn't give away any of your secrets. I lied for you as shamelessly as you lied to them. And me. But not for your sake. For your father and mom's sake. I didn't have the heart to smash the illusion they harbor about you."

"Did you tell them you're my wife?"

Katarina is quiet for a while. "I didn't dare, Matej. I was afraid you would never forgive me for that. But it seems to me they guessed."

They are silent for almost a whole minute.

"And?" Matej gets up his courage after a while. "What will we do now?"

Katarina gently takes his hand. "You'll have to part with your dreams."

"Hah!" Matej pushes her away.

"You've grown into something that is neither dream nor person."

"Katarina, I tried! But I couldn't admit that it was all in vain. I wanted to stay in the clouds."

"With me on the ground, holding you by a string. Like a kite, so the wind doesn't carry it away."

"No one can run you over in the clouds."

152

"But you can still run over those on the ground," Katarina adds.

"I have lost the ground under my feet," Matej says. "I'm waiving my arms trying to grab onto something."

After a long pause, Matej says: "I'm not worthy of you."

"You can't stand me, that's the problem." Katarina is about to cry. "I remind you too much of your defeat. Which you probably attribute to me."

"I don't attribute anything to you," says Matej.

"I remind you too much of what happened before we came to London. And met again."

"Do you wish we hadn't?"

"I don't know, Matej. It's too late now to wish for anything else. There are moments in life when you have to resign yourself to the fact that it's too late for some things."

"Probably for us, too," says Matej.

"I hope not," Katarina says and takes his hand.

"Shall we stay here a few days?" she asks him.

"Why?"

"Go for walks? Talk? The weather is supposed to get better."

"The sun will shine and then everything will be right? Tell me another fairytale."

"We're together in what's happening. And we'll come out of it together."

"I told them you're English," Matej admits.

"Are English women worth more than Slovenes?"

"You probably never hated me as much as right now."

"Shall we go to the beach?" Katarina asks him. "To the pier?"

"Why?"

"Just because. Sometimes you have to do things just because."

Katarina and Matej go up the steps to their London studio. The neighbor opens the door and comes into the hallway.

"Where have you two been all this time?"

"In Brighton, Mrs. Winter," says Matej.

"Didn't you know your parents were coming?"

"My parents?" Matej says with surprise.

"They were here. I opened up for them with the extra key. I couldn't just leave them in the hallway. The old gentleman had no strength left. They came twice. Yesterday they waited in the studio for two hours, all four of them. This morning only your father and mother. They sat in the room for three hours. You were nowhere around!"

"Thanks, Mrs. Winter," says Katarina and pulls Matej along.

She unlocks the door, and they quickly disappear into the apartment.

Inside, Matej steps to the window and stares out at the treetop in front of the building. Katarina puts the kettle on to make tea.

"Aren't you going to say anything?" she turns to Matej.

"What can I say?"

"They left. But I'm here."

She catches sight of her reflection in the mirror. "Look at me. I'll soon be thirty-one. My life with you is all I have. And a lousy job."

"They're gone, and they left five hundred pounds on the table," says Matej and pushes the notes to her across the table.

Katarina calmly counts them. "Five hundred fifty," she says. "That's good. We'll at least have money for the rent."

She picks a piece of paper off the table. "What's this? 'I promised you a reward.' Underlined. From your brother?"

"Probably," Matej acts clueless. "One of his jokes."

Katarina puts the paper down and sits on the edge of the bed. "I'm tired. I have to get up early."

Matej turns and looks at her. "Is a life without dreams worth living?"

"Is it worth sacrificing your life for dreams?"

"What if anything is left then?"

"You and I," says Katarina wearily. "Just you and I."

She stretches out on the bed, pulls up her legs, folds her hands, and lies motionless.

"Do you think there's a place we go after death?" Matej asks.

"That place is here," says Katarina and wipes away tear that fell on the blanket.

The water boils, and the kettle noisily turns off. Silence. Katarina doesn't move.

Matej comes close, sits on the edge of the bed, and looks at her. He lies down next to her. He cautiously puts an arm on her waist. She puts an arm over his shoulder.

Matej sobs. Katarina hugs him with both arms and pulls him close.

Matej is crying inconsolably.

"Did you tell them that my ex-husband shot us and it's a miracle we're still alive?"

"No. Did you?"

"No. Because then they'd want to know why he shot us."

"We made a big mistake."

"Yes. Especially me. But the one you've just made is much worse."

"So it's over between us?"

"I don't know, Matej. Every end is the start of something new. Maybe I'll go home."

"Why?"

"I have a feeling that I'm falling down slippery stairs into a dark cellar in which nothing but putrid rottenness awaits me."

"Decline and fall," says Matej. "No one escapes it."

Part 3

FOG

There's not much of a crowd in the waiting area at Ljubljana Airport. Following a chime, a female voice announces the departure of an Adria Airways flight for Paris; it is the last call for passengers to board. Damjan and Katarina are sitting near the downstairs bar, their carry-on luggage alongside. Katarina is paging through a magazine. Damjan just sat down with a glass of whiskey in his hand.

"To see Paris and die, isn't that the name of some film?" Katarina looks at him sideways.

"How about seeing Australia and living?" Damjan replies.

Katarina looks at the glass in his hand. "If you keep this up, you might see Australia, but the state of your liver may not allow you to enjoy it for long."

"It's barely my second," Damjan objects.

"But not the last," Katarina buries herself in the magazine again.

"You know what most affects my liver?"

"Alcohol," Katarina responds.

"No," says Damjan. "That you keep nagging me about it."

"Maybe because my father died of cirrhosis."

"Oh," Damjan sighs, "why do we have to keep arguing about this?"

"Will you promise not to drink on the plane?"

"Adria doesn't even give you water. But it's too long from Frankfurt to Sydney not to. Sorry."

"You won't find work in Australia if you're drunk," Katarina says after a while.

"The bigger question is whether *you*'ll find work."

"And why wouldn't I?"

"Because you enjoy being on people's backs."

"Right," says Katarina and closes the magazine. "Let's stay home and be unemployed. You drunk, and me bitter."

"It's too late," says Damjan. "The luggage is already on board."

"How much extra did you have to pay?"

"Don't ask. I don't know why we have to haul along everything we own."

"Because we're going for good," says Katarina.

"What if they have enough architects and nurses in Australia?"

"We checked."

Damjan looks at the clock. "You think there will be a delay?"

"There already is. But we have two hours to change planes in Frankfurt."

Damjan looks around the waiting area. "Where are all those people going?"

"To Brussels," Katarina says. "Look at those gentlemen, how well they're dressed. In elegant black, with ties. Not in jeans, like you."

She starts paging through the magazine again.

"You think I won't be permitted to enter Australia without a tie?"

"That's not what I said," Katarina shakes him off.

"But the insinuation was clear: I dress sloppily."

"Me, too," Katarina admits. "But if someone demanded you wear a tie for a good job, would you put it on?"

"Who would demand that? The days of formality are over."

"The days of jobs, too."

"We should have become government employees," says Damjan. "They go to Australia for holiday, not to look for work."

"Stop complaining, Damjan," Katarina reproaches him. "You can get up some optimism if you try."

"Only if I see it in front of me. Right now all I see is pessimism."

"It's the tension, Damjan. Are you at all aware what we're getting into?"

"Haven't we thought everything through?"

"Except for things we know nothing about."

The loudspeakers announce boarding for Frankfurt. Katarina puts the magazine down on the next chair and gets up.

"Shall we go?"

Damjan gets up, too, but more slowly. "We don't have to be among the first ones."

"Why not? Here we can. Everywhere else we're among the last."

"Sorry, but that constant negativism of yours gets on my nerves a little."

"I have a life behind me, Damjan. A life, the worst of which you know nothing about."

"Because you don't want to tell me."

Katarina's cell phone rings. She pulls it out of a pocket in her purse.

"Not now," she gets angry. "Who can it be?"

She takes the call and listens.

"What?!" she almost screams. "When...? That's impossible... That's *not* possible!"

"What is it?" asks Damjan.

Katarina grabs his hand and turns around. "Come on, we're getting the luggage back!"

She lets go of him and hurries to the waiting area entrance.

"Are you crazy?" Damjan screams after her. The other passengers look at them with surprise.

Damjan grabs Katarina's arm and pulls her back. "Can you tell me…?"

But Katarina isn't listening to him. She frees her arm and hurries on.

Damjan steps in front of her. "That's enough. What's going on?"

"Mom fell down the stairs!" Katarina blurts and starts sobbing. "The neighbor called me. It's bad. She might not live!"

"But we can't… the luggage is on the plane that will soon take off. And what about the tickets?"

"Should I let her die?" Katarina screams so loudly that everyone in the lobby looks at her. "Is that what you want? For me to leave Mom to die?"

"Your sister can come from Prague," Damjan tries to convince her. "Prague isn't far, and we're on the way to Australia!"

Katarina turns around to go on. Damjan grabs her by the arm and pulls her back to the middle of the waiting area. He shoves her down on a chair and sits next to her.

"We've been getting ready for more than half a year. Because of emotions we're not going to…"

"You really don't understand? Mom fell down the stairs!"

"The luggage is checked for Australia. We've packed everything we own!"

"We can still get the luggage off if we don't waste time!"

She wants to get up, but Damjan pulls her back down. "We let the apartment for a whole year! Where will we live? We're both out of work. What will we live on?"

"For my mom it's a mater of *whether* she will live."

"Mom, always Mom," Damjan says resignedly. "Since we met."

"Good for you that you never had real parents and don't know what a mom means!"

"I'm at fault for not having real parents?"

"Sorry. But…"

"Katarina, whatever happened, you can't help her."

"Maybe she's already dead. Will you at least let me go to her funeral?"

She tries her utmost to get out of Damjan's grasp. Damjan lets her go.

"Fine, I'll go myself."

"Go ahead," Katarina retorts. "But don't ever think that I'll follow you."

She grabs her bag and hurries towards the exit.

Katarina leans on the counter, behind which the airline representative is phoning. He reads the luggage number from the boarding pass to someone on the other end. Katarina feels Damjan join her from behind.

"Sorry," he whispers in her ear.

"This will be hard to forget," she shoves him with an elbow.

"I panicked," he tries to explain.

"And I didn't?" Katarina is even less pleasant.

"Yes… Yes…" the representative repeats in the phone. "Alright, you'll have to tell Frankfurt to send the luggage back. The main thing is that it doesn't go on the plane to Sydney. So, you'll take care of it."

He puts down the phone and looks at Katarina, then at Damjan. "I'm sorry but that's all we can do."

"When can we expect…?"

"As soon as the luggage is returned, we'll deliver it to your house," the representative assures her. "What is the address?"

He gets ready to type the address into the computer.

Katarina turns to Damjan. "What address?"

Damjan shrugs. "We don't have one."

"Our apartment," Katarina decides. "We'll ask the renter to let us know."

Damjan agrees.

"I'm going straight to Kočevje. Are you coming with me?" Katarina asks.

"I'd rather stay in Ljubljana," Damjan decides without thinking about it.

"Where will you be?"

"I'll find something."

"Look, I simply have to find out what happened. I'll call you. We can take a taxi together to Ljubljana."

Katarina turns to go.

"Ma'am!" the representative stops her. "The address."

"Will you take care of that, Damjan?"

Katarina hurries off. Damjan stays there.

The representative waits. "Yes?"

The apartment Damjan and Katarina rented out is on the twelfth floor of a high rise with a clear view to the castle. The renter, a man of about forty, cradling a baby in his arms, offers Damjan a seat on the couch.

Damjan sits down. The renter stands and rocks the baby so it doesn't wake up.

"It's good that her mom is okay," he says.

"A broken hip, left arm, and collarbone, and concussion," Damjan lists for him the results of the fall down the stairs.

"I didn't know it was that bad," says the renter, who is trying not to sound indifferent.

"They took her back from the clinic to her flat in Kočevje. Katarina decided to take care of her until she is back on her feet."

164

"That could be a while," the renter frowns.

"That's why I came," Damjan seizes the opportunity. "Mom's apartment is too small for me to be there as well. Even Katarina has to sleep on a mattress in the kitchen."

"An awkward fix," the renter agrees.

"Maybe, considering the situation," Damjan suggests cautiously, "we could agree..."

"Wait, you don't really expect a renter to offer you a mattress in the kitchen!"

"I was thinking..."

"We signed an agreement. For a whole year!"

"That's true..." Damjan agrees, "but..."

"I have a family, for heaven's sake. It's a good thing my wife is at work and isn't hearing this."

"I was thinking..." Damjan mumbles.

"It's a legal agreement, you can't break it."

"I only came to check whether maybe your situation had changed..."

"Mine hasn't. Yours has."

"Yes," Damjan hangs his head, "quite a bit."

"Look, I'm sorry it turned out this way, but I'm the last one who can help you."

Damjan gets up. "I knew I shouldn't have come. When a man's in trouble, he can't think soberly."

"You must have relatives who can take you in temporarily. Or friends."

"I don't have relatives," says Damjan.

"There's an ocean of rental ads in the classifieds," the renter reminds him.

"I know." Damjan nods.

"It's true you don't have a job, but you're not without money. I paid the whole year's rent in advance."

"That's true, too," Damjan agrees. "No offence intended. Good-bye. If the luggage comes…"

"I'll call," the renter assures him.

"They'll probably call me first," says Damjan.

"Well, then it's not a problem."

The apartment of Damjan's friend Rok is in an old building beyond Bežigrad. A rented room and a half, musty, with worn and dusty furniture. Damjan rolls his small suitcase (the carry on he was going to Australia with) through the living room door.

"God, you're worn out," says Rok.

"Confused," says Damjan. "The whole thing still doesn't seem real to me."

"I can hardly believe it either," says Rok. "My God, a coincidence like that happens only once in a thousand years, and to only one in a billion people."

"I don't know," Damjan shakes his head. "What is life if not a series of coincidences?"

"Yeah," Rok agrees, "but not that kind. I don't know what you did in the last life, but you must have done something outrageously bad to be punished like this."

"Maybe I killed someone," says Damjan. "Or will."

"You want me to open the day bed right now, so you can rest?"

"Let's have a drink first," Damjan suggests.

"Right," says Rok. "Let me see what I have."

"I have something," says Damjan. He pulls a bottle of whiskey out of his suitcase and puts it on the table.

"Still can't do without?" Rok looks at him.

Damjan shrugs. "I try, but… sometimes I just can't."

"I understand. There are moments when…"

"First I lost my job," says Damjan. "Then they fired Katarina."

"You're not the only ones."

"Now this…"

"We live in interesting times, the Chinese would say," Rok tries to joke.

"Screw the Chinese," says Damjan. "Screw the whole world. Who benefits from it anyway, the way it is?"

"Some do," says Rok and puts two glasses on the table.

Damjan pours them both a whiskey.

They toast.

"It's dumb of you to have paid for a hotel room for two weeks," says Rok.

"What should I have done?"

"You could have come here right away."

"I didn't know you're on your own. We haven't seen each other in over a year. And if we hadn't met today by accident…"

Rok empties his glass and puts it one the table.

"Sonja moved out. I knew all along it would happen."

"How did you know?"

"I saw we're not compatible."

"I'm sorry," says Damjan. "When did she leave?"

"A week ago."

"Just like that?"

"One day she came home and started reproaching me for working all the time. That all I do, day and night, is work. And that she gets nothing from me. That I don't even have time to watch a movie with her."

"That's what women are like," Damjan nods and pours another whiskey.

"But you know yourself what it's like in an architect's office. They'll suck your blood."

"At least you have a job," says Damjan, not without envy.

"The question is for how long. The boss keeps complaining that there's less and less orders. I'll probably be the next one to go."

"And if that happens?"

"I'm thinking of Austria," says Rok. "At least it's close."

"Too close," says Damjan.

"You won't be offended if I tell you something?" Rok looks at him. "The decision you two made…"

"Australia?"

"Wasn't the smartest."

"Why not?"

"I'd understand if you would have gotten a work permit in advance. And a residence permit. That's what the majority of intelligent people do. But no, you two set off to the other end of the world like tourists! In the hopes of finding a great job the first week, with your employer taking care of the formalities."

"I know three such cases," says Damjan.

"And where is it written that you two would be the fourth?"

"Sooner or later we'd find something," Damjan insists.

"I know at least ten other people who went there as tourists. And they got nothing. Some of them have already come back."

"We did visit different agencies," say Damjan. "But they're all crooked: they want money but guarantee nothing."

"Why don't your try in Austria?"

"I already said, it's too close."

"That's just it. You can drive across the border. Or in Germany?"

"The language," says Damjan. "I don't know and can't stand the language."

"You'd learn it as you go."

"I don't have the talent," Damjan says. "There wouldn't be anything temporary available in your office?"

Rok shrugs. "I'll ask." He gets up. "I have a meeting. Make yourself comfortable."

He goes to the door.

"Thanks, Rok," says Damjan. "Nice of you. Really nice. I won't forget it."

Rok turns around. "There's something else I have to tell you."

Damjan looks at him and waits.

"Regardless of what you think about it, Katarina made the right decision. I'd do the same. Wouldn't you?"

"I don't know," Damjan says.

The lost luggage office at the airport. Damjan is standing at the counter; a representative is behind it.

"But that's impossible," Damjan explodes, "it's been three weeks!"

The representative agrees. "I've been working here five years, and nothing like this has ever happened."

"What should I do?" Damjan spreads his arms helplessly.

"I have no idea," the representative spreads his in a like manner.

"Aren't you here to help people?"

"Listen," the representative replies. "We're not at fault the people in Frankfurt loaded your luggage to Sydney despite our communication."

"I know, but..."

"We're not at fault," the representative continues, "that it was lost after they sent it back to Frankfurt from Sydney. It has to be somewhere, but they can't find it."

"We had everything in the luggage," Damjan tries to explain. "Clothing, medicine, toiletries, shoes, a camera, personal keepsakes, letters, books, and house plans. We're left with nothing!"

"It's an awkward situation," agrees the representative. "But there's still a possibility of the luggage suddenly turning up in Ljubljana."

"What's the possibility of that?" Damjan demands.

"Frankly speaking," replies the representative, who has had enough of Damjan's anger, "very small."

"None, you mean."

"The first mistake was yours," the representative points out. "You checked the luggage for Australia, and then you didn't board the plane."

"You don't understand..." Damjan keeps trying to convince him, but the representative has had enough.

He turns and goes through the door into the back.

A kiosk at the Three Bridges in Ljubljana. The cashier hands Damjan the classifieds through the window. Damjan pays and turns. He almost runs into Darja, who is standing behind him.

"Oh," Darja lets out, hardly believing that she's seeing him.

"Oh," Damjan reacts similarly.

Both are surprised, both slightly embarrassed. They step to the side.

"Buying or selling?" Darja glances at the classifieds.

"Looking for work," says Damjan.

"You!?" Darja is surprised. "Don't joke with me."

"Work and a room," says Damjan. He can't help but add a noticeable hint of bitterness to his tone.

"Don't you two have an apartment?" Darja asks in disbelief.

"It's a long story."

"What about… Katarina?"

"And you, you still have a job?" Damjan tries to change the conversation.

Darja nods. "You know I can't lose a job my father arranged just like that."

"Especially if the father is as influential as yours," says Damjan, perhaps even with a slight reproach.

"Do I have to apologize?" asks Darja, who doesn't miss Damjan's tone.

"If we were still together," Damjan jokes bitingly, "he could arrange a job for me, too."

"Now Katarina's father can do that," says Darja, likewise with some reproach.

"Who's dead twenty years already," says Damjan. "And he wasn't capable of getting one even for himself."

"What about Katarina?" Darja asks again.

Damjan looks at her. "I see you're still mad at me."

"No. Anger passes after two years. And I wasn't mad at all, I was crushed."

"But you picked yourself up, I see, and now you're alright."

"And you"—Darja looks him in the eyes—"are you happy?"

Damjan looks at his watch. "Time for coffee?"

"You think that's a good idea?"

"We'll see."

"By rights I should say no," says Darja.

"By rights I should have a job and be happily married."

"You are. Aren't you?"

"You said we're going for coffee."

"I don't know…" Darja hesitates.

"Please," says Damjan and looks her in the eyes.

Katarina's mother's apartment in Kočevje is small and modest. Outside is the noisy main street. Her mom, in a vice of three different pieces of cast, is lying on a bed, behind which is the kitchen door that opens onto a corner in which Katarina is making coffee.

"Are you mad at me?" her mom cackles.

Katarina doesn't hear her. Her mom yells: "Of course you are! I know you are!"

Katarina leans towards the door. "What?"

Her mom turns her head towards a beloved little statue of the Jesus crucified hanging on the wall above her bed. "You're the only one who understands me. You know I didn't do it on purpose. You did it. For me. So I wouldn't be left alone."

Katarina brings the coffee and puts it on the table by the bed. "Who are you talking to?"

"To the only one who hears me," says her mom. "Because you don't. You act as if I'm not here."

"You know what," says Katarina, "I've had enough of this." She goes to the kitchen.

Her mom waves her right hand, which isn't in a cast, and knocks the coffee off the table. The coffee spills on the rug. "There you go!" she yells. "Now you can take the rug to the cleaners. Since you don't know how to take care of me. You don't know how to take care of your own mother!"

In the kitchen, Katarina enters a number on her cell phone and raises it to her ear.

"Damjan?"

Damjan and Darja are sitting at a table on the Ljubljanica embankment sipping coffee. Damjan has just put his cell phone to his ear. "Yes?"

"Is that you?" Katarina asks him.

"Could it be someone else?"

172

"Your voice is strange," says Katarina.

"Why?"

"You're the one who should know, but your voice is strange," Katarina repeats.

"And how should I change it so it stops being strange?"

"Did you find a job?" Katarina asks so as to avoid an argument.

"No," Damjan replies, almost with pleasure.

"Are you even looking for one?"

"I'm ready for the reproaches," says Damjan. "Go on."

"I'm not reproaching you at all, but you'll have to find something, anything. We can't touch our savings."

"What about you?" Damjan asks her in an aggressive tone. "Are you looking for a job?"

"In Kočevje?" Katarina raises her voice. "Next to Mom, who can't move and has turned me into a door mat, I'm supposed to find a job in a place where half the people are unemployed?"

"Why are you calling?" Damjan wants to know.

"To ask you why you don't visit me!"

"I did. A week ago!"

"Ten days ago."

"A day here or there."

"Damjan, what's going on with you?" Katarina wants to know.

"Why do I have to keep justifying myself? For every little thing!"

"Oh, come on," says Katarina, already close to despair.

"Ever since we met! Nothing is right with me! Everything always had to be your way!"

"Only when you couldn't make a decision," Katarina corrects him. "And when you could, your decision was in most cases wrong."

"One for sure."

"You mean the decision to marry me?" Katarina wants to know. "Is that what you mean?"

"You really don't see it?"

"What?"

"That what you hear from me even now is self-defense? That I have to defend myself all the time?"

"You never reproached me for that," says Katarina. "Why now all of a sudden?"

"Because I realized you'll never stop. I'm tired."

"Shall I tell you how my mother tires me out?"

"That's what you wanted, my dear. That's what you sacrificed Australia and the future for."

"Not the future. As soon as Mom's better, we'll go."

"To look for the lost luggage?" Damjan laughs.

"I can't go on like this," says Katarina. "Not on the phone. Please come so we can talk face to face."

"I don't have time, I'm looking for a job," Damjan announces coldly.

"Are you still at Rok's?"

"Where else should I be?"

"I'm only asking. Why do you feel accused right away?"

"And when is your sister coming from Prague?"

"It doesn't look like too soon," Katarina admits bitterly. "She keeps saying she has exams."

"Of course, it's nicer in Prague than with her boring mom in Kočevje."

"I don't know, Damjan, I don't know what I'm going to do... I'd like to kill myself!"

Katarina ends the conversation, slumps to the floor, and starts sobbing.

"Didn't I tell you to avoid the man?" her mom calls from the living room. "I warned you he's a coward and you can't trust him. But you did it your way. Always your way."

174

"Mom, I inherited all my bad traits from you, if you happen to be interested."

"From your father, my dear, who loved his flask more than me!"

"Mom, I'll leave if you don't stop," Katarina threatens.

"Of course, you'll leave your own mother to die. I know you. You're just as mean as your lush of a father. It's no wonder your first husband shot you."

"You know what," says Katarina, "more and more it seems to me that you didn't fall down he steps by accident, but on purpose. You didn't want me to go to Australia."

"You didn't want either. Otherwise you wouldn't have come back."

"Mom..."

"I'm not surprised that your Damjan holds that against you. He'll never forgive you."

"I don't remember you ever being so mean."

"Look in the mirror if you want to see real meanness," her mom shoots back.

Katarina reaches for her cell phone and enters a number.

"Alenka...? Yeah, I know you have exams, but you'll have to come now. Mom just died."

She puts the phone away.

"If you intend to slaughter me," she hears her mom's voice from the living room, "use a butcher's knife. You'll find it in the drawer under the counter."

Darja's studio isn't large but it's tastefully furnished. The wide couch is opened into a bed, which doesn't have sheets on it.

Darja goes in first. Damjan follows her with his carry on and a large shopping bag.

"Excuse the mess," says Darja. "You know how it is when you live alone."

"Only too well," says Damjan.

"You didn't clean up either when I visited you. Before…"

"Before what?"

"You met Katarina and said good-bye overnight." Darja wants to cry.

"Look," says Damjan, "I don't think it was a good idea, really."

He takes the handle of his carry on and turns to the door.

"Damjan, please," Darja tries to reason with him.

"I'm grateful for the offer, but… And where is it I'll sleep?"

"You're really funny. If we slept together a hundred times as lovers, we can probably sleep together as friends two years later."

"Are you sure?"

"We don't have to touch!"

"All the same…" Damjan hesitates.

"You said you're in Rok's way. I wanted to help you. But you decide. If it's unpleasant for you, go to a hotel."

"That's not it. I couldn't take the reproaches…"

"There won't be reproaches," Darja raises two fingers.

"Are you sure?"

"There won't be any more. I'm glad to see you, glad I can help you. I'm glad of the company. I don't like being alone."

"You probably didn't live alone for two years?"

"No," Darja admits. "But it wasn't good. We ended it."

"As long as he doesn't think…"

"He can think what he likes," Darja waves.

"I wouldn't want him to see in me…" Damjan goes on.

"That's his problem," says Darja. "I'll make room for your things in the closet."

176

"I bought some fresh underwear," says Damjan and puts the plastic bag on the bed. No one could miss the symbolic meaning of this gesture.

"All my things are…"

"Yeah, you said that," says Darja.

"I doubt I'll ever see them again."

"You can take a shower if you want. The towels are on the top closet shelf."

"Super," says Damjan.

Darja finishes changing the bed, undresses, puts pyjamas on, and crawls under the covers on the far right. Damjan comes out of the bathroom in his pyjamas and crawls under the covers on the far left. There is a half-meter between them.

"No touching," says Darja.

"No touching," Damjan repeats.

"Good night."

"Good night," Damjan repeats.

"Can I turn off the light?" asks Darja.

"Already?" Damjan is surprised.

"What do you want to do? Stare at the ceiling?"

"I remember you would often read before bed."

"And I remember you didn't like that. You couldn't fall asleep with the light on."

"And you couldn't fall asleep without a book in you hand."

"Although I read mostly stupid things."

"And now you can fall asleep without a book?

"I changed. I changed a lot, Damjan."

"I see."

"You did, too."

"For the worse?"

"In general. You were always in a good mood. Now you're bitter."

"Can I give you the reasons?"

"If you want."

"It would take too long," Damjan reconsiders.

"I know. You're out of work. And the thing with Katarina, and Australia. You're taking the whole thing well."

"I have no idea what to do."

"You can stay here until things come together," she says and automatically touches him with her hand. "Ooops! No touching."

"No touching," Damjan repeats, although there's less certainty in his voice. "How fast and unexpectedly a person's plans fall apart," he adds.

"That's exactly what I said to myself when you left me."

"I'm sorry," says Damjan. "That's one of the two big mistakes in my life."

"And what was the other one?"

"Marrying Katarina."

"You loved her," says Darja.

"Maybe I did, but differently than you."

"Is there more than one kind of love?" Darja asks with surprise.

"I subjected myself to her will," says Damjan. "You have no idea what a manipulator she is."

"Why?"

"She didn't even tell me that her first husband shot her and she almost died. And that she then lived in London for several years with her former renter. I found all that out from other people."

"And despite that..."

"You have no idea how often I thought of you," Damjan lies a little but not completely. "I missed you."

"Damjan, stop being nice to me. We said no touching, and that's how it will be."

"I'm not trying to be nice, I'm talking about my feelings," Damjan finds a suitable way out of the jam.

"When you left, it seemed to me that men don't have feelings at all."

"What about your new guy, does he have them?" Damjan wonders.

"He's not new, but ex-. I'd prefer not to talk about him."

"I wonder who you were with. Was he better than me?"

"In what sense?"

"Well... let's say... in bed," says Damjan.

"I'm not going to talk about that."

"What about in other senses," Damjan continues.

"Would I have let him go if he was?"

"I don't know," says Damjan. "Women are capable of anything. I still don't understand you."

"You don't understand me?"

"Not you. Katarina."

"Why?"

"Everything has to be her way. Every little thing. Without exception."

"That obviously suits you," says Darja. "Otherwise you wouldn't have been going to the other end of the world with her."

"Maybe it suited me sometimes, but now things have gone too far. What about yours? Why did you break up with him?"

"Because with him I was alone," Darja says simply and clearly.

"How alone?"

"Lonely. He was always working, all the time. He didn't even have time for a movie."

"Strange," says Damjan, "that's why Rok lost his girl. She reproached him for the same thing, for working too much."

"Obviously all men are alike. The ones who have a job."

"You mean we're conscientious? Maybe that's only true of architects. We let ourselves be used. What was yours?"

"You won't believe it."

"Don't tell me he was an architect!"

"Unfortunately. When I lost one, I wanted another."

"Then I must know him. Can you trust me with his name?"

"You don't know him; he's not from Ljubljana."

"Maybe we were in school together."

"I asked him, but he said he doesn't know you."

"And the next one will be an architect, too?"

Darja is quiet for a while. "There won't be the next one."

"Are you going to a convent?"

"I've gotten used to life alone. And the only one I could live wih is you."

Some minutes of silence, longer than they ought to be, follow those words.

"You never know what the future may bring," says Damjan.

"Can I turn the light out now?" asks Darja.

"That's fine with me," says Damjan.

Darja turns out the light. "Good night."

"Good night, Darja," Damjan replies tentatively.

"No touching," Darja warns him.

"No touching," Damjan repeats.

When the morning sun breaks through the fog and shines through the window onto the couch opened into a bed, Damjan and Darja are sleeping naked, in a tight embrace.

The mess in Mom's apartment in Kočevje gets worse by the day. Katarina can't keep up. Her mom is still lying in the same position. Katarina comes in from the kitchen and puts a plate of sausages cut into pieces along with pieces of cut up bread on the table by the bed.

"I wanted hot cereal," says her mom.

"I don't have time to feed you with a spoon," Katarina answers. "And you throw it all up right away."

She goes back to the kitchen. With her right hand, her mom takes a piece of sausage from the plate, puts it in her mouth, and chews. She looks at the little Jesus statue on the wall.

"Isn't it terrible that God, your father, punished me with such a daughter? The other one is better, but she's not here. She would make me hot cereal every day. But I don't know, maybe I'm mean. Tell me, Jesus. Am I mean?"

Katarina comes out of the kitchen, phone in hand. "The day after tomorrow you have a check-up in Ljubljana."

"Will they take off the casts?" her mom cheers up.

"All I know is that you have a check-up," says Katarina. "An ambulance will come."

"I'm not going alone."

"I'm going with you. What are you getting worked up about?"

Katarina goes back towards the kitchen. Mother hits her in the back with a piece of sausage. "Maybe that's it! Maybe I'm worked up because I'm going with you instead of with your sister!"

"My sister?" Katarina tosses over her shoulder. "She won't even come to your funeral."

"I hope no one does. I don't want people to pretend how sorry they are that I'm gone. Especially you!"

Katarina sits on the floor and leans against the closed door. There are tears in her eyes. She calls a number.

A telephone rings in Ljubljana, in Darja's apartment, where Damjan is lying on Darja's bed, naked to his waist.

"Yes?" he answers.

"Damjan, where are you? Come down, I can't take it anymore!"

"I can't either."

"I need support, Damjan. *Moral* support!"

"Me, too."

"At least come and visit. At least for an hour or two. What's going on with you?"

"I'm working."

"You're working as what?"

"In Rok's office."

"Nice," says Katarina, "but it's temporary. When Mom's casts come off, we're leaving."

"Where?" Damjan asks calmly.

"Where? For Australia! Isn't that where we were going?"

"Were, but you didn't want to leave."

"How can you still not understand?"

"You left from the airport for your mom's. Everything we were taking with us vanished in thin air."

"And I'm to blame."

"No, I am, because I didn't leave by myself."

"You would do that?" Katarina can't believe it.

"I should have, but it's too late."

"I don't want to stay here. I'd rather die."

"Get yourself a job. I did."

"I had to take some of the savings, because Mom's pension isn't enough for everything. So it's good you're working. We'll need money for new plane tickets."

"Sorry," says Damjan, "I have to go…"

"Wait! The day after tomorrow Mom and I are coming to Ljubljana. To the medical center. Can we get together for a coffee somewhere nearby? At least that?"

The silence that follows is chillingly long.

"When?" Damjan finally asks.

"I'll let you know."

"I've got work to do," says Damjan and ends the conversation.

"Right," Katarina says to herself. "Work. You don't have to worry about me slowly dying."

She enters another number and waits. A recording informs her she can leave a message.

"Listen, dear sister, having a good time in Prague," Katarina begins. "When do you intend to come home and take on part of the responsibility for Mom, who is your mom, too? I have to warn you that she intends to change her will and leave absolutely everything to me. And I'm not joking. The apartment, the woods in Kočevska Reka that are worth heaven knows how much, and the three fields in Mačkovec. So you know. So you don't reproach me in the future for not telling you."

A nurse's aid wheels a hospital bed down a long corridor in the Ljubljana medical center. Katarina's mom is lying on it. Katarina walks after them.

Damjan and Darja come through a door into the corridor and right in front of the bed. Damjan is limping.

"Move," the aide unpleasantly directs them.

Damjan stands there and stares speechlessly at Katarina. Darja tries to hide behind his back, but she doesn't manage.

"Well, at least you came," says Katarina. "I'm glad you know how to keep your word. Why are you limping?"

"I fell down the stairs."

"You, too? Did you break your leg?"

"I sprang my ankle," says Damjan.

Katarina looks at Darja. "That's Rok, right? Unusual how people change in two years."

"It's not what you think…" Damjan tries to explain.

"I've heard that in a hundred films. Can't you at least be a little original?"

"I'm asking you once again to move," the aide commands.

"Did she push you down the stairs?" Katarina looks at Darja. "Why didn't you do it a little harder?"

"Didn't I tell you to stay away from that liar?" her mom says.

"Listen," says the aide, "if you don't move, I'll call security."

Damjan and Darja step aside, and the aide pushes the bed past them down the corridor.

"As soon as you turn your back, he's with someone else," her mom says.

Katarina turns around while following the bed. "See you. Husband."

"And you were going to go to Australia with that whore-aholic," her mom sounds off again.

Darja's studio. Darja and Damjan are lying on the bed and staring into space. A bottle of whiskey is on the table by Damjan's side. Damjan fills a glass and downs it.

"Can I have some?"

Damjan pours her some and hands her the glass.

Darja sits up and slowly sips it. "What are we going to do?" she asks.

"I don't know."

"Maybe I'm to blame. I shouldn't have invited you here."

"No one is to blame," says Damjan. "Things happen."

"Or not," says Darja.

"There's not a person in the world who is in control of his life," Damjan states sorrowfully.

"Do you think she knows?" asks Darja.

"Katarina? She's not stupid."

"Will you go back to her?"

"I have no idea."

"I'm surprised she hasn't called you yet."

Damjan empties another glass of whiskey. "She did. She wanted to have a coffee with me tomorrow."

"What does that mean? That I've lost you? Again?"

"Let's wait and see what's over the horizon," says Damjan.

Katarina and Damjan are sitting at a table in the Union coffeehouse. She is drinking coffee; he has a whiskey. There's an awkwardness between them. For a time they're silent. Damjan finishes his whiskey and raises his glass.

"Waiter? Another, please."

"Does she drink, too?" asks Katarina without looking at him.

"Look... I'm under stress. The project is over and I'm without a job again."

"She can't support you? I hear she has a good job in some ministry."

"How can I explain to you that I'm just staying at her place? I sleep in my own room. There's nothing between us."

"I didn't know there's more than one room in a studio."

"How do you know she has a studio?"

"I know a thing or two, Damjan. A thing or two."

"She took me in when Rok's girl moved back. She's doing me a favor."

"And you expect me to believe that?"

"I don't expect anything, I'm stating the facts."

"Can I state one, too?"

"Go ahead," says Damjan. "You'd like a divorce."

"I hope you said that in jest." She looks at him sharply. "Because if you didn't, that means *you* are thinking of a divorce."

"What reason do we even have to think about a divorce?"

"Darja, for example."

"Katarina, I told you the truth, and I'm not going to repeat myself. Because I'm not guilty of anything. I don't have to prove anything."

"Then listen."

"I'm listening."

Katarina takes her time before speaking. "I'm pregnant. A month and a half."

Damjan is silent and tries to hide his shock.

"Aren't you going to say anything?"

"What can I say?"

"Aren't you going to ask me who the father is?"

"Come on," says Damjan.

"That's good. Because if you asked me that, I'd get up right now and you'd never see me again. Or your child."

"And what do we do now?" asks Damjan, rather indifferently, it seems to Katarina.

"What do we do now?" Katarina says so loudly that the waiter turns his head. "We'll thank God for this blessing. A child born in Australia is automatically an Australian citizen. And because of that the parents receive residence permits."

"Are you sure?"

"They confirmed it at the embassy! Do you understand what that means?"

"No," Damjan shakes his head.

"That means we have to go to Australia before I'm showing."

"What about your mom?" asks Damjan.

"I managed to convince my sister. She'll be back from Prague in three days."

Damjan is silent.

186

"Don't you want to go to Australia anymore? It was you who was in such a hurry to get there."

"That's not it," says Damjan.

"Is there a reason we shouldn't go?"

"No reason," says Damjan, "but…"

"But Darja. That's the reason, isn't it?"

She gets up, takes her purse, picks up her glass and splashes the water in Damjan's face.

Then she leaves.

Darja is standing by the gas cooker with a wooden spoon in her hand and looking at Damjan, who is stretched out on the couch with his hands under his head, lost in thought.

"Did something happen?" she asks him.

"Nothing special," he shakes his head.

"Something must have."

"The project at Rok's office is over," Damjan decides to tell her what is bothering him. "There's nothing more coming along. Katarina would like to leave for Australia as soon as possible."

Darja is silent for a while and busies herself cooking. Then she asks: "Did they take the casts off her mom?"

"No," says Damjan. "Her sister is coming back from Prague."

Darja is quiet again. Then she looks at Damjan. "Do you promise not to be mad at me if I tell you something?"

"I wont' be."

"This idea about Australia seems to me… no offence…"

"What?" Damjan wants to know.

"A mistake."

"Why?"

"Are you aware how far away it is? Things here will straighten out sooner or later. You just have to be patient."

"You have a job in the ministry for environmental affairs, so you can be patient," says Damjan.

"That's exactly what I wanted to say to you. I can easily support you while you're looking for a job. I have a good enough salary."

"And where will I find a job?"

"My father can set one up for you without any trouble through his connections. After all, he's the head of a construction company."

Damjan shakes his head decisively. "I don't want to get a job like that."

Darja is genuinely surprised. "How do people get jobs nowadays? Would you have gotten a job in Rok's office if he hadn't put in a word for you?"

"I don't know," Damjan admits.

"I do."

She puts down the spoon and reaches for her phone. She enters a number.

"Dad?"

An empty, neglected apartment with two chairs and a mattress on a dirty floor doesn't inspire the impression that it would be possible to convert it into a comfortable living space.

But Darja's father is an optimist. "It needs some remodeling. That shouldn't be a problem for an architect." He looks at Damjan and pats him patronizingly on the shoulder.

"I don't think so," says Damjan with no apparent sign of actually believing him.

"Why should you squeeze yourselves into a studio when you can make a spacious family apartment here," says Darja's father.

188

Damjan is silent.

"Damjan?" Darja pokes him.

"I'll put up the necessary means," her father says. "Don't worry. I know what your situation is like. You probably know how to handle some tools?"

"Won't be a problem," Damjan replies without enthusiasm.

The father turns to his daughter. "Well, you see. Isn't it good he came back? Watch out he doesn't get away from you again."

"I will, dad," Darja promises, unable to hide her embarrassment.

Her father turns to Damjan. "As far as work goes, I know full well how hard it is for architects nowadays. But I still have a few friends and almost every one owes me. I suggest you start your own firm. It will be easier that way. Darja will help you. You're familiar with those things," he turns to his daughter, "after all, you're a lawyer."

"Of course, dad."

Darja's father quickly looks at his watch. "I'm in a hurry to a meeting. You two go ahead and stay here and think about how you'll arrange your nest. The key is in the door."

He leaves.

"What do you say?" Darja asks after a while.

"He's generous, your father," Damjan admits.

"What do you think about this space?" she wants to know.

Damjan looks around. "With a little work and a lot of money it could be turned into one of the most beautiful apartments in Ljubljana."

Darja jumps up to him and hugs him. "Shall we celebrate? There, on the mattress? The first time in *our* apartment?"

Damjan hits the mattress twice. The dust that comes up almost chokes him. He looks around the space.

"There's too much filth around us," he says.

189

Katarina is standing in the kitchen, cutting cooked sausage into pieces on a plate. Her mom is lying on the bed in the living room, her arm still in a cast.

"Hot cereal, I said, hot cereal," she cackles in the direction of the kitchen door. "Not sausage again."

"Why not?" Katarina replies. "It's easier to hit me in the head with a sausage; cereal would fly all over the room."

"I can hardly wait for Alenka to get here from Prague. She'll know how to take care of me."

"You won't believe it, Mom, but I'm a hundred times more impatient for her to come!"

"So you can go to Australia? With that coward of yours who has someone besides you? Maybe even two? He probably changes them every other day. More often than his underwear!"

Katarina adds a piece of bread to the chunks of sausage and takes the plate to her mom's bed, where she puts it on the table.

"Lunch is served."

"When Alenka gets here, there won't be room for you any longer. You'll have to move out."

"There's no room for me as it is, so I'm moving out right now," says Katarina.

She goes back to the kitchen. She reaches for her cell phone and enters a number. "Damjan?"

Damjan answers in the new apartment, in a dirty t-shirt, with a brush in his hand.

"What's up?"

"Why are you so out of breath?" Katarina asks, who has an image of a nude Darja before her eyes.

"I'm working," says Damjan. "I got a job."

"Nice. What are you doing, digging ditches?"

"Why are you calling?" Damjan wants to know.

"Alenka told me she's coming only in a week. Australia will have to wait a little."

"That's alright," says Damjan, "I got a job remodeling an old apartment. I have to finish it, so at the moment I can't go anywhere. Anything else?"

"You know very well what!" Katarina loses her patience. "The child can become an Australian citizen only if we prove he was conceived there!"

"How can we prove that? And was it even conceived? Does a child even exist?"

Damjan ends the conversation, shoves the phone in his pocket, and keeps on working.

Katarina puts a piece of sausage that was left on the counter in her mouth. She slowly chews. Tears crawl down her cheeks. She catches sight of her reflection in the mirror and for the first time in her life sees wrinkles of hate on her face.

When they meet again in the Union coffee house, the hate is gone. An expression of pragmatic decisiveness has replaced it. Damjan is drinking whiskey, as usual, and she coffee.

"How much do you drink a day?" she asks him.

"As much as I like," he denies her the right to interrogate him.

"Does she buy it for you?"

"Among other things," he tries to ruin her mood.

But it doesn't work, because Katarina has come with a plan.

"Look," she says calmly and falls silent, as if wanting to double check in her mind what she intends to say. "I'm prepared to overlook this fling of yours, but under one condition. That we leave right away."

"What about Mom?" asks Damjan. He gets the feeling that they're repeating the same conversation they had at the same table a while ago.

"Alenka keeps delaying, but she'll be here in a week."

"And if she's not?"

"If not," Katarina says decisively, "I'll dump Mom off on the social services. Now tell me: are we going or not?"

"So the child will be able to become an Australian citizen?"

Katarina opens her purse and puts a piece of paper in front of Damjan.

"Read it. It's a confirmation of pregnancy. Issued by the Kočevje clinic."

Damjan reads the confirmation. He even turns it over as if he doesn't believe it's authentic.

"Matic Pograjc, my classmate, became a doctor?" he can't contain his surprise.

"He shouldn't have?"

Damjan puts the confirmation down on the table. "Wasn't there something between you when he was in high school and you were in medical school?"

"Yes," Katarina admits. "Bad math grades."

"And why exactly did you go to him?"

"I didn't. I went to the clinic. It happened he was on duty."

"And you two brought back old times."

The corners of Katarina's mouth droop, and she tries to stifle the tears she feels inside.

"Damjan, what's going on? Until now, everything between us rested on mutual trust. Now this. What have we sunk to? Whose fault is it?"

"Yours," Damjan says sharply. "When will you admit it? If you hadn't taken off so stupidly from the airport, we'd already be in Australia. And nothing would have happened because of that."

"But," Katarina holds back the tears as hard as she can, "it seemed to me then I had no choice! Now I'm sorry. But now it's too late. I see you won't forgive me for that."

She gets up, grabs her purse, and leaves. She leaves the confirmation of pregnancy on the table. Damjan folds it up and puts it in his pocket. Then he turns to the waiter.

"One more whiskey, please."

Darja is standing by the bed and methodically folding things into a large suitcase. Damjan stands and watches her.

"How many days are you going for?"

"Five," says Darja.

"You need that many clothes for five days?"

"You don't know how people dress in Brussels."

"And so suddenly. You didn't even know about it yesterday."

"Someone cancelled, and I had to jump in," Darja explains a little impatiently, as if Damjan's lack of trust bothers her.

"How many of you are going?"

"Eight, I think."

"Well, at least I won't be bored," says Damjan. "There's more work in the apartment than I thought."

Darja closes the suitcase; Damjan picks it up and puts it on the floor.

"One more thing," says Darja. "Sit down, please."

Damjan sits down next to her on the edge of the bed.

"I feel bad that things are evolving in this direction, but the matter is out of my hands."

"What are you talking about?"

"About Father," Darja explains.

"I don't understand."

"More than likely he won't be able to find you a job. He's under investigation."

"In connection with what?"

"In connection with deals he made with the ministry for environmental affairs. His partners are turning their backs on him."

"I'm sorry," says Damjan, not knowing how to take the news.

"It's still not clear how it will end, but just in case, you have to look for work yourself. You promise?"

"I'm already doing that," says Damjan. "When I have time."

He suddenly appears downcast and confused. Darja hugs him. "But you love me, right?"

Damjan nods weakly.

"Say it out loud," she asks.

"Please don't order me. It's bad enough that Katarina does that."

"Sorry. I wouldn't want you to displace disappointment in my father onto me."

"Now you, too, are treating me like a child," he reproaches her.

"I'm not. But I know you drink and you're not completely stable emotionally."

"And you are?"

"Far from it," says Darja and moves away from him. "I'm off."

She gets up and reaches for the suitcase.

Damjan is painting a wall in the new apartment. It seems to him someone is knocking. He listens. Silence. He keeps painting.

194

The door opens, and Katarina comes in. She comes up and stands behind his back.

Damjan is suddenly aware of her presence and turns around.

"How did you find me?"

"Are you hiding from me?"

"Should I?" asks Damjan.

"Then why does it matter how I found you?" She opens her purse and hands him two newly issued plane tickets to Australia. "Sydney. The return date is open. We can go at any time. Tomorrow, let's say."

Damjan handles the tickets as if he doesn't know what to do with them.

"Darja is in Brussels. She'll be back in five days. I can't leave without saying good-bye to her."

"Why not?"

"I'm remodeling the apartment for her."

"For her or for the two of you?"

"For her. Her father hired me."

"So that's how it is," Katarina says. "Family ties are arranged. Who did she go to Brussels with?"

"With a whole team, eight people."

"With that undersecretary of hers?" Katarina looks him right in the eyes.

"What undersecretary?"

"The one," Katarina informs him almost with pleasure, "who hired her without posting the job by agreement with her father. And who is about to be sacked. Together with her."

Damjan is confused for a moment, then calms down. "Where did you get that information?"

"I have friends."

"Friends who spy on your husband?"

"Not on him. On his ex-, who he left for me and who he now prefers to his lawful wife and child!"

She turns and marches towards the door.

Then she suddenly comes back and hands Damjan a photo.

"It might be of interest to you."

This time she leaves.

Damjan stares at the photograph. The brush falls from his hand.

Damjan and Rok are sitting at the living room table in Rok's apartment, sipping whiskey.

"Sorry for barging in like this," says Damjan.

"Come on, you know full well that you're welcome any time," says Rok, pouring him another glass. "Tina is on the night shift, she's a nurse. We're alone, just go ahead."

"How many nurses are there in the world?" Damjan says with surprise.

"A lot," says Rok, "although I keep reading in the newspaper that there's a shortage."

"And how is the thing with Tina coming along?" asks Damjan.

"I could talk to you about her all night," Rok gets animated. "I don't know what she sees in me, but what the fuck, she's mine. And she even mentioned marriage."

"Come on."

"I'm on the right path to becoming normal. Like you."

Damjan laughs bitterly. "Things have gone in the opposite direction for me."

"Can't be," Rok is surprised.

Damjan hands him the plane tickets. Rok reads the information off one of the e-tickets. "Ljubljana-Frankfurt-Singapore-Sydney. So you're going!"

196

Damjan hands him the confirmation of pregnancy. Rok looks at it carefully. "Damn! Congratulations!"

Damjan hands him the photo.

"This is Darja," says Rok. "In your arms. No, wait... Who is this guy?"

"I think he's an undersecretary at the ministry of environmental affairs. Darja is his assistant."

"Hmm," Rok covers his face. "That's awkward. But maybe it's from the time when you were with Katarina. You can't hold that against her."

"Does it look to you like it could have been photoshopped?" Damjan wants to know.

"I'm not familiar with those things, but it looks believable to me, sorry."

"What would you do in my place?" Damjan asks.

"What any man would do, who's worthy of the name," Rok replies without a bit of hesitation. "I'd go to the ministry and confront the guy with the photo. If he's in his office, there's a chance it really is touched up. If he's also in Brussels, it will quickly be clear to you what time it is. Although even then you could be mistaken. Who did you get it from?"

"From Katarina."

Rok shakes his head. "I don't know. I really don't know."

The undersecretary is sitting at his desk in his office at the ministry of environmental affairs, buried in papers. Damjan comes in without knocking, comes up to him, and sits down on a chair in front of the desk.

"Who the hell are you?" the undersecretary looks at him slightly confused.

"I see you're not in Brussels," says Damjan.

"I see you're not blind, which is good," is the answer.

197

"I have a few questions," Damjan continues.

"Really?" says the undersecretary. "You won't be offended if I call security?"

He reaches for the phone. Damjan puts the photo in front of him. The undersecretary takes his hand off the phone.

"Who's that?" he asks.

"My girl," says Damjan. "And next to her, in a very intimate embrace, you."

"I don't deny that it's me," says the undersecretary. "That Darja is your girl is news to me and of no interest at all. The photo is, no offence, an amateur touch up."

He shoves it back across the table to Damjan.

"Maybe," says Damjan, and leaves the photo on the table. "But you can't deny that Darja got a job because of your deals with her father, who is the subject of a criminal investigation."

"Are you a police officer?" The undersecretary looks at him without fear.

Damjan shakes his head.

"Have you come here to put pressure on me?"

"Far from it," says Damjan.

"Then I have to inform you that the distance from your chair to the door is exactly three meters. If that's too far for you, perhaps security can help."

He again reaches for the phone. Damjan takes the photo and gets up.

"Don't you think that this is the end of it," he says.

"I'm afraid it really isn't," agrees the undersecretary. "Darja won't be happy when I tell her how stupidly you're carrying on."

"We'll see," says Damjan and turns to the door.

"If you need help, I know a good psychiatrist."

Damjan is in the kitchen nook of Darja's studio preparing a modest supper. The doorbell rings. He goes to open.

Katarina tries to squeeze in. With a suitcase.

"What are you doing here?" Damjan stares at her, shocked.

"Are you going to shove me out in the hall?"

Damjan moves aside and allows her to roll her giant suitcase into the studio.

"Alenka unexpectedly came back from Prague today already. I have nowhere to go. Will you take me in until your dear returns?"

Damjan doesn't know what to say.

"I can sleep on the floor," says Katarina, "or in the entry if you're repulsed by sleeping with the mother of your child. Or I'll go to a hotel."

She turns around.

"But only for two days," Damjan stops her. "Darja is coming back the day after tomorrow."

"By then we'll already be on our way to Australia," Katarina replies.

She sits down on the opened couch as if she's at home in the studio. "Or do you still want to stay with a woman who's cheating on you?"

"Where did you get that photo?" Damjan asks.

"Does it matter?" asks Katarina.

"That's what matters most."

"I took it myself."

"I don't believe it," Damjan shakes his head. "And if you really did, it wasn't honorable."

"Oh, no? And it's honorable that I'm fighting for my husband and the family so the child has a father when his father lost his parents when he was five and grew up without direction, which he constantly proves by his behavior? And it's honorable for you to cheat on me with another woman, lie to me, and not trust me? Sorry I can't figure that out, perhaps I am stupid."

"I don't know what to say," Damjan is embarrassed.

"Nothing. Better offer me a glass of whiskey."

Damjan bends over, puts a half empty bottle of whiskey on the kitchen counter, and fills two glasses. He hands one to Katarina.

"Cheers, my lawful drunken husband," says Katarina and downs her glass. "It's not bad, maybe I'll get used to it."

"Whiskey is expensive," Damjan replies.

"By law you have to support me," says Katarina. "Now tell me, when is the last time you did your marital duty?"

Damjan looks at her. Katarina starts to undress and toss her clothes on the floor.

Damjan looks at her.

"What?" Katarina challenges him. "Do you and Darja do this kind of thing fully dressed?"

When the morning sun shines in the window, Damjan and Katarina are sleeping half-naked on the opened couch. The doorbell rings.

"Damjan!" Darja's father yells in the hall.

Darmjan, startled, awakens. He looks at his watch: it's ten.

"Damjan, are you home?"

Katarina wakes up, too, and is going to say something. Damjan covers her mouth with his left hand and puts his index finger to his. He pulls the cover over her head and goes to the door in his briefs. He unlocks it.

"What's going on?" asks Darja's father in the hall. "I was looking for you in the penthouse, you're not there, I call on the phone, and you don't answer. What's going on?"

Damjan assumes a repentant pose. "I'm sick. Some virus. It's better you don't come in."

"Have you talked with Darja at all?" her father wants to know. "I call her, but she doesn't answer. She doesn't call back either."

"I talked with her only once. She says everything is okay."

"Call her," Darja's father orders. "Call her and tell her to call me back for God's sake. It's urgent! Will you do that?"

"Yes," Damjan promises.

Darja's father heads to the elevator and turns around.

"Look... The job I promised you..."

Yes?" says Damjan, knowing full well that he can only expect an excuse.

"I didn't forget. It won't be right away, you'll have to wait a while. So long. Get better."

He leaves. Damjan closes the door, locks it, and comes back into the room.

Katarina is sitting on the couch with her legs crossed, looking at him triumphantly. "Well?" she says.

"What?"

"I knew they'd want to bribe you."

"Ah, come on, what would they get out of that?"

"For you not to raise a stink. That guy in the ministry is married."

"You poke around too much in things that are none of your business."

"Oh, no? Everything," Katarina straightens up, "everything that concerns my child's father is my business! Absolutely everything!"

"Darja is coming back tomorrow, maybe even today. You can't stay here."

"I won't. Tomorrow we're going to Australia. I reserved the seats."

"I'm not going anywhere," says Damjan, "until I clear a few things up. You understand?"

"No," Katarina objects.

"As soon as you can, this morning, go to the penthouse Darja and I are fixing up. You can sleep there, on the mattress. You can buy a sheet on the way. No one will bother you there."

"Right," says Katarina. "I'll sleep on the mattress. While you lay the whore, who's laying her boss behind your back."

Katarina starts getting dressed.

"If only for once you'd understand me!" Damjan grips his head.

"It's impossible," says Katarina, "to understand you, dear. Since I don't want the child to grow up without a father, I'll have to get used to it."

Katarina can't fall asleep on the mattress in the penthouse that Darja and Damjan are fixing up. The dust bothers her, and so does the dankness of the half-painted walls, the rotten wood, and the fog coming in through the broken windowpane. It seems to her that the fog that has been hanging over the city for ten days has come inside her, spilled into her veins and crept into all her membranes and organs, saturated and softened her brain, blurring her thoughts, which are dull, unfocussed, lazily woven memories of flames of a life that never was really hers.

It actually seems to her that she had been living in such a fog most of her life.

She remembers how in London her co-worker Mary told her that in 1952 such dense smog covered the city that you couldn't see more than a meter, and twenty thousand people died, and more than fifty thousand went to the hospital for help. She saw on the small TV screen in her mom's apartment how a similar smog envelopes, wraps, and engulfs Beijing, New Delhi, Singapore, and even London. More and more of the world. And that one of the main causes is salt from sulfuric acid, which comes from sulfur dioxide produced by coal burning power plants and factories.

Maybe it's true, she thinks. But not in Ljubljana. Here, she thinks more and more, it is the confusion in her soul that causes the real fog, at least the one she can see. It seeps out and covers almost the entire surroundings in which she finds herself, follows every decision she makes or it seems to her she makes, because she often has the sense that her phantom double makes decisions about her life. It is not within her but without her, and it decides for her so she can avoid the consequences of the decisions. For it's obvious—even children know this (adults often forget)—that decisions have consequences. And what we call life is only consequences, while the decisions retreat into the inaccessible depths of memory. We might only become aware of them on our deathbeds.

Is it possibly just a matter of being difficult to be a woman in society as it is? Is it easier for men? She knows from experience that it can't be; men, too, bear the consequences of their actions, which are possibly even worse, although it's hard for women to admit this. Hardest of all for her, it seems, because there were always men in her life from whom she expected firm convictions, which eluded her. Why hadn't it befallen her to run into at least one who could convince her of this and instill enough confidence to follow him? Lieutenant Colonel Osterc? Brane? Matej? Damjan? Brane exuded the most confidence, but fate had brought him to her to entice her into an abyss and expose her true inner nature. Had she known how to resist him, had she had enough strength to do that, her life would have been different.

Would it really have? On the dusty mattress in the musty penthouse in which her husband is fixing up an apartment for her predecessor and in all probability successor, Katarina's soul is consumed by the question of whether it's not an illusion if we imagine we know where we're going and where we were destined in the past, and that others reached their goals because they knew where they were going. Did others, like tourists aimlessly wandering the world, know how to turn new information into knowledge and change their plans accordingly? And again? And again? Or were they, like her, stuck with a fixed itinerary that couldn't be changed without worse consequences than they would have had if they were loyal to the originally conceived program?

Katarina can't find an answer to the question. It seems to her that she wasn't included in the travel plan she signed in her half-remembered childhood, but that she had been changing her destinations based on information she continually received from life. Perhaps it would have been better had she remained committed to the original plan, stable, less a victim of events and more their initiator and director. Is there actually anyone in the world who can do that? For whom a fog doesn't blanket life? Where does the conviction that we know what we're doing and where we want to go come from? That we know today what tomorrow's preferences will be, and that those who cross our path and with whom we enter into relationships know where they're going and won't want to go elsewhere tomorrow?

Was she expecting more from others than from herself? That they wanted what she wanted? That they wouldn't want something else tomorrow? Why was Damjan, who she never really got to know, a suitable life companion, as cold and reserved as he was? Would he have changed had they already been in Australia and her duty to her mother had not seemed more important than remaining loyal to their goals? Was the duty like a feeling of guilt because she had shoved it aside and ignored it in the past? Hadn't she withdrawn her loyalty from Damjan at a key moment? Did she now have the right to reproach him for retreating to the place from which with cunning persuasion she had enticed him into an illusory hope that he was the right one for her and she for him?

Why do the answers to all those questions lie in the poisonous fog covering the city and choking her as nothing in the world ever had? Why is her life made up mostly of questions? Why are there so few answers? And why are most of them wrong? Is it just her fate? Or the fate of everyone she runs into, partially visible, partially reachable, and partially recognizable in the fog of life?

Rok and Damjan are sitting in the waiting room of the Kočevje clinic.

"He won't admit it," says Rok.

"Leave it to me," says Damjan.

"Do you know what it means to falsify a medical document? Loss of license and possible jail. He would be crazy to admit it."

"He'll have to," Damjan is convinced.

"How do you even know she's not pregnant?" Rok asks him.

"I hope she isn't."

"Damn it, life has really mixed things up for you! I'd go crazy."

"I have, didn't you notice?"

"Considering that I drove you to Kočevje for nothing at all, it's me that's crazy, not you."

Damjan looks at his watch.

"He probably escaped out the window."

"Actually it's not me that's crazy," says Rok, "it's you."

A doctor in a white gown steps out of the office. He looks at Damjan, surprised.

"Damjan? It really is you."

"My friend Rok," Damjan introduces his friend.

"I couldn't believe it when the nurse told me you're waiting," says Dr. Pograjc.

"Why not?"

"I couldn't think of a reason for a high school buddy to visit me all of a sudden."

"There is a reason," says Damjan.

"After all, you're not my patient. Or maybe you are? Let's sit down."

All three take seats.

"Nice to see you after all this time, Damjan. How many years has it been?"

"Quite a few."

"I thought you're living in Ljubljana," says Pograjc and looks at him with concern. "Is there a problem?"

"Katarina has one."

"Yes," Pograjc says after a short pause. "How is Katarina? I haven't seen her for years either."

"I came to ask you," says Damjan, "just between us, as old friends, whether it's too late for an abortion."

He pulls the confirmation out of his pocket, unfolds it, and hands it to Pograjc, who reads it with surprise.

"But," he says, "my stamp is at the bottom! And my signature!"

"Why are you so surprised?" Damjan asks him.

"Because it's not my signature," Pograjc insists. "It's forged!" He puts aside the confirmation and pulls out his cell phone. "I have to call the police right away."

Damjan takes hold of the hand Pograjc is holding the phone with. "Wait. Who in this building could issue a confirmation with a stamp and forge you signature?"

"Any one of the nurses. They all have access to the stamps."

Damjan pulls the confirmation out of his hand, folds it, and puts it in his pocket.

"No," Pograjc wants it back, "this is a very serious crime, it has to be investigated!"

"You go ahead, everything is clear to me," says Damjan, gets up, and turns towards the exit.

Rok follows.

"Damjan, wait a few minutes. I have to get to the bottom of this." Pograjc pulls him back. "Please. I'm asking you as a school buddy. You can't think that's really my signature."

"How am I to know," Damjan shrugs. "It might be. Maybe she's pregnant. Maybe not."

"Did she use Clearblue? She can get it in any drugstore. She can find out in a few minutes whether she's pregnant."

"She came to you because she knew I wouldn't believe her. She wanted official confirmation. It's not important whether she got it from you or from one of the nurses."

"It is to me, Damjan," says Pograjc. "It's a punishable offense. Please wait."

Damjan and Rok sit down again. Pograjc goes into the clinic.

"Do you think he's bluffing?" asks Rok.

"I'd say no," says Damjan.

"I don't think so either."

Damjan thinks for a while, going over things. "I think I know what happened. Katarina's cousin works here as a nurse."

"Damn..." says Rok. "But she wouldn't..."

"You don't think so?"

"On the other hand…" Rok allows for the possibility of the opposite.

"On the other hand, she might have," says Damjan. "And did."

"But why would Katarina bring you a false confirmation that she's pregnant? She surely doesn't think that she can hold on to you like that. She's experienced enough."

"She wanted to force us to go to Australia."

"But you intended to!" says Rok.

Damjan gets up. "Let's go."

Rok gets up as well. "We're not going to wait?"

"There's no sense. We'll go back to Ljubljana. Wait… Do you have a smart phone?"

Rok pulls out his phone and hands it to Damjan.

Damjan searches and checks information on Google. Then he shakes his head.

"Did you know that a child born to foreigners in Australia can become an Australian citizen only if at least one of the parents already has a residence permit?"

"No," Rok shakes his head.

"Well, now you know. And so do I."

"She was even lying about that?"

"Unfortunately."

Darja's studio. The couch is put back. Damjan is sitting on it, a laptop on his knees. Darja is taking things out of the open suitcase on the floor and putting some away in the dresser. Others she throws in a laundry basket.

"And how was it?" asks Damjan.

"Painfully boring. You know how these things go."

"I don't."

"But it was more interesting here, no?" Darja looks at him.

"How do you mean?"

"My boss called and told me you were at his office with some touched up photograph."

"This one?" Damjan reaches into a pocket in the laptop case and hands Darja the photo.

Darja looks and it and gives it back. "And you thought it was real."

"No. But I was confused."

"Did it come in the mail?"

"Katarina gave it to me."

"Nice of her."

"And that's not all. She lied that she's pregnant. She wanted us to leave for Australia before you got back."

"She obviously loves you," Darja observes sincerely.

"Is that called love? I didn't know."

"Women who love too much are capable of the worst things. They can forgive and they can murder."

"Do I have to be afraid of you, too?" Damjan looks at her.

"I don't love you too much. I love you just enough."

"How much is enough?"

"If you love someone just enough, you see his mistakes and you love him just the same."

Again Darja reaches for the photo, which Damjan is holding in his right hand. She looks at it closely, then gives it back to Damjan.

"I think I know the author of this masterpiece."

"Who?"

"Your friend."

"Which friend?"

"Rok."

"Don't be silly," Damjan waves.

"He's a photographer. Didn't you know?"

"An amateur. With a little digital camera. Like me."

"He obviously didn't tell you he has his own studio."

"Rok is an architect."

"When he has work. When he doesn't he's occupied with photography."

"How do you know?"

"Because I know him," says Darja. "Very well."

"Why didn't he tell me that? We're friends."

"He would tell a friend on whose orders he fudged the photo?" Darja is surprised.

"Friends trust each other."

"Not always. And not all."

Damjan is totally confused. "But that's... that's..."

"On the one hand, I understand her. Because..."

She can't finish the sentence. Someone is at the door.

"Darja," her father's voice is heard, "open up! I know you're home!"

Darja puts a finger on Damjan's mouth.

"Why don't you want..." Damjan whispers.

"Shhhh!"

Darja's father bangs on the door. The next minute Darja's phone rings in her purse. She quickly shoves the purse under two pillows on the couch. The phone rings quite a few times. It finally quiets down. Darja's father loudly curses at the door and leaves. After a while they hear the sound of the elevator going down.

"I forgot to tell you he was looking for you," says Damjan. "He wanted to know why you didn't answer his calls."

"Do you remember what I told you before I went away? About the investigation into a corrupt contract?"

Damjan nods.

"Father wants me to give false testimony for him. To lie in court. I won't do that."

Damjan nods.

210

"And your job?"

"I don't have a job anymore, dear," says Darja and closes the empty suitcase. "I found out in Brussels already that they suspended me. The firing will come in a few days."

"I'm to blame," Damjan says contritely.

"Why you?"

"Because I went to your boss."

"Don't be silly. He's on his way out, too. It's an ugly story. I'd like to forget the whole thing. And go off somewhere to hide. Somewhere far away."

"There's something else," says Damjan, as if he doesn't dare tell her. "I let Katarina sleep on the mattress in the penthouse. Her sister is back and there's no room at her mom's."

"Nice," Darja praises him.

Damjan gets up. "I must go and throw her out."

Darja shoves him back on the couch. "Let her stay there. She has to be somewhere until things are sorted out. Try to understand her."

"After everything she did?" Damjan can't believe it.

"She was fighting for something I would fight for, too," says Darja. "I forgive her. You should, too."

Damjan hangs his head. "It's hard…"

"Kindness is always repaid with interest."

"I'll think about it," Damjan promises.

"Most of all, you're forgetting one thing," says Darja.

"What?"

"That you cheated on her. With me. Are you any better than her on account of that?"

"That's something else," Damjan objects.

"She was fighting for something she had lost, and she didn't want to admit it," Darja goes on defending Katarina.

"She lied!" Damjan is emphatic.

"I did, too, as long as we're on it," Darja admits. "I wasn't as open as I would have liked to be."

"How am I supposed to take that?"

"Do you remember what I said about the guy I lived with for a while when you left me?"

"The one who worked all the time and didn't have time for you?"

"Didn't Rok tell you that his girl left him for the same reason?"

"Yeah," says Damjan. "Sonja."

"No, her name was Darja. And my boyfriend was Rok."

Damjan is silent for a while. Then he says: "You have to be joking."

"No, Damjan, I'm not."

"Why didn't you tell me?"

"I wanted to. But I didn't dare. I was afraid of hurting you. And you would leave. I wanted you to stay with me. By me. And be mine."

"Nice," says Damjan after a short silence. "All three of you were lying to me."

"You're completely unfamiliar with lying, of course. You could never tell a lie."

"I'm not claiming that, but…"

"But what?"

"I don't understand anything anymore," Damjan says, crushed.

"Me either. And I never did. But it doesn't bother me. And never did."

Damjan sits still for a while, staring into a void.

"What is it?" Darja asks him.

"Do you remember that old mattress in the penthouse?"

"Very well," says Darja. "That's where you refused to have sex with me for the first time."

212

"Do you remember the dust that came up when I hit it?"

"That, too."

"Do you remember," Damjan goes on, "what I said to explain to you why I didn't want to have sex on it?"

" You said there was too much filth around us."

"It turned out that we're all filthy."

"I didn't create the world," says Darja. "I don't direct the times."

"No."

"I'm only an actor in a drama that none of us has read to the end."

Damjan gets up and stares out the window for a while. Fog stills covers the roofs, but life goes on in different ways for different people. But why does life, too, remain in an even denser fog than the one enveloping the city for over a week? Why didn't Katarina ever confess to him where the scars on her stomach came from? "My past is mine, yours is yours," was her answer when he tried to find out. He didn't press it. In the end, he didn't tell her either that his parents had committed suicide and he had grown up in a foster family.

And who did she have in mind when she told him—not exactly him, but thinking out loud—that she had seen two people from afar in a Ljubljana crowd, one of whom should have been dead and the other in London? She said it might have been a hallucination or a fleeting similarity, and didn't want to say anything more. And who did she have in mind when she said another reason they had to go to Australia as soon as possible was that someone she was very afraid of was getting out of jail? The unspoken secrets didn't help them. Every successive lie, small or large, ineluctably drove them to where they were now. To this moment.

"What should we do?" he finally turns around.

"We're not the only ones in this world who are putting that question to themselves," says Darja.

"You said you've had enough of it all and want to go somewhere far away."

"I probably will." Darja nods.

"I think you will, too."

He reaches for the laptop case and takes out the plane tickets. He hands one to Darja.

"Wait," says Darja, "this is Katarina's ticket!"

Damjan pulls his cell phone out of his pocket and enters a number. "Travel agency? Can you tell me whether Singapore Airlines permits the transfer of a plane ticket to another person...? I thought so. That's alright, I'll come in and buy another one."

He puts away the phone. Darja looks at him. First with fear, then her features form into a hopeful smile that is yet filled with the stress of uncertainty.

"You're crazy," she says. "Aren't you?"

"No. Only someone who would like to escape the story of his life."

Darja hugs him. "Like me?" Then she pushes him away. "What about Katarina?"

"Would you rather be in her place?" Damjan asks her.

"I know it sounds stupid, but I'd like to be her *and* me."

"Unfortunately we both have to remain who we are," says Damjan.

"And what will happen to her? We can't just throw people away."

"We all make our choices," says Damjan. "We have to. She did, too. And we all have to live with the consequences."

"Where did you read that?" Darja asks him. "Have you suddenly become original?"

They embrace. Darja stares out the window over Damjan's shoulder.

"My heart hurts so," she says. "It's so foggy outside. And in my head. What will happen to Katarina?"

Damjan is silent.

Part 4

SUMMER

The little village by the forest is bathed in summer sunlight. It's humid, and a thunderstorm is gathering behind the mountains. Tonko, a longtime career officer who was promoted from intern to chief of the tax bureau, leaves the white-hot kitchen and sits down at a table by the window.

There's a new laptop on it. For the third or maybe fourth time he checks the contents of the message he sent the day before to the address katarina231@yahoo.com.

"Dear Katarina," the words he chose jump smilingly at him from the screen. "Mom left for Hvar with the retirees. The house I was born in and in which I dreamed of you so many times is empty. I'll show you the room I slept in, the bed in which I marveled at your photo by flashlight with the covers pulled over my head. You know, the one with braids! Let it finally happen here, in that bed! Fate has blessed us and chosen us to experience a miracle…"

Aren't there too many phrases in the message that might be more at home in a romance novel? Which Katarina surely doesn't read? And which he himself leafs through only occasionally? And only because his secretary leaves them on the office table?

But now it's too late. Now Katarina has already read the outpouring of ecstasy so ill becoming a man of his age, and one so serious on the surface. And with a government job! Heaven knows what kind of opinion she has formed about her ill-fated lover from the distant past.

Maybe she's laughing at him. And she won't come.

Tonko nonetheless returns to the kitchen to check whether the great feast is all set. They would begin with grilled wild mushrooms for initial associative arousal (he noticed when he was cutting them in long pieces that they have the form of a phallus). They would continue with hot Indian curries that are supposed to be (as he was able to learn by googling them) an effective aphrodisiac. They would conclude with a local pastry to remind them how sweet a workout between freshly laundered sheets can be.

Tonko, who was never married, had devoted quite a bit of time to honing his culinary skills. As a sworn gourmet, he didn't want to dine in cheap taverns. Therefore he wasn't worried that Katarina, his little girl from long ago, wouldn't like his lunch.

He had thoroughly straightened up the house the day before to create optimal conditions for the event he had mulled over a hundred times already. He had brought in twenty bottles of French wine, new sheets, and a CD-player with a collection of CDs in which he included popular songs from the time Katarina and he had been in grade school. Enya's songs were on most of the CDs. Katarina had begun to be infatuated with her in the eighth grade.

Early in the morning he had gone to the store in nearby Kočevje one last time and bought five big candles. Then he bathed, shaved, and dressed nicely. He had become quite systematic during his long years of government service, and was capable of thinking of every detail. He did more than would a thousand men in his place. So he didn't see any reason for everything not to turn out as he planned.

Katarina shows up two hours late. She parks her car by the water well near the road and goes to the house on foot, without a suitcase, just a purse, although they had agreed she would stay over. But perhaps she left a traveling bag in the trunk, Tonko tries to comfort himself. When he sees her coming through the orchard towards the yard, it dawns on him that this isn't the Katarina he wrote hot letters and even poems to in school, but an unfamiliar, almost middle-aged woman, though she is two years younger than him and so can't be more than thirty-two. Her unfashionable suit, which reminds even the conservative state functionary of times past, evokes the impression of serious and old-fashioned propriety, far from the passionate lover he yearned for.

But when he hugs her at the threshold, she is once again the girl of his dreams, the red thread of all the fantasies that accompanied him through his boring life. Her closeness strikes him like a whirlwind, his stocky figure almost wavers. Her panting mouth near his, the fresh softness of her thighs, which he fleetingly feels against his, the scent of her hair, the moist heat of her palms—all of it fills him with a quaking feeling he can't name.

Tonko could spend the rest of his life like that, in an embrace that would remain a promise and unfulfilled hope.

And it seemed to him that she, too, would like to freeze the feeling instead of risking that the outcome wouldn't fit expectations. To freeze the dreams in a moment when they still promise everything—isn't that a temptation he had succumbed to a thousand times already? Hadn't they both at some key moment? Isn't the temptation even greater now, when they've decided to freeze the moment?

Only when she takes a step and his hip accidentally touches hers again does Katarina uncertainly push him away and ask whether he intends to leave her on the doorstep. He offers her his arm in a gallant gesture and accompanies her into the room, where at the sight of the white tablecloth on the table Katarina smiles mysteriously. A popular song they often listened to while holding hands is blasting from the CD-player on the windowsill.

Who can say where the road goes...

Katarina's face darkens, her upper lip nervously twitches, and she moves away from him a little.

"Can you turn off the music?" she demands in a tone of voice one might use to reprimand a naughty schoolboy.

Tonko complies without objection and does nothing to show what a wave of devastation has rolled over him. He had hoped that "her song" would transport her to a time she was in love and awaken feelings she may have forgotten, but that he never had.

Katarina quickly realizes that she had chastised her host too sharply, so she makes it up with a sweet smile. Tonko immediately uses it for his next maneuver: he steps up and awkwardly kisses her on the lips. For some time they stand close together, quivering. Tonko senses how the onetime schoolgirl's and now nurse's heart is beating. It pleases him that it's beating faster than usual. Katarina, still uncomfortable with the tone of her words, doesn't remove her lips as quickly as she otherwise would have.

This is proof to Tonko that she likes the moist pressure of his lips, and so, emboldened, he tries to insert the tip of his tongue.

At that, Katarina pushes him away decisively and asks, "What about the soup? It will get cold!"

Tonko is so excited during lunch that his hands are shaking. He only becomes aware of it when he raps his spoon on the edge of his bowl. In her faultlessly ironed white blouse, her manicured nails, and the measured movements with which she cuts the chicken thigh and carefully places pieces in her mouth, she gives the impression of having calmed down after her initial irritation and gained control of the situation.

222

Tonko fears the initiative has slipped away from him, even though he is aware she might be pretending. The more it seems to him his guest is exerting control, the more the awkward handling of his silverware reveals that he is turning into a bumbling adolescent the schoolteacher is about to put in the corner. His heart jumps anxiously.

This can't be allowed to happen.

At first the conversation is shaky. They try to make a connection and find safe ground. After spinning words about the benefits of their work, she suddenly asks him to tell her something about his friendship with Damjan, her husband. Had they really been that close? Why hadn't they been in touch for so many years? And why all at once did he decide to visit him?

"Oh," Tonko defends himself, "you know how it is with friendships. A thing or two linked us in high school. Then Damjan got a job in Ljubljana, and I in Maribor. Although I was transferred to Ljubljana not long after, to the Tax Office. It was a coincidence that led to the visit."

It seems Katarina only half believes him. She asks whether he knew she was married to Damjan. For an instant he's seized by the desire to tell her the truth. Then he changes his mind and says he had no idea. It had struck him like lightning when he saw her at his apartment. And at that moment he was also overcome by a powerful love.

"Love at second sight," he adds, sure she will like the phrase.

Katarina responds with surprise. How had he recognized her? Because she must have changed a great deal over the years and after all that had happened. Intuition, Tonko lies. Her eyes, mouth, and freckles. And he had never really forgotten her. He saw no difference between the schoolgirl and the mature woman who had unexpectedly come out of the bedroom during his visit. When he introduced them, Damjan had even said, "You might know each other." And she blushed slightly. Just as she is blushing now.

Tonko takes two sips of French wine and asks directly: "Did Damjan know about our love in school?"

Katarina wordlessly nods and takes three sips of wine. Then she defiantly straightens up and empties her glass. Tonko leans over the table and refills it.

He asks whether it bothers her that he and her husband had been high school friends. Katarina replies that in the beginning it didn't. But when he visited, and she saw him again, mature and successful, and even more when he called afterwards and said he had dreamed only of her his whole life, something stirred in her.

It was as if two tectonic plates had slid by each other and caused an earthquake. It was as if she had felt the opportunity of renewed youth. That is why she sent him those childish, silly e-mails. It was only a few days ago that her conscience started to bother her. In sum, she couldn't break off with Damjan just like that.

Tonko feels the ground shift under him again. She probably hadn't come simply to tell him it was a mistake to come?

"Me, too," he launches into a counterattack out of uncertainty. "I sensed an opportunity for renewed youth, too. Do you remember? We wrote that we're fated for each other, and that five thousand horses couldn't keep us apart."

Katarina shifts anxiously and looks out the window at the orchard. "You saw to that, not the horses."

Tonko thinks it best to overlook these words. She probably didn't come just to make an issue of his mistakes so many years ago. After all, they were both children, and if they hadn't touched on that childish slip-up in months of e-mail correspondence, it would be senseless to go into it now.

"We waited too long," Katarina says suddenly and with a finger starts to draw circles and squares in the wine spilled on the table.

"That's what you wanted," Tonko says, trying not to let his words sound like a reproach.

Now he, too, starts to draw circles and squares with his finger, on a dry spot.

"That must mean"—he painfully prepares to express his fear in a minimally fateful tone—"that your feelings are no longer those that I discerned from your messages?"

Katarina averts her eyes.

Then she tosses her hair, pushes her chair back, and gets up.

"I don't know, Tonko, I don't know," she says and anxiously paces the room. "I don't know any more what is and isn't. So much has happened to me in recent years that I'm completely confused."

Tonko hurries to get up and goes to her. He puts a hand on her shoulder from behind and breathes in her ear, "Katarina…"

He tries to turn her around, but Katarina pushes him away decisively.

"Let's go somewhere," she says. "I can't breathe here."

Tonko locks the house and they head through the orchard towards the forest. He puts an arm around her waist, and Katarina doesn't push it off. They wander through the unmoved grass towards the road below the orchard. The thunder that a little while ago was rumbling over the mountains had moved off together with the clouds beyond the forest and humid heat filled the entire space that could be seen.

They turn off the road onto a path leading through currant bushes between the pines, firs, and beeches. Broken rays of sun fall through the branches and change the ground into a blinking pattern of squares and circles recalling the ones they drew on the table a little before, a kind of unstable chess board over which they moved their feet in an unconscious game that would decide their—his, or her, or both of their—future.

To whose advantage? Was it all just a maneuver to decide which of them, once again after all these years, would triumph and which would lose?

Tonko suddenly slows his pace, draws Katarina close, and kisses her. He is surprised when he feels she doesn't resist. He half expected her to push him away again. But no, she wraps herself around him, her tongue glides into his mouth, and she licks his. The taste of onion gravy on hers and bitter wine on his flow together into something pleasant, even arousing, which brings them together more closely than words had divided them before.

Tonko gets his courage up and whispers in her ear that maybe they should try and find the hollow in which they secretly met when they were in school. Katarina nods.

"If you can," she says. "I can't find my way in the forest."

Hand in hand, like school kids in love in some far off times, they set off through the hornbeams and pines towards the hollow with low brush that was once, long ago (although it seems barely yesterday) the hiding place for their love, their safe corner in a world they didn't yet know. Her eyes are suddenly submissive and promising, and Tonko is enjoying

226

the exhilaration of a suspicion that she, too, desires what he has his entire life.

For it to happen there, where they first kissed. On the moss, under a roof of aromatic acacia.

When they're already close, Katarina asks him why he never married. He jokes that he was waiting for her, because she was the only one with whom he would dare step on the path of no return. It was her image with which he passed the hours of insomnia that tormented him from the very moment when his infatuation condemned him to eternal yearning for her.

Katarina wanly smiles and repeats: How is it possible that at his age, with a prestigious position, relatively wealthy, a guaranteed and far above average pension, interesting if not exactly attractive (that belly is a formidable hurdle in women's eyes)—how is it possible that despite all this he is still single? After all, there must be at least a hundred women who would happily bear the yoke of a family for him. Might he still be the Don Juan he was in school, flitting from one to another like a bumblebee?

Not for a long time anymore, replies Tonko, stupidly flattered but at the same time bitter at the thought of what a gulf had opened over the years between his reputation and the life that fate had bestowed on him. He bends over and picks up a forked stick, part of a beech branch that had crashed to earth during a storm and begun to rot.

"Are you afraid of wolves?" Katarina asks him.

"Wolves don't bite each other," he jokes acidly, "especially if both are loners."

They go slowly ahead over moss, tangles of sticks, and roots. Tonko both supports himself with the stick and rakes the ground and moss around him, and slaps the bushes and trunks. It seems to him that they're accompanied by a shadowy threat. Perhaps they shouldn't have come to the forest in which the stillborn hopes of their love lay buried.

Suddenly something rustles in the bushes in front of them. Katarina spontaneously rushes into his embrace. A doe leaps by.

"Oh," she whispers in his ear, "I thought it was something dangerous!"

Tonko presses her close, but she quickly frees herself and says: "Do you feel how my heart is beating?" She takes his hand and puts in on her breast. Tonko quivers and starts to massage it spasmodically.

"Ouch!" Katarina steps back, "can't you be gentle?"

Tonko wants to whisper to her that he can, of course he can, because he hadn't had a chance in his life to be crude, except with himself, but that's another story. Gentleness with everything but himself, even clients in his government position, had almost been forced on him. If life passes you by without noticing, you have little else left but politeness, caution, and meekness. Perhaps an obsession here and there, like religion, to awaken something in life that has long rested in the grave of squandered time.

But why should he explain all that to her? Why should he expose the secrets of a conspiracy she, too, is part of, although possibly without being aware?

Katarina pulls him ahead through the forest as if she were in a hurry. Yet another doe leaps off through the blinking network of sun and shadows. When it noisily disappears into a cluster of trees, something inside Tonko shifts, and memories batter him.

There, beyond the forest, was the school where it all began. Which girl was first? Silva Meglic? Silva Tratnik? In any case, a Silva. Or Slava. He loaned her a workbook and put notes inside with declarations of how he wanted to kiss her. For a time she responded encouragingly, but then, when he didn't know what to do next, she returned all twenty notes and curtly wrote that he was a dope and that she would file a complaint if he didn't stop it.

Not long after he met Katarina. She had very light hair, was in the seventh grade, had a face full of freckles, and laughed in a special way. Her laugh was Tonko's torment and pleasure, as her movements and slightly hoarse voice were an even greater torment and pleasure, as well as her blouses, which couldn't hide the quivering of her barely noticeable breasts.

They agreed he would loan her a book, and he stuck a passionate love letter among the pages. Dear, dearest, beloved Katarinčica, he wrote, and so on in that style for five pages. He begged her not to torment him, to say yes or no. The day when he was waiting was "a day of life and death, a day of birth and death, a stormily sunny and hot day, full of hail, cold, and snow" (that's approximately how he described it in his diary).

She returned the book with her answer. I love you, I've loved you a long time, I desire you, and so on in such a style. She had not escaped the influence of trashy literature, and she knew how to sigh as ecstatically as he.

So began the serenade, which was full of heart spasms and stresses, full of daring desires and fear, full of exultation and exhaustingly abundant happiness... (and so forth, all described in detail in Tonko's diary). They would meet in the wooded hollow (the one they were now making their way to). There he kissed her for the first time. He covered her eyes with a hand, since at decisive moment he was seized with shaking. The kiss was short. She didn't open her mouth, and he felt coldness in her thin, bloodless lips—not just lack of will, but almost resistance.

Nonetheless, after the event he didn't dare admit that he wasn't divinely happy. The feeling didn't stem from pleasure but from triumphing in the feat accomplished; from the consciousness of finally joining the ranks of lovers. He carried her photograph in his pocket, secretly looking at it under his school desk. He swiped his father's pocket flashlight and hid it under his pillow so that at night he could take pleasure in his chosen one's freckled smile.

He started writing poems to her. The verses that boiled up from his exultation seemed to him so superb that he frequently compared them to the best penned by Petrarch, Prešeren, and Rilke. In the summer, he went to camp on the sea and was afraid he would greatly miss her. But then the experience of the pounding waves and the smell of fish and taste of salt on the wind that blew from behind Velebit Mountain swept him away and he forgot about her. The days were overflowing with all kinds of new things! Her image faded and retreated into a time of life that seemed lost in the past and meaningless to him.

The vacation lodge was brimming with pretty girls. He was first in love with one, then another, and there was no end to his arousal. And since some of them were much more beautiful than Katarina, deep inside he began to be ashamed of his attachment to her. When she popped into his mind, he felt a bothersome attachment, which he wanted to end in the ecstasy of experiences at the beach. The experiences weren't love, they were only the sum of impressions that later, when he had drunk them in, started to multiply and undermine everything that was but a memory, the sediment of a time that had passed.

When he got home, he straightaway wrote Katarina a short letter, ending it with a quotation from Levstik: "Time is a wind that blows off the chaff and leaves only the grain."

With that pompous declaration he retreated into enjoying his inflated self-worth. For the first time in his life he had ended a love affair and he was sated with the conviction that now all the girls were available to him. He saw the measure of his attractiveness in the insensitivity with which he had gotten rid of his first love.

Therefore the greater his astonishment when he cast a hook into the fishpond of female flirtatiousness, and none bit.

He was overcome by the feeling of being wronged. The failures kept coming. He lent books to girls at school and stuck love letters in them. It wasn't long before he had promised "heavenly moments" to all the girls in the class. Not one responded. When he got to the last one, he was seized by despair. The thought that the girls were mocking him was a torment. One day he got to school a little later; the class was at their desks waiting for the teacher, who was late. When he came in, he felt all their eyes following him. Someone coughed meaningfully, and snickering broke out behind him. He sat down.

And then he saw it. Someone had written in chalk on the board: "Don Juan's confessions." His love letters were taped underneath. The worst part of it was that they were all identical, down to the last word.

He heard the history teacher's rubber soles squeaking down the hall. He rushed to the board and started ripping down the letters and sticking them in his pocket. The minute the teacher entered, there was an explosion of hellish, derisive laughter. Tonko flew into the hallway and ran towards the stairs. He met the principal, who asked him whether he had been stung by a wasp.

He dashed out the door and into the street, running to the edge of the village and through the fields towards the forest.

He turned into the bushes, lay down on the moss, and cried in a fit of shame. It seemed impossible that he would ever return to the class. He thought of his mother and father. Being shamed in front of his classmates seemed less terrible that being shamed before them, should they find out how he had dishonored himself. He had his cry and slunk back.

The principal was lying in wait for him in the hallway, and took him into the office. He told him he was to blame. Why didn't he just pinch the girls on their behinds, like all the other boys? It was true the class had gone a little too far. He led him back to the classroom. When Tonko took his seat, his head hanging, the principal authoritatively looked around the room and threatened that the first one to open his mouth would have to write a hundred times: "I'm a fool who won't forgive my classmate Platonic love."

Tonko didn't forget the shaming. He decided he had to erase it at all costs and prove to his classmates they had wrongly made fun of him. To this end, it seemed to him natural to use the girl he had actually conquered and then jilted. In a gently worded letter, saying he had changed his mind, he invited Katarina back into his "embrace."

He was convinced she would jump for it. But no, she had another boy. When he recovered from several days of dizziness, he started pleading. He reproached her for betraying him. He begged her to consider his yearning. In the end, he threatened to hang himself.

She was silent. He had an anxious, emotional summer, full of anger and tears and thoughts of revenge. Again he wrote her poems and once again thought of himself as a genius.

"I know that each one of the girls desires me, but my heart can't love them, because it is an extinguished candle that only you can light. But you, my maiden, don't respect my love, you destroy my heart."

He wrote her long, bombastic letters with quotations from Aškerc, Jenko, and Prešeren. On the one hand, he promised her eternal loyalty; on the other, he threatened to become a famous movie actor, and then it would be too late. She had to decide now.

It was in vain. He finally grew weary of the fitful wooing and began to forget about it. The speed with which the whole thing sunk among bad memories quite surprised him.

In the end, it seemed to him it had been nothing more than a kiss, one kiss, which was too cold to remember forever. Everything else was an illusion he had devised in his passion to avoid his classmates making fun of him.

Katarina suddenly calls, "Catch me!", and runs between the trees. Tonko hurries after her, but she is fast and nimble, as if she had turned into a taunting young girl. And he is heavy and awkward, having grown stiff from long years of sitting still at his desk.

Katarina looks back and ambiguously jokes: "Oh, what a fat stick you have, help me!"

The sun's rays catch the waves of her hair and then grow dim in the trees, in the flickering spider web of sun and shadow, which seems to have cloaked time like a spider does a fly, forcing it to be still. Staff in hand, Tonko stumbles after her.

"After all, she's finally here with me, in front of me, I've caught up with her, I've caught up with my desire for her," goes through his mind. He's convinced that now it will happen; there's no way back.

He wouldn't have caught her, of course, had she not stopped and waited. After having spent a decade trying to fill the void in his soul with fatty foods, he was quite stout.

"Katarina," he wheezes more than breathes. Completely out of breath, he presses her to himself. "Do you know how long I've been waiting for this moment?" He sloppily puts his mouth to her, onto her mouth, her neck, and shoulders. He shoves his fat fingers under her blouse and struggles to loosen her bra.

"No, Tonko!" she hisses into his face almost venomously and sticks a nail in his hand. "Why can't you wait? We said there, where you kissed me the first time."

"I can't wait," the tax inspector answers lasciviously, "we might not find the place, the bushes have overgrown it."

"Yes," Katarina replies and gives him a shove, "the bushes have overgrown quite a bit. Don't be aggressive, I'll scream!"

They continue on through the aromatic summer forest. Their feet crunch over the piles of sticks and rustle last fall's leaves. They brush aside branches in their way, prickly currant branches, and gradually go down into the hollow they still remember, although it seems to them smaller and less mysterious than it was. Katarina goes ahead of him, carefully looking for firm ground in her dress shoes, which though low-heeled are unsuited for walks in the forest. Tonko lurches after her, leaning on the staff with which he would like to thrash the whole world, the indifferent world that has denied him everything it has lavished on others.

Observing Katarina from behind, he has to admit that time hasn't passed her by either: although she acts young, her hips have widened and become almost formless. Many years have passed since they kissed in this forest.

And suddenly the tax inspector feels a pain more despairing than any he has ever felt. It's as if burning concrete were being poured into him and was flowing through all his limbs, down to the capillaries in his fingers. So many years have passed! And he's still here! He's just the same as always. He's just older and has things: a position and things.

234

But his dreams and desires are still the same.

Why does the body age but the soul is stuck in a traffic jam of unrealized yearnings? Tonko leans against the nearest beech and starts to sob. He hugs the tree and slides down its trunk to his knees.

Katarina crouches by him and puts a hand on his shoulder. He feels her breath in his ear.

"Tonko," she urges him, "don't be childish, why are you doing this?"

Tonko lets go of the trunk, shudders, and embraces Katarina. He buries his head in her embrace and wets her skirt with his tears, while she crouches on the leaves and uncertainly pats his head.

"I'd like," he sobs to her, "do you know what I'd like? I'd like to be a beech that the wind strips yellow leaves from and blows them away, and then new, fragrant ones grow. I'd like the wind to blow away my life and leave me only the trunk of childhood with a fresh future. There's a child in my heart, and only the child in me is what I truly am. Everything else is contrived and false."

Katarina is silent. The hand with which she is patting the hair on his head—once wild, almost sticking out, but now flat and reduced to a few wisps—loses its tenderness and vigor. She suddenly calms down and withdraws. She seizes his head with both hands and pulls him up.

Tonko bashfully casts his eyes down.

"Why did you come?" he asks her and gets up all his courage to look at her.

Sparks from the afternoon sun behind her head, behind the swaying chestnut, beech, and fir branches dance with the wavering shadows on Tonko's distorted face.

"If only I knew," Katarina replies quietly. "I, too, dreamed about our love becoming something purifying. A wind that would blow away the rotten leaves and leave only the innocence I still feel inside. But there is no such wind. Choices come up only once, Tonko. You can't relive love. Actually, it wouldn't be love. It would just be sex. We're old enough to realize that. My ability to love has evaporated. Too much has happened to me. I don't know what I want anymore. I only know I don't want what you're offering."

She gets up and walks through the trees, drained. The sunny, dancing web under the trees wraps, envelopes, and distances her.

"Dear, dear, dear Katarina," Tonko writes her a last letter in his mind. "Which of us made the bigger mistake? You with your pride or me with my fantasizing? Or was there no mistake, and life is only the result of the total of our misunderstandings?"

He adds in closing: "But sex, Katarina, is something that at my age I haven't yet tasted! Because of that I feel like a paraplegic! Could you really not muster enough understanding to have mercy on me?"

T onko returns to the house. First he cleans up the kitchen table. He notices that Katarina left two carrots on her plate. He shoves them in his mouth and slowly chews: he imagines he's chewing her saliva with them.

When he's cleaned up the table and stacked everything in the sink and on the kitchen counter, he turns on the player and listens to Enya. He drops the idea of sitting right down at the computer and writes Katarina a letter in which he would list all of his trials—this time actual ones, not made up—and goes to the bedroom, where there is a two-meter mirror on the wall. The store delivered it a good year ago.

Why did he even order it? He placed it so as to reflect the bed and anything that would happen on it. But what he wanted to happen there stubbornly remained a part of his dreams and refused to become reality. The woman he imagined to be his last chance for his dreams to come true had just driven off in her car.

He steps up to the mirror and views the image of a man contemplating him from within. It starts to dawn on him that he does this at least three times a day and that he has been doing this since he ordered the mirror. If he felt the need, he could list a hundred reasons for looking at himself, from checking how fast he is losing weight and how it affects his appearance to searching for reasons that women continually turn down his attempts to get them into bed.

He is also dimly aware of the fact that all of his attempts to lose weight have gone awry. Dimly because he confronts the fact every time he steps in front of the mirror. How is it possible that fate cast him such an unhappy fate? As a child, teenager, and young man he was quite pleasing, though in no way handsome, but appealing enough for girls not to avoid him. In his own eyes, however, he was so attractive that he had haughtily and cruelly jilted Katarina, perhaps the only girl in his life who really loved him.

Time is a wind... Hah, hah, it had blown away his grain and left him with the chaff.

Why had he started putting on weight a little after twenty? Too little physical activity? But that went for others his age as well, who despite sitting in front of a monitor fourteen hours a day maintained a normal figure! Did he eat too much? It's true that he had tried to assuage some of life's pains with food, actually not just pains but often hardly noticeable aches that he could have ignored. Was it genetic? His mother was slender; his father sturdy without being fat; his sister, married with children, had a normal figure, although she liked to cook and to eat even more. Something had gone terribly wrong in his case.

"Why, why, why?" Tonko asks himself for the hundredth time.

He looks at his unusual figure, a man with a large belly, but evenly bulging, as if he had been drawn by a cartoonist, with a shirt on which the bottom buttons won't button, and pants he had to let out at the waist in order to fasten them. He looks at his arms sticking out of the short sleeves and giving the impression of being swollen because of some unknown disease. He looks at his three fleshy double chins and cheeks creased with fat, and the eyelids so filled with fat that they are puffy and hang over the eyes so that he can barely see the world. He looks at his knees, which have become so thick that they stick out in his pants, even though they're the widest you can get. He looks at the entirety of his figure and asks himself why something so unnatural had to happen to him, a normal person with a sensitive nature, a kind hearted and talented civil servant with a good salary who is, insofar as possible, forgiving even of people who have made some mistake on their tax return, even a serious mistake, thus breaking the law, which for the loyal government representative he considers himself to be, is further cause for the stress that pressures him from morning to evening and even in his dreams.

He recalls trying a number of diets that were supposed to reduce his girth and most of all change his grotesque face into something normal, unnoticeable, and acceptable. He found everything and carefully studied it on Google, along with all the contradictions, because he had long ago concluded that Google was mainly created so that the majority of people would not agree about most things. But no solution really worked, although with some it seemed that he had hit on the right one—for example, a radical three-day diet American doctors in a Birmingham hospital were using for patients to lose weight quickly before an operation. But three days after ending the diet he concluded that his weight had gone up by two kilograms.

Standing in front of the mirror after Katarina, Katka, Katarinčka's departure—the only one he really desired to introduce him to the world of sex—Tonko realizes that his physical appearance doesn't bother him as much as the fact that as a result, at his age, he hadn't lost his virginity.

He had been explaining to himself for years that that can't be normal; it can't be tied only and exclusively to his appearance. There must be natural or unnatural forces in play, which have also to do with his character, his attitude towards women, and his attitude towards himself, sex, life, and the world in all its aspects.

All the same, when he delved into intensive and often cruel research of those possibilities, he couldn't find an answer that would relieve him or point the way forward. As a man of his age, he still desired something completely normal: a relationship with a woman that would also include sex. Is there anything wrong with that?

It's true that besides that, perhaps even more, he also desired a purely sexual experience—the feeling of shoving his penis, of a suitable size, not too large or small, into a vagina and experiencing something that is given to almost the complete majority of men in the world. But what is wrong with that? Is it a sinful, dumb desire?

"No, no, no," Tonko repeats in his mind standing before the bedroom mirror. It's a normal, very normal desire. That's how we procreate, that's how humans continue the race. And why are some given to keep doing that until they drop, while he has not one opportunity? Whom did he offend? Who is driving him so far as to lose self-control and do something he would never do in his right mind?

Rape?

Of course, Tonko the tax inspector, caught up in balances, adding, subtracting, concessions and tricks large and small isn't seriously thinking about any rape. He only thinks about something like that in the worst moments of despair.

He did, so to say, everything that enables a man of his age to become familiar and acquainted with sexuality: he joined quite a few websites, where he introduced himself as someone who has a "big one," answered print offers and internet ads offering sexual services, and even placed quite a few himself, but everywhere the answer was the same: dead silence.

And then he stopped. He withdrew into himself, into his character, and his values, and left off visiting pornographic websites that helped him have an orgasm—actually more like an ejaculation than an orgasm. He swore he wouldn't visit them anymore (and to his great surprise he didn't once break that promise to himself). He redirected his attention to the real, physical world. He wanted life, experiences, and reality.

Why then, he had asked himself several times, be alive? Why not be a virtual person? He didn't want that, he only wanted from life what belongs to a human, and his desires were modest. Only one desire pursued him throughout the years of advancing in his career: to lose his virginity. So at a tavern he could unhesitatingly answer his colleagues' question, "How many have you had?" without hesitation: "Unfortunately only one, but the right one."

But that's not it, Tonko says to himself when he looks in the mirror with heavy heart, as if always hopeful of finding an answer there. His appearance couldn't be the only thing that repulsed women, including women who weren't much themselves. The reason must be elsewhere. Are women afraid of tax inspectors? He should have lied, fibbed to them that he is a doctor, maybe a gynecologist, a history teacher. Or a psychotherapist?

He would surely get enough clients as a therapist, and the majority of them would surely be women, and at least one of them would perhaps form the illusion that therapy is more effective if conducted in bed once in a while.

Unfortunately, Tonko long ago concluded that he doesn't know how to pretend convincingly, and most of all he is incapable of lying when people look him in the eye. Even if he became familiar enough with other occupations at least to talk about them, it would be written on his face that he isn't what he is passing himself off as. He was simply too open, almost as if afraid the tax administration would catch him in a lie.

He really was open, for years to his own detriment, but he wasn't stupid. He knew full well that you can buy sex, and for not much money if you're satisfied with the average offering. He had a good enough salary to visit one of the girls who offered their delights in the classifieds and on the internet at least three times a month. And he would have a relatively normal sex life.

But besides openness, Tonko had another characteristic that brought him more grief than good, and that was the firm conviction that as a government official in a very responsible position he had to maintain his dignity. If he decided to visit one of those girls that charge money, he wouldn't lose his virginity but would forfeit it forever.

He didn't want to risk that. Of course, no one would know, it would all remain hidden, and most men in his place would do it without a second thought. But he would know. And he would be ashamed of himself. He was also deathly afraid of sexually transmitted diseases and it seemed to him almost impossible that he wouldn't contract one given all the bad turns that had accompanied him in life.

No, Tonko yearned for something completely different than emptying himself into a female sexual cavity into which ten or more men a day shot their sperm. He was convinced he couldn't even get it up if he were conscious of doing something dirty. And even if by heaven knows what miracle he did the deed, the smell of the woman would stay with him his whole life. He didn't doubt that for a minute.

Tonko was obsessed with physical cleanliness. He regularly showered two or three times a day; everyday he put on fresh underwear and a fresh shirt. Ironing, which over the years he had turned into a real art took up a great deal of his free time. He even enjoyed it, bending over the ironing board. He was a regular customer at the nearby dry cleaners, where they were glad to see him, because he brought in profits. But he never left the place without the feeling that they were giggling behind his back and asking whether something was wrong with him.

Perhaps he expected too much. He dreamed of losing his virginity in a way that would in all respects remain "pure," with a woman who was in love with him at least half as much as he was with her, or if not half, then at least ten percent. If she couldn't do that, she would at lest have to enjoy it a little, get into the act, stroke his hair and back and moan a little along the way, even if it was barely audible, which would be proof to him that she was not giving herself out of sympathy and that he was satisfactorily executing his task as a man.

He was convinced that that's how it would be with Katarina, his only true love, whom he had so stupidly jilted in a moment of youthful exaltation. He was surprised she had even visited if she had not been prepared to stay the night and relieve him of the burden of bitterness that had expanded in him over the years. Was it possible that she had come with that intent, and he was the one who ruined the opportunity with his inappropriate behavior? Did she know, did she maybe suspect that he had lied at least a little to her, although it was out of consideration for her feelings?

Tonko moves away from the mirror with a feeling of revulsion at the figure he had stared at for so long, and still with a bit of hope that the mirror deceives at least a little and that there is at least some small thing about him that a woman, a half-blind one, would find attractive.

The only thing he had left was not to lose hope. He was more and more aware of this, more determined to try everything possible before, as he suspected, answering one of the ads in the end. Or before jumping headfirst into the well in front of the house, which also seemed to him a possibility.

Tonko notices that while he was staring in the mirror evening had reached the threshold of the house, and that night was not far off, another night of loneliness and masturbation, which he almost always did with tears in his eyes, despairing at the thought that he, Tonko, the tax inspector, a once slim and appealing boy, is forced to do something like this. What is left for us in life when dreams disappear? The sober, empty repetition of the same movements from day to day, experiencing oppressive feelings that are so familiar that we shouldn't be aware of them? A dead life? How unusual that death's shadow can cross the road we're traveling before we die.

Tonko turns on a light. At least it can be light around him if he can't chase the darkness from his soul. He opens another bottle of wine, fills a glass to the brim, sits down at the computer, turns it on, opens his e-mail, and starts typing what he had already decided would be his last message to Katarina. One of the last, for it seemed to him he had a lot to say. And much of what he had to say to her was not necessarily so thematically connected as to go together. In any case, he thinks that he will decide how to send his thoughts to her when he's at a loss for a word and it's obvious that their conversation is over.

How to begin? How to preserve that youthful, almost childish infatuation that suffused his last messages? But it wasn't necessary to preserve it; in the end it wasn't suitable for the sober, unvarnished truths he wanted to convey to his last and only love.

Tonko finishes the glass of wine, takes a deep breath, and starts typing.

"My dear, dearest, forever but never my Katarina. I know it's too late and that you'll perhaps never forgive me my mistakes, but when you were here and when it was about to happen, that which despite everything I was firmly convinced was intended for us, and I even understood from your messages that you thought the same, that you were promising exactly what I most wanted all my life, perhaps the only thing I really wanted, for everything else came of its own accord, our meeting didn't end as I expected (and perhaps how you expected, for a desire I couldn't overlook was burning in you), because you felt (and how couldn't you) that I was as open as I should have been with you. You'll understand if I write that I kept some things to myself, because I didn't want to hurt you, open wounds that may have healed, question the fate that befell you, for each of us has the right to keep to themselves some things, painful things, to bury them in the depths of forgetting, and not only you, but me, too. How else could we keep on living? But I can't take it anymore, I feel a duty to confide everything I know about you, for everything between us, if not between others, has to be clear. That's the only way we will remain friends, if we can't become lovers.

The fact is, Katarina, that I've been following your life from the time you turned me down (after I, immature and full of myself, turned you down). Don't ask me how I managed to remain close to you and follow your steps and your fate, because that's not important (perhaps I should have worked for a news agency and not the tax office). But now I'd like to admit that almost every important aspect of your life and your fate is known to me. I know that the young man because of whom you refused to renew a bond with me became a soldier, advanced quickly to become a lieutenant colonel, while you wanted to be a doctor, but you were stuck being a nurse. I know that when you both had jobs you got married and moved into a beautiful house in one of the best parts of Ljubljana, into a house his uncle had left him. I know he was very jealous, and you felt confined and wanted to overcome that feeling with affairs when he was in Afghanistan. I also know how the matter ended. It was in the newspapers. It's a real miracle that after the gunshot wounds you suffered all three of you lived, albeit with consequences that didn't improve your physical beauty, nor did it do any good for your souls, but in one way or another changed and marked you for your whole life.

I know your lieutenant colonel is in jail now, I also know that you went to England because you felt vulnerable, got a job as a nurse's aide in a gerontology unit, met one of your renters there who was shot with you and his friend, and as lonely as you were, you set up house with him, then married him, even though he was more homo- than heterosexual, and tried to have a normal life together. He disappointed you greatly, like all the men in your life, there was too much lying, so you left him and went back to Ljubljana, where you met Damjan, our architect friend, and decided to start fresh with him. But Damjan was cold, very, very cold, I also remember that, but you were trying to make amends for all your past sins with exaggerated worry about your mom, you wanted to balance your moral compass, although your mom couldn't stand you. Despite that, when you and Damjan were already leaving for Australia, you aborted your departure at the last moment.

Then Damjan went to Australia with his old girlfriend, but you stayed home, alone. Not long after that your mom died. You couldn't get a job. What's worse, you gave birth to a little boy. Since you didn't have Damjan's address, you couldn't prove you hadn't lied to him. That's what hurt most. And it still hurts.

When I visited Damjan, Katarina, I knew everything about you and your life up to that moment. I came to save you from his cold embrace, the unreliability that caused him to one thing today and something else the next. I seemed to me I could pull off that feat. But no, you were married to an architect with whom you were planning to go to Australia; after England where things went bad, you wanted to start a new life far from Europe, on the other end of the world, where no one knew your husband had shot you because, drugged up and with a mask on your face, you were having sex for a porn film.

I think you made the worst mistake of your life that time at the airport before departing for Australia. Despite his coldness—I dare say that's what all architects are like—you would have quickly gotten used to the bounds of normalcy with Damjan in Australia, in a more or less ordinary relationship, forgetting about the bad cards fate had dealt you.

When you finally visited me today, I didn't dare tell you how much I know about your life. I pretended to be convinced that you're still living with Damjan, otherwise I would have had to admit everything I'm admitting now: that I followed you through life and witnessed your gradual fall into the depths of existence with sorrow, as I'm witnessing my own descent into the hell in which I'm forced to live. The question for us two, Katarina, is extremely simple: is it worth continuing the lives we've made for ourselves with a series of bad decisions? I'm not sure about me. You have to go on, you have no choice. I don't know if it ever seemed to you that someone was following you. That was me. I'll stop now. We'll never see each other again. Mostly because I don know why you responded to my invitation. You were looking for a potential partner with a good job who would take care of your child. You can't imagine how humiliated I am because I didn't appear to you to be suited even for that role. Despite that, I sincerely wish that you find someone who will be a good stepfather to your child."

Part 5

NIGHT

A lamp near the park bench automatically comes on at the same time as the others arrayed along the path. The warm summer evening gradually turns into night.

Matej hurries up from the right and drops breathlessly on the bench. He takes a deep breath. He puts a sandwich half wrapped in paper down on the bench.

"Damn..." he curses quietly.

Soon Gugec hurries up from the same direction, likewise out of breath. He's holding the same kind of sandwich. He's going to sit down and extends a hand to push Matej's sandwich aside, changes his mind, and remains standing.

"Son of a bitch..." he breathes fitfully. "I won't even be able to eat."

"Me neither," Matej chokes. "I lost a lung on the way."

"I'm telling you," Gugec brags, "no Ethiopian is going to win the next marathon."

"Did he see you?" Matej answers.

"Who?"

"The sandwich man! Did he see which way you ran?"

"He didn't even move! He stood at the counter and staring up as if it wasn't clear to him what was happening."

"He's probably not used to someone ordering a sandwich and then taking off without paying."

Gugec is happy with the little raid. "Isn't it great to eat even if you don't have money?"

Matej dampens his spirits. "The only problem is, we can't go there anymore."

"Why not?" Gugec is surprised.

"Because now they know us and the next time he won't go for it!"

"But he didn't even get a good look at us! And if he did, next time we'll put on fake mustaches and he won't have a clue."

"Can you be quiet for five minutes? So I can pull myself together?"

"You're not okay?"

"I can't breathe!"

"Maybe it's asthma," Gugec observes empirically. "Or cancer. That's how it starts."

"Quiet, I said!" Matej repeats. "Otherwise I'll whack you."

"Man, are you friendly," Gugec moves away. "As always."

"One more word and I really will," Matej threatens him.

"Right, I'd better eat."

He takes a bite of the sandwich and chews. "Son of a bitch... It's really good...! Not like the one yesterday."

"The one yesterday wasn't at all bad," Matej disagrees.

"It was disgusting. Tasted like rotten fish. We're not going there anymore."

"I thought it was really good," Matej repeats.

"Because you're used to eating shit," says Gugec.

"Me?"

"Because you've been eating it a long time. I've just started."

"Oh, yeah? What did you eat before? Pork cutlets?"

"I can't stand them," says Gugec.

"How much did you even earn when you were working?"

"500 euros."

"A tycoon! You could have saved some."

"Son of a bitch, don't you know my mother's unemployed?" Gugec gets angry. "And my old man, who lost his job a year before me?"

"And now?" asks Matej. "Who's supporting them?"

"Ah, the government, no?"

"I didn't know it exists," says Matej.

"Fuck, that's the way the world is. That's the times. Are we to blame?"

"Maybe God is, who allows it."

"Let God sleep," says Gugec. "My old man says he's sleeping, pleased with himself ever since he created the world."

"Created?" Matej sits up straight. "More like a sick cow gave birth to it."

"And who was the father?"

"More like this world dropped out of someone's ass."

"That's a great way to put it. It should be published. We'll put it in graffiti. On the parliament building, a church, bank, and everywhere criminals get together. Why don't we enjoy a little social protest?"

"It's senseless," says Matej. "The papers are full of it. And does it change anything?"

"My old man says everything's mixed up. Everything is made of something else..."

"Didn't I ask you to be quiet for five minutes?" Matej leans back.

"And you know what's the worst?" Gugec keeps it up.

"I asked you as a *friend* to keep quiet!"

"You know..."

"I can't breathe! My heart's pounding!"

"So you won't eat your sandwich?"

Gugec nods at the package on the bench.

"You didn't eat yours yet."

Gugec swallows the last bite, crumples the paper, and misses the trash can next to the bench. "You really don't want it?"

Matej closes his eyes. "I'm not even going to listen to you anymore."

"Well... I think, if you're sick..."

Matej grabs his package and holds it out. "Under one condition. That from now on you steal sandwiches for both of us."

"Wait..." Gugec shifts his feet. "Is stealing suddenly a problem for you?"

"It's a problem if I have to run... I can't... My head is spinning, my lungs balloon... and my knees..."

"Why even steal if you don't eat it?"

"I eat. But I can't now."

Gugec takes the sandwich out of his hand.

"You agree to the condition?"

"There's just one problem," says Gugec and unwraps it.

"I knew you'd find something," says Matej. "Give it back." He puts out his hand.

Gugec holds onto the sandwich. "I'm serious. They only sell sandwiches in five places. They know us all over."

"You're the one who suggested fake mustaches."

"That's not enough. We'll need plastic surgery."

"I know a hairdresser who can make you a wig."

"You want me to die laughing?" Gugec barks.

Matej holds out his hand. "Return the sandwich."

Gugec takes a step back. "Son of a bitch, we don't have to eat just sandwiches! It's not good for you. Don't you watch TV? Every day they serve you the drivel about how you have to have balance, a little of this, a little of that, and mostly vegetables."

"Then what?" Matej asks. "Are we going to take a cart to the grocery store?"

"We can try," Gugec agrees.

"And take it overflowing past the check-out?"

"You don't think it would work?"

"And 60 mph down the main street?"

"Listen…" says Gugec. He starts eating Matej's sandwich. "Why should we steal food if we can pay for it?"

"Did you hit the lottery?"

"I've told you a hundred times! Purses!"

"We'll eat purses?"

"Son of a bitch, why make fun of a friend? The only one you have."

"I have more than enough." Matej looks down.

"Yeah, those crazy ones. Where you were. And where you'll have to return sooner or later."

"One doctor was very nice to me," says Matej.

"Listen," Gugec goes on. "Each of us swipes a bike some-where… Then… we wait."

"For judgment day?"

"For the day people go to the bank to get their pensions! And we ride around a little. I'm telling you, on every street there will be some old woman limping to the grocery store."

"What will they live on if we steal their pensions?"

Gugec is silent for a while. The he says: "You know what your problem is. You're too honest. You won't get by like that."

"I won't anyway," Matej hangs his head.

"Listen," Gugec suddenly raises his voice, "some people stole millions and don't care if someone has a pension or drops dead tomorrow. And you're worried about old ladies? Who you don't even know and you'll see only one time and never again?"

"My grandma is an old lady."

"She must be if she's your grandma," says Gugec as if he doesn't understand what Matej is trying to tell him.

"And what's her pension? Less than three hundred a month. How much bread do you think she can buy after she pays the bills?"

"Not much, I'd say."

"And you'd take even that?"

Gugec grasps that he has to change the topic. He tries to push a piece of sandwich into Matej's hand. "At least eat half of this junk. Yours is worse than mine. Mine was great."

"Throw it in the trash if it's no good," says Matej.

"Listen," says Gugec. "How long have we been friends?"

"Long enough that it's beginning to get on my nerves."

Gugec throws the rest of the sandwich into the trash can by the bench and turns to go.

"Where are you going?" Matej yells after him.

"My mother's cunt. That's where you told me, no?"

"Come on," Matej softens his voice, "come back."

"No."

"You're acting like a five-year old."

"Now I'm really going." He disappears behind the trees.

Matej gets up and yells. "Okay, okay! I'm acting like a child. Sorry, alright!"

Gugec comes back; Matej sits back down.

Gugec sits next to him. "Can I tell you a few things?"

"Go on," Matej agrees.

"You're not going to tell me to be quiet for five minutes until you get yourself together?"

"No," Matej promises.

"Are you alright?"

"As much as I can be."

"I'll have a five-minute speech. Will you hold up?"

"One minute," says Matej.

"That's not enough," Gugec shakes his head.

"Damn, we're not representatives in the chicken shit parliament! We're not paid for the time we declaim. You can give me the history of the world in one minute!"

"I want to tell you something else."

"Right," Matej agrees.

"Will you listen?" Gugec wants assurances.

"If you talk so as I won't fall asleep."

"When do I talk like that?"

"Usually."

"Are you aware that I was a member of the debating team in school? And even the advisor wasn't as good as me? Do you know I have more gray cells in my brain that Schwarzenegger has muscle mass?"

"I believe it," says Matej. "Your bank balance is proof of it."

"Since when do you equate intelligence and money? Even the greatest geniuses died poor."

"The same is going to happen to you."

"I said I would give a short talk, and you're fucking with me."

"I'll listen. Can I at least yawn a few times?"

"You've been doing that since I met you. Only one thing interests you in the whole world: eyes up and arms and legs spread."

"Whose fault is that?"

"Yeah, I know," Gugec agrees.

"I'd go to work, find me something!"

"You'll have a hard time getting job with your mental defects."

"Wait, now you're offending me?"

"Since when are facts offensive? You really do have mental defects. You're getting treatment."

"Taking into consideration everything I lived through…"

"You're in for a while, then out. You've been out now for quite a while, so they'll soon grab you and you'll go back in again."

"You really are a good friend," Matej moves away.

"I don't mean anything by it. I have mental defects, too. The whole world does. Really. The world is kaput. No one can save it."

"My grandma says the Church teaches otherwise."

"You grandma is senile."

"Don't offend her, she's the only one in the world who cares about me. Father and Mother are dead, my brother and sister want nothing to do with me. Even though they could give me something. Grandma is all I have."

"I'm not trying to steal her from you."

"If she knew I'm a thief, even a petty one, because I don't dare to be a big one, she would die of shame."

"She'll die anyway. How old is she?"

"Didn't you say you'd give a five-minute talk?"

"I don't feel like it anymore," says Gugec.

"No, really, I'm curious," Matej insists.

"Why?"

"I'm curious what in this fucking world is so important that you can't tell me in less than five minutes!"

"You know what's the matter?" says Gugec. "It's that I forgot what I wanted to say."

Matej gets up and says, "I'm going."

"Wait, would you…"

"I promised grandma to make her lunch. Buckwheat dumplings. She got the flour from charity."

"She can wait. Sit down. Come on." He puts out a hand to pull him back on the bench.

"I'd rather stand," Matej retreats. "I have to move. Otherwise…"

Gugec gets animated. "Listen, some people stole millions. Didn't they? They stole millions, threw the people out on the street, not only my old lady and old man and you and me, but another hundred thousand people. And they're still wolfing down steaks. For breakfast, lunch, and dinner. And they empty half their refrigerator in the middle of the night. What about us two? We swipe a sandwich, because we're hungry as dogs, and it's shit we'd like to vomit, and what happens if they catch us?"

"I don't know, because they didn't."

"Arrest, court, sentencing. A record."

"We already have one," says Matej. "Both of us."

"Isn't something wrong with this?"

"What?"

"Son of a bitch, why are you playing stupid? You have mental defects but you're not stupid. The problem is you can't free yourself from you grandma's apron strings."

"Leave my grandma alone!"

"Listen." Gugec is a little confused. "Why in general... Son of a bitch, we're friends, not... We're both worked up... We'll end up... You know where...? Where they treat *you* every other month."

"And that's your talk?"

"Listen... Someone is to blame for us having to steal!"

"We are," says Matej.

"You don't understand at all."

"And you do?"

"We're living in total shit...! But, son of a bitch, most people are pretending that everything is okay... That everyone has enough! I don't know... are people blind?"

"What is your speech about?"

"Do you know anyone who's prepared to do something about it?"

"Are you?"

"Matej, listen..."

"Let's leave this crap for some other time. I'm really worn out."

He sits down on the bench, leans back, and closes his eyes.

"You're worn out because you're underfed. But God forbid you protest. You're humiliated, offended, run over, pissed on, and get it up the ass from all sides, but you don't care."

"I'm sick," says Matej.

"I don't understand why you didn't stay in there. To be cared for. Regular meals. You could take the crazy people. I could. Who couldn't for three square meals a day?"

"I would. But grandma..."

"Put her in a home."

"My brother and sister put Father and Mom in a home. And they died there. Grandma is staying with me. She's the reason I came back to this subalpine paradise. She would miss me in a home. And I her. We have no one else. She stumbles and falls a lot."

"For that reason. They'd care for her in a home."

"Blessed are those without feelings," says Matej.

"You have too many, and look where they've gotten you."

"Better that than a heart of stone, like you."

"Fuck it," says Gugec, "that's how it is when life hits you on the back of the head and spits on you for good measure."

"You're fine. You have your parents."

"Athletic ones. They walk regularly."

"Really?"

"Yeah, to the Red Cross. For food."

"Soon everything will be okay," says Matej, as if to comfort him. "The night of the world is coming."

"It's already here."

"That's only a scout," says Matej. "The real one is coming. It will wrap everything in darkness, and then there will be peace. It will deprive us of speech. There will be no more writing. No more words. Can you imagine? No arguments. No lies. Only darkness and silence."

"What are you talking about?" Gugec looks at him.

Katarina comes down the path and stops. "Where's Face?" she asks in a disturbed tone of voice.

"Katarenka, hey!" Gugec greets her and whistles. "Pussy who gives herself to nobody unless they pay!"

"Face said we're supposed to meet here. Did he leave?"

"Face isn't for you," says Gugec. "If I took care of your business, you'd be rich by now."

"Just like you," says Katarina without even glancing at him.

"Face is a thief, he's using you all day long."

Katarina looks at Matej. "You're completely green. Are you sick?"

"Of course he is," says Gugec. "I mean... he steals a sandwich... and what does he do? Throws it in the trash."

"You did that," says Matej.

"Only half of it. I had to eat the other half."

"Was Face here?" Katarina worries. "Did he leave?"

"He wasn't while we're here," says Matej.

"We agreed to meet a client."

"Maybe he was and left with the client," says Gugec. "Because you know, Face is a fag."

"Good thing he didn't hear you," says Katarina.

"Everybody knows that. Right, Matej?"

"If he heard you," says Katarina, "you'd be spread out here on the ground."

"He would be. I'm a black belt. I bet you didn't know."

"I'm serious," Katarina warns him. "Don't provoke him."

"How much of what he takes in does he give you? Or do you take something in yourself? On the side?"

"Cut it out."

"But I was the first. I had everything arranged, a whole network, and I rented a studio. Then that damn Bosnian lick-ass comes along and steals you."

"Face isn't Bosnian," says Katarina. "He was born in Ribnica."

"Yeah, but to whom?"

"His parents, fuck you!" Matej butts in. "His name isn't even Face, it's Brane."

"Son of a bitch... I had ads all over. You know how much they cost? Twenty clients lined up. And she..."

"She preferred him," says Matej.

"You joking? He forced her with a knife to her throat."

"Gugec," says Katarina, "those ads of yours weren't worth shit. Excuse the expression."

"You hear that, Matej? She spreads her legs ten times a day, and I have to excuse her for saying shit?"

"But your ads really were just that," says Matej.

"How do you know? Were you looking for a whore?"

"I read them, because I knew they were yours."

"And? 'I lick, massage, vibrate, bang, am real handy and treat it like candy.' Find me a better ad and I'll blow you right here."

"I'd rather Katarina did that," says Matej.

"She will. And me, too. She never denied her services to a friend." He looks at her. "Right?"

Katarina bows her head. "Face would kill me if he found out."

"He doesn't have to find out," says Gugec.

"He does, everything."

"He can't. He doesn't have a camera in the trees."

"Absolutely everything," says Katarina. "And then he whoops me."

"Well?" Gugec turns to Matej. "Is it clear to you now what filth Face is? She's afraid of him. She's so afraid she can't even breathe. Son of a bitch... I'll put an end to this."

"You can't," Katarina shakes her head.

"Does he have you on a chain? By the way, I'm curious about something. Is he there when you bang hairy old fat guys?"

"Gugec, stop," Matej warns him. "We're friends."

"Were," says Gugec.

"We still are," says Katarina. "But..."

"Now you have to charge friends, too."

"We can still be friends without that."

"Well, sure," says Gugec snootily, "don't think I have to pay for sex. I get it for free... As far as that goes, I have enough... Married women cook something for me now and then. And I can tell you, some are very good cooks."

"Bon appetit," says Katarina.

"Do you have any hash?" Matej comes close to ask her.

Katarina looks in her purse. "You need something to eat more than hash." She offers him a sandwich in a paper sack. "You're completely pale."

"I think I'm going to die soon," says Matej, calmly, as if he were talking about the weather. "I honestly can hardly wait. Eternal peace. Something better. That's just what I'm waiting for, for grandma to die, and then I'll go. Right after her." He starts eating the sandwich.

"Is it good?" Katarina asks.

"Great. Where'd you get it?"

"At the grocery store. They make them to order."

"If you have money," says Matej.

"Look at that," says Gugec. "He didn't like the one we stole, but he's devouring this one as if he hasn't eaten in a hundred years."

Katarina ignores him and continues talking with Matej. "Grandma okay?"

"She's worse."

"But you're taking care of her?"

"For sure. When I was small, she took care of me."

"You have a heart of gold," says Katarina and pats him on the head. "Despite everything."

"Don't let me shit myself from laughing," Gugec laughs.

"Step into the bushes," Katarina advises him. "So you don't do it in your pants when Face gets here."

"If anyone does, he will. And once and for all. Once and for all you'll see what I'm made of. Katarina, I'll rescue you from his Bosnian claws."

"Dream on," says Katarina.

"And then... listen... Then you'll have top shit clients. You'll have... the elite...! Bank directors... Tycoons!"

"I can hardly wait," Katarina laughs.

"I mean, on the wet grass behind the nearest bush... Or in some alley... For thirty euros, son of a bitch, like you're the cheapest hooker... I'll rent you a studio!"

"I have a studio," says Katarina.

"I'll rent you a bigger one. A one-bedroom. Two-bedroom!"

"I didn't know you're that rich."

"Look... we'll agree on it," says Gugec.

"I know what that means. That you'll rent an apartment with my money."

"Son of a bitch," says Gugec, "whose money does Face use to pay for the studio?"

"Let it go," says Katarina.

"You know he drives a Ferrari?"

"I didn't know a five-year old Peugot is a Ferrari."

"You think he has just one car? He has five. At least."

"You're crazy," says Katarina.

"You think so?" Gugec looks at her. "How many like you do you think he has listed? Twenty for sure. Ukrainians, Filipinos, from the Dominican Republic, all kinds. Can you imagine how much he earns? And he gives you the crumbs. Enough not to drop dead."

Katarina is silent.

"And not to get fat."

"Can you be quiet for a few minutes?" Matej interrupts. "I'd like to eat the sandwich in peace."

"Wait," Gugec starts to object.

"You talk too much," Matej interrupts.

"Son of a bitch... you keep telling me to be quiet... What's with you?"

"He's right," Katarina sides with Matej. "You talk too much."

"Son of a bitch, that's just... I don't know what to say."

"Nothing," Matej suggests.

"I'm aiming to provide our friend with a little more dignified life... At least a *little* more dignified... And what thanks do I get?"

"Now I really think you should stop!" Katarina warns him.

"How much of the receipts does Face give you? Ten percent?"

"I won't say."

"Not more, for sure. I know him. But listen... I would *take* ten percent... You'd get how much...? Ninety!"

"You'd take from me? For what?"

"To protect you! Don't forget my black belt… And to supply clients… And for the ads!"

"Ads?"

"Yeah, the ads, which wouldn't be as shitty as the ones Face puts out."

"Or as stupid as the yours were, the ones we heard before."

"Every artist develops. He learns from his own mistakes. And I did. Can I give you a few examples?"

"Yes, give them to us!" Matej yells. "Give us a few examples! Night is coming, darkness descending, we're short on time!"

He gets up and starts nervously circling the bench.

"Katarina, listen to this," Gugec continues. "Twenty-three year old student with depraved eyes, seductive body, please respond, I'm in a sexy little outfit, and will give you 100%."

"Twenty-three years old?" Matej exclaims. "She was twenty-four ten years ago, when I rented from her!"

"That's true." Katarina nods.

"Yeah, but… son of a bitch… you can't say that! You don't give personal information to get a job! You look for clients. Everyone lies, from the top to the bottom, why shouldn't you?"

"There's already enough lying around me," says Katarina.

"As for the eyes"—Matej leans over the back of the bench and looks her in the eyes—"they're not depraved but dead. I know, because death has taken over my soul, too."

"Matej, please…" says Katarina.

"Don't listen to him at all," Gugec advises her. "You know he has mental defects. Wait a minute while I put my brain into fifth…"

"That's hard," says Matej, "seeing how you have only two gears."

Gugec ignores him. "Listen to this... Twenty-eight year old doe with appeal, passionate seductress and teaser, seeks a man for a pleasant date and unforgettable experience. I'll fulfill all your secret fantasies from A to Z."

"That has nothing to do with me," says Katarina. "My rule is: shove it in, spit it out, and take off."

"But listen," Gugec almost gets angry, "you'll never get more than fifty euros like that!"

"Then I'm a cheap whore."

"Son of a bitch, Katarina... Face undervalues you."

"He sells me for what he can."

"Then you're undervaluing yourself. Do you ever look in the mirror?"

"Not often. I'm ashamed to see what's become of me."

"Wait," Gugec recalls. "This is the best. Want to hear it?"

"Yeah, go on, let's!" Matej yells, more and more excited and confused.

"Thirty-year old long-legged, blond exclusive kitten with supple thighs, a loose party girl, pleasantly simple and a stunning beauty who likes to do forbidden things and conjure up moments of passion making you dizzy seeks a stable man for whispering between the sheets."

There are a few minutes of silence. Katarina and Matej look at each other.

Matej crumples the paper sandwich wrapper and nimbly tosses it in the trash can near the bench. "Score!"

"Well," says Gugec, "I finally convinced you."

"Not you," says Katarina. "Matej did. He scored."

"Then I don't know," Gugec waves his hands. "I don't know what to do."

"Can I tell you?" Katarina asks. She searches her purse, finds her wallet, pulls out a twenty-euro note, and offers it to Gugec. "Go to the stand, the one across from the park entrance, and bring three beers. I'm thirsty." She looks at Matej. "You'll have one, right?"

"Make it a Laško," says Matej.

"Make it a Laško," Katarina repeats.

Gugec handles the money. "You're sending me for beer?"

"No, we're asking you to go to the store and bring it."

"But..."

"Will you buy it with your own money?" asks Matej.

"I don't like people sending me for cigarettes."

"She's not sending you for cigarettes!" Matej is getting loud and aggressive. "She's asking you to buy three cans of beer on *her* money. One of them is for *you*!"

"Why are you barking at me?"

"Doesn't a friend ever run out to get beer for a friend? Do you think that's so special?"

Gugec dithers for a while and then goes. He turns around. "Will you two be here when I get back?"

"No," says Matej. "We'll fly off into the darkness that's descending and disappear forever into the universe."

"But..." Gugec hesitates.

"One more 'but' and I'll come after you!"

Gugec goes down the path. Katarina and Matej remain alone. They're quiet for a while. Then Katarina searches in her purse.

"Want a chocolate? You have no idea how pale you are."

"The sandwich was enough."

Katarina drops the chocolate back in her purse. "Can you even stand me anymore?"

"When didn't I?"

"Oh, there were moments!"

"I always did and always will."

268

"Despite what I'm doing?"

"You're doing what you always did. And happily. Before it was for free, now it's for pay."

"I remember what we had."

"Us two?"

"It was pure. What I'm doing now is dirty."

"Sex is sex. Dirty or pure is just what we feel."

"What we felt was far from what I'm now doing."

"That's gone. Night came and took it all away. The one that's coming will swallow the world. And us. And not only us. Everything."

"Why everything?"

"Don't you see that the world has caved in?"

"It's true everything has gone wrong. If I didn't have responsibilities, I'd as soon die right now."

"You have responsibilities?" Matej looks at her.

"You do, too. Your grandma."

"They took away her supplement!" Matej gets angry. "They took away her disability allowance! She gets a 280-euro pension!"

"Matej…"

Matej calms down and sits back down. "Do you have a smoke?"

"I told you I don't."

"You said that when Gugec was here. You always have one."

"I have something better."

"Heroin?" Matej shakes his head. "I wouldn't go that far."

Katarina searches in her purse and offers him a pill. "Ecstasy."

"Oh, Katarina," Matej says. "Do you remember how we started with that?"

"With Brane. In the house where we were shot."

269

"And then we quit."

"That's true. We were clean in London. I was clean with Damjan, too. Although when he left for Australia I felt the urge to start again."

"And you did. For Brane. Who's now called Face."

"Who's now called Face," Katarina repeats. "Why do people keep changing?"

"Evolution," says Matej.

"Why so fast? So much? Why for the worse? Never for the better?"

"Because the night of the world is coming. Darkness will cover everything. Our hearts, our thoughts, our wishes. We'll become animals. We'll kill each other."

Katarina swallows the pill. "I couldn't make it... without this," she explains.

"You mean fucking ten disgusting men every day?"

"They're not all disgusting," says Katarina.

"You get some dishy ones?"

"Some show up because they're unhappily married."

"Then you're doing socially useful work."

"That's just what your older brother told me in Brighton, when I said I wipe old people's asses in the gerontology unit."

"My older brother," says Matej, "wrote me off as soon as Father and Mother died. And I him."

"You're not in touch?"

"Not at all. Or with my sister. All I have left is grandma."

"You lost your brother and sister because you lied to the family. For five whole years."

"The same reason I lost you."

"Not only that. And you didn't totally lose me. You're still my friend."

"Who can't help you."

Katarina offers him the pill again. "Want it?"

Matej shakes his head. "Never again, Katarina. It's good to start with. Then comes the punishment."

"The feeling of happiness outweighs the punishment."

"The feeling of happiness is brief, the punishment is long."

"You can shorten it. You take another one."

"The road to destruction."

"At least it should be without fear. If you're on the road to hell and in a good mood, you have nothing to fear, right?"

"Except the moment you reach your destination."

"I don't believe in hell. I believe in death, which will come when it comes. To tell the truth, I've been dead for some time. But you know that."

She offers him the pill one more time. "You really won't?"

"When grandma departs for the next world."

"Maybe I will before she does," Katarina hangs her head.

"How would you do that?" Matej looks at her from the side.

Katarina swallows the pill. "I'd take twenty instead of two."

"But you won't," says Matej. "I know you won't."

"I would," says Katarina. "But I can't."

"Face won't allow you."

"Forget about Face. I could get rid of him quick. I can't, because I have responsibilities."

"Responsibilities? Your mom died, your first husband is in jail, the second, me, gets periodic treatments in the nut-house, the third ran off to Australia, you're involved with Brane again, which I'll never understand, what responsibilities are you talking about?"

"You wouldn't be interested," says Katarina.

"I'm interested in everything about you."

"Matej, we're not going to dig up corpses."

"What responsibilities, Katarina?"

"Let's drop it."

"I demand an answer."

"You have no right."

"I'm *asking* for an answer," says Matej.

"I can't give you one. Because it has to do with you."

"Me?!" Matej sits up straight.

"You. But I don't know if you can keep it to yourself."

"Damn, Katarina, you know what... Not to trust a person with whom you had a close connection, even marriage... for how long?"

"We went through different phases, Matej. We're no longer what we were."

"Katarina..."

"*Will* you keep it to yourself?"

"You know what..."

Katarina is silent for a while. Then she takes a deep breath and says: "I have a child."

"You have a child," says Matej after a short pause.

"He's two and a half years old."

"Cool."

"His name is Matej."

"Why?"

"Because that's what I wanted. My aunt is bringing him up, because I can't."

"Why not?"

"Because Face swore he would throw him in the river if I stopped working for him!" She breaks down crying. "He said he would cut him into four pieces!"

Matej gets up and nervously walks back and forth. "That's what he said?"

"That's what he said," Katarina replies and starts to sob loudly.

"Then there's no solution but for me to kill him," Matej decides.

"Don't be crazy!"

"It's the only way."

"That wouldn't change the fact that I have a child," says Katarina.

"And he's Matej," says Matej.

"He's Matej."

"Why isn't his name Gugec?" Matej stops in front of her. Katarina bows her head. "Because it's less likely."

"But possible?" Matej wants to know.

"Hardly," says Katarina.

"Hardly?"

"Ah…" Katarina hesitates, "once, when we met, he came and… almost raped me."

"Almost."

"Yeah, because… in some way I… I don't know what was with me… I…"

"What, Katarina?"

"I let him."

Matej is silent for a while, walking back and forth in front of the bench with his hands in his pockets.

"Wait a minute," he says. "We were friends, and you went to bed with Gugec?"

"Not to bed. It was in the car, on the back seat of his junker… really uncomfortable."

"The junker he drove into a tree?"

"Yes."

"And?" Matej looks at her. "Did you enjoy it?"

"I don't know," says Katarina, her head bowed.

"Yes or no?"

"Maybe."

"After you husband went off to Australia and we met again in Ljubljana?"

"I don't want there to be secrets between us."

"You mean to say that you were a whore before you *officially* became a whore?"

"We were friends, Matej."

"Isn't it enough that you fuck Gugec on the back seat of his junker without me knowing about it?"

"You were in treatment, Matej! When you got out, I didn't dare tell you because you would right away go mad again. Anyway, it was just one time."

"Enough for a child."

"I had protection."

"We also did it only once. In London. And only because I asked you nicely. Because I got curious."

"And once here. Did you forget?"

"I would rather. I don't even know why we…"

"Matej, it happened."

Matej is silent. Then he quickly gets up, jumps to the trashcan and starts to vomit. Katarina looks at him. Matej vomits for a while, then straightens up and wipes his mouth.

"And what do you expect now? For me to raise the child?"

"I want you to know, that's all."

"Why can't you leave some things unsaid?"

"Because I've left too many things in life unsaid, Matej. And because of that I'm here, where I am. I decided I want to be different."

"No matter what you do to others because of that?"

"I wanted you to know why I have to obey Face."

"I'll kill him," Matej decides after a brief silence.

"He'll kill you first."

"You don't know me. The night of the world is coming. On such a night, I'll become a wolf."

"You want my advice? Avoid him."

"And as far as Gugec goes… You know what I'll do to him? I'll nail him to a tree with a spike."

"You should have nothing against him. I'm to blame. I was in a fix. He said he could help me."

Matej rushes to the trash can again and vomits.

Gugec comes back with three cans of beer. "How old was that sandwich you gave him?"

"Give me a beer." Katarina holds out a hand.

Gugec hands her a can. He offers one to Matej.

"Just drink them both," Matej chokes.

"Son of a bitch, it was you who made me get them."

"Move!" Matej pushes him. He grabs his stomach and squats, staring at the ground.

"Right, I'll drink two," says Gugec. He puts one can on the bench. He opens the other and drinks.

Katarina opens her can and drinks. She puts the can on the bench, presses a button on her cell phone, and raises it to her ear. She drinks, then puts the can down. She puts away the phone. "Strange. It rings but there's no answer."

"He wrote you off," says Gugec.

"I should be so lucky."

"Won't take long. Count your wrinkles."

"You're very kind."

"You know who ages fastest? Whores and politicians. When you pass your use by date, he'll kick your butt."

"That's what I'll do if you don't quit," Matej threatens him.

"Vomit a little more," Gugec advises him. "You'll feel better. It's always good to vomit it all out."

"Now you're both getting on my nerves," says Katarina.

She gets up, takes another gulp of beer, puts the can on the bench, picks up her purse, and goes off.

At the same instant Face pedals up from the left on a woman's bike.

He stops. "What's going on here?" He looks at Matej and Gugec.

"Where were you?" Katarina wants to know.

"What are these two doing here?"

"Ask them. They were here before me."

"They're always where they don't belong."

"Nice bike," says Gugec. "Did the Ferrari break down?"

"Watch you tongue, or you could lose it."

"Empty threats. You won't do shit. You never do."

"We're going to have a face-to-face talk," says Face.

"Right now is fine."

Face looks at Katarina. "Who bought the beer?"

Katarina sits back down. "Gugec," she says finally.

"Was it you, Matej?"

"I did," says Gugec.

"With whose money?"

"Mine," says Gugec.

"Did it fall out your ass?"

"That's possible. I don't have a bunch of pussy to sell and make money off them."

Face looks at Katarina. "Was it you who gave him the money?"

"Only for beer," says Katarina.

"How much?"

"How much was the beer, Gugec?"

Face holds out a palm to Gugec. "Give me the change."

"But I didn't..." Katarina tries to explain.

"Be quiet," Face orders her.

"She gave me ten euros," says Gugec. "The beer was..."

Katarina suddenly raises her voice. "I gave him *my* money."

"Your money isn't to give to others."

"I'll do what I want with my money!" Katarina disagrees and gets up.

Face slaps her while still sitting on his bike. Katarina drops her head, sits back down on the bench, and curls up inside.

Matej gets up. "Do that one more time and..."

"Yeah?" Face stares at him.

"You'll see."

"I'm shaking with fear," says Face. He winks at Katarina. "Give me that beer."

"That's mine," says Matej.

"Then why aren't you drinking it?"

"Because it makes me vomit!" Matej almost yells. "Because I'm sick! Because we're all sick! Because the night of the world is coming! Because the devil is preparing a grill on which we'll roast!" He pulls his hair as if trying to yank it out.

"Give it to me," Face winks at Katarina.

Katarina reaches out a hand and gives Face Matej's beer. Face opens it and drinks.

"I called, but you didn't answer," Katarina half reproaches and half informs him.

"I left my phone in the car."

"Where's the car?"

"It's gone."

"Towed?" Katarina asks.

"No. I called. Stolen. When I get the bastards, I'll toss them in five different bio recycling bins."

"Where did you get the bike?"

"At the library. It wasn't locked."

"Just think," says Gugec, "where the world's gone to. Just a year ago we were all honest."

"Good thing I don't know how to laugh," Face frowns, "or I'd die laughing."

"I'm serious."

"You've been a degenerate as long as I've known you. That's the way you were born. You even did time, didn't you?"

"Watch out you won't. Not for a month but several years."

"You're thinking of turning me in?" Face looks at him challengingly.

"You never know what a person will do under pressure," says Gugec.

"Where's the pressure? Tell me and I'll massage it."

"Can you two stop?!" Matej yells. "And admit you're both sick?"

"Sick, why?" Face asks him.

"That's the only way to save the world," says Matej. "We have to admit we're sick."

Face shakes his head. "I don't understand those doctors. Why did they let you out? They should keep you locked up all the time."

"They let me out because I have to clean up the trash that is choking the world!"

"Hard job," Face shakes his head again. "It doesn't look like they gave it to the right person."

"Son of a bitch, why wasn't I born a thousand years ago?" Gugec interrupts them. "I would have been a crusader, gone to Jerusalem to rob, and returned with a ton of gold and silver."

"Others do the robbing now," says Face, "and then they go to Jerusalem as tourists."

Matej stares through the trees and over their crowns at the sky. "Still, we should…"

"What?" asks Face.

"Maintain our… dignity."

"Do you know what he's blathering about?" Face looks at Katarina.

Katarina nods.

"Then explain it to me… Because I have no clue."

"You can't maintain your dignity when they take it away and you're a piece of shit on the street," Gugec gets angry.

"We're somewhat to blame ourselves," says Katarina.

"We're to blame for being pieces of shit on the street? And like shit, they want to throw us into a ditch so no one steps in it."

"That's true, but…" Matej starts and falls silent.

"What?" Face demands.

"We have to draw the line somewhere."

"I'd draw it here," says Face. "Because this philosophizing is going nowhere. My rule is that you have to take care of yourself. The ones on top know it, but we have a hard time with it. Everyone according to his ability."

"I remember the times when it was different," Matej falls to thinking.

"You mean before they hauled you in. Or when we were still friends and living at this whore's place? Girls I remember waited a while before they spread their legs. This one did it right away."

"You said something else," Katarina objects. "Girls I remember didn't hesitate. That's what you said."

"You didn't either. You jumped me."

"No I didn't."

"I knew right then that sooner or later, after all the mistakes you would make, I'd have to rush to your aid."

"I would laugh," says Katarina, "if I didn't have a sea of sorrow inside."

"Go ahead and laugh," says Face. "Did that guy even show up?"

"What guy?"

"The one," Face gives her a mean look, "we agreed with!"

"No one was here," says Katarina.

"He probably was but left when he saw these two. What are they doing here?"

"When did you buy this park?" Matej takes a step towards him.

"That's right, son of a bitch," Gugec joins him. "Who gave you the right to take over a public place?"

"I told you they were here before me," Katarina repeats.

"You're going too far," Gugec tells him.

"Don't shoot off your mouth," Face warns, "or you'll get it right there."

Face pulls out a cell phone, looks at the list of calls, touches one, and puts the phone to his ear.

"Don't let him come here," Katarina asks. "Let him go somewhere else."

"Good evening, sir," Face speaks sweetly into the phone. "We agreed... No, not that bench... not on the main path... On the one to the right... Fifty meters from the entrance and to the right... Yes, were waiting for you here... Agreed."

He shoves the phone in his pocket.

"Don't let him come here," Katarina repeats. "Let him go to the studio."

"He's a government official," Face explains. "If he has an address, he can cause a bunch of trouble. I know the type."

"Face," Gugec speaks up, "how much do you charge... one of those... official types?"

"Why? Are you one of them?"

"Son of a bitch, you won't believe it... I had ambitions."

"Me, too," says Face, "but the devil stole them and gave them to others."

"Son of a bitch, we all had some," Gugec gets angry.

"And then the world showed up and trampled them with its big boots," Matej stares at the clouds above the trees.

"You need a woman," Face says to him. "How many years have I been telling you that? Here she is. And since you know each other, you have the right to a discount. Fifty euros."

"Wait." Matej can't believe it. "You sell Katarina to friends?"

"Your price is actually higher. Nuts can be dangerous. Five hundred euros."

"Why would I pay you for something I got for free?" Matej laughs.

Face looks at Katarina. "What's he talking about?"

"I have no idea. You know he has problems. They let him out yesterday."

"It's a crime to let out nuts."

"He's not crazy," Katarina disagrees, "he's sick."

"Why are you defending him?"

"Because you wronged him. You were friends."

"Where have those times gone!"

"Listen, Face," Gugec interjects. "That super bike of yours... Would you lend it to me for, oh, twenty minutes?"

"Why?"

"To try it. I'm thinking of buying one like that."

"A woman's?"

"No... Listen, here's the thing... I have an urgent errand. I'm back in half an hour."

"I've heard promises like that."

"Don't you trust a friend?"

"Since when are we friends?"

"Since we've known each other."

"You joking?"

"Then from now on," Gugec suggests.

"I can rent you the bike. How much did you say, twenty minutes?"

"Son of a bitch, I can't believe…"

"Have you heard of the market economy?"

"You're going to charge me for a bike you stole?"

"Such are times," shrugs Face.

Matej starts running around the bench in a circle. "I need a gun…! That's what I need…! A gun! A machine gun…! Tat-tat-tat-tat… Tat-tat-tat-tat…"

"What's wrong with you?" Face asks him.

"He'll have to go back in soon," observes Gugec.

Face shakes his head. "Just to think, once we were living at this whore's…"

Matej starts pulling his hair. "I'd like to kill someone… Anyone… To do at least something that'll have results."

"You already did," Katarina tries to remind him.

"What do you mean by that?" Face steps up to her.

"Nothing," Katarina bows her head.

"Do you think I'm a fool? I'm repeating: what did you…"

"Nothingggg!" Katarina yells in his face.

"Wait a minute," says Face, not at all angry. "Let's get one thing straight."

"Someone's coming," says Gugec.

Tonko comes slowly down the path, dressed as if to go to Mass, so rotund that he's almost round, and appearing to be more frightened than confident.

Everyone looks at him.

"Good evening," he pleasantly greets everyone. Since everyone is looking at him, no one notices that Katarina has paled, then blushed, then made a move as if to run, and then dropped her head as if she wanted to hide her face.

Several seconds pass before Tonko recognizes her. But he's a tax inspector, so he knows how to control himself.

He continues on.

Matej wishes him a "good evening" when he's already passed.

Gugec adds his "good evening".

"Wait," Face raises his voice. "Didn't you and I..."

Tonko turns around. "I don't understand."

"Fifty meters from the entrance and turn left?"

"Some mistake," says Tonko, turns, and unhurriedly continues on his way, like someone who has set off for an evening walk in the park.

Face gets out his phone and presses a button. A phone rings in Tonko's jacket pocket. He stops. He pulls out his cell and puts it to his ear.

"Yes," he says, his back to the company.

"Can you turn around?" Face says.

Tonko finds himself in a difficult quandary. "I didn't know if I'm in the right place."

"My instructions were very precise."

"I didn't know a... crowd would be waiting for me," Tonko waves a hand.

"It's not a crowd. It's two cretins who happen to be here. They're leaving."

"I'm not," Gugec objects.

"And me neither," adds Matej.

"The main thing is that she's here," Face gestures at Katarina, who's head is still bowed. "Why in the world do we have to talk on the phone?"

Tonko obediently puts away his cell phone. Face puts his away, too.

"Well? Have a look at her."

Tonko slowly returns and has a quick look at Katarina, whose head is still lowered.

"I think there's been a mistake," declares Tonko and swallows as if he has a lump in his throat that's making it hard to breathe.

"What mistake?" Face demands almost aggressively.

"You sent me photos of another person," Tonko insists despite the threat. As a tax inspector, he's used to aggressiveness from people who owe.

"I sent you a photo of a nude woman with her legs spread," says Face. "You don't recognize her because she's dressed and because her face isn't in the photo."

Tonko looks Katarina over again, stunned and sad. Katarina keeps hanging her head, although it's apparent he has recognized her.

"It really is a mistake," Tonko repeats and turns to leave.

Face pushes the bike away onto the grass by the path and grabs Tonko by the collar.

"Face, what are you doing?" Katarina raises her head.

"Dear sir, although it's not customary in this country, we at least are going to honor agreements."

"I didn't promise anything," Tonko asserts, convinced no one can do anything to him.

"Oh, no? Then what are you doing here? Gugec, help me and I'll loan you the bike."

Gugec steps up to Tonko and grabs the front of his shirt. "Promises are to be kept, sir!"

"Let him go," Katarina tries to intervene. "He doesn't like me."

"I sent him a photo, we agreed on a price, and now he wants to back out," Face rages and grabs Tonko by the collar from behind.

"Son of a bitch," says Gugec, "all government workers are alike. The fact that they look for sex with whores says it all."

"Can I ask you to stop choking me," the badly frightened Tonko barely gets out.

Gugec steps back. Face pushes Tonko ahead and forces him onto the bench. He seizes his head and turns it violently towards Katarina. "Have a look at her."

Then he orders Katarina: "Turn your head and look at his face."

Katarina obeys, although unwillingly. Her eyes are still shut.

"No violence," Matej interferes. "No violence. The night of the world is coming and it will be bad! It will by veeeery bad for all of us."

"What's wrong with her" Face demands of Tonko.

"I didn't say…" the unfortunate and demeaned gentleman starts, but Face interrupts him: "Does she have tits?"

"Probably," Tonko shrugs.

"Probably?! Show them to him," her orders Katarina.

"No," Katarina objects.

"Pull up your blouse and show him your tits!"

"Look," Katarina tries to dissuade him, "if he doesn't want to, so be it!"

"Are you deaf?" Face screams. "Do I have to smack you to get the wax out of your ears?"

Katarina turns her head to the left, stares into emptiness, quickly lifts her blouse and bares her breasts.

"They're not that great," Gugec observes, "they hang a little, the years take their toll, but, son of a bitch, it's not like a man wouldn't still rub them with pleasure."

"Does she have tits or not?" Face demands an answer from Tonko. "She has a tongue and a mouth? Go on, show him your tongue," he orders Katarina. "Lick your chops like you want to blow him."

Katarina licks her lips with obvious distaste.

"Son of a bitch," says Gugec, "I'm already hard. Something's wrong with this guy."

"I'm going to vomit again," Matej announces, but doesn't move. He stands, legs together, and stares dumbly in front of him. "Maybe we really did die that time, all three of us. And what we're living is hell."

"For me for sure," says Katarina.

"Can she lick it for you?" Face asks Tonko. "Can she suck your shaft?"

"Shaft?" Gugec laughs. "Government workers have little ones. That's why they want to be chiefs."

"Can I ask you to loosen your grip a little?" Tonko wheezes. "I'm choking!"

Face removes his hand from his client's collar. Then he shoves his head from behind. Tonko coughs a few times.

"I'm going to vomit again," Matej announces, but doesn't move. He stands, legs together, and stares dumbly in front of him.

"Go there behind the bush," Gugec advises. "It already stinks enough here... He sniffs the trash can. "Son of a bitch, now I'm going..."

"Show him your pussy," Face orders Katarina.

"No," Katarina objects.

"Look," Tonko sighs. "I can't..."

"No problem," Gugec jumps in. "I can get you Viagra in less than half an hour. Face, will you lend me the bike?"

"She carries it in her purse," says Face. "Nowadays no one can do it anymore."

He looks at Katarina. "It's not like you forgot it?"

"No," Katarina answers.

"Well, sir?" Face turns to Tonko. "You'll be taken care of in all respects."

"I wanted to say that I can't under such conditions," Tonko tries to explain. "I expected something else. Something more… civilized."

"And now you're going to start preaching to us?" Face says with surprise. "You can be glad I'm even calling you 'sir.' It's an effort for me. I'm not in the habit of being respectful to clients who are prepared to pay for sex. I'm saying 'sir' because you're a well-known person."

"I'm not well-known," Tonko disagrees.

"That's true," Face admits. "As far as the media goes, you're anonymous. But, dear sir, you're a tax inspector. I know all about you. You risked quite a bit when you answered my ad, no?"

"Yeah, and the horses are out of the barn," Gugec tags on.

"I could blackmail you, for example," Face continues. "Like you blackmail people who owe taxes. Right? But I won't. Why not? Because I'm honest."

He looks at Katarina. "Aren't I?"

Katarina lowers her head. "I don't know."

Face slaps her. "You don't know?"

Katarina tries to hide the tears. "You are."

"Well?" Face turns to Tonko. "There's confirmation. Now see to it that you act honest, too."

"I don't understand," Tonko frankly admits.

"That you'll pay what we agreed on."

"Pay for what? There was no…"

"The girl is here."

"There was a misunderstanding," Tonko insists.

"Hand over a hundred euros," Face holds out his hand.

"That's not enough," Gugec intervenes. "A hundred and fifty."

"Hand over a hundred," Face repeats, "and you can go."

"But nothing happened," Tonko disagrees.

"How not? She's here, she's yours. There, behind the bush. We'll watch out no one sees. She'll do whatever you want. You won't find anyone better than her."

He holds out his hand. "A hundred euros."

"I don't have it," Tonko admits.

"Listen," says Face. "You really are stupid. You have a half hour, and say an extra ten minutes, the girl will give you Viagra…"

"I don't need it," Tonko replies immediately.

"She has it in her purse," Face goes on, as if he doesn't believe him. "It's expensive, Viagra… An hour? An hour and a half?" He holds out his hand. "A hundred euros."

"I forgot my wallet," Tonko tries to get out of it.

"Gugec, help me," says Face. "Check Mr. Tax Inspector's pockets and give me his wallet."

"Glad to," says Gugec and sets to work.

"No violence!" Matej yells. "No violence! Because violence is coming. The final, great one. The night of the world. Violence is becoming god. And I can't stop it."

Face pulls a knife out of his pocket and hands it to Matej. "Please. Stop the violence. If you dare."

Matej takes the knife and shoves it into his jacket pocket. "I can't… All my strength is gone. And my will."

"Then give me the knife back," says Face.

"He doesn't have anything in his pockets," Gugec announces, having searched Tonko.

Face forgets about the knife and grabs the tax inspector by the collar. "Listen, you fat whore-aholic! After everything we talked about on the phone, you come without money? What were you thinking? That she'll give it to you for free?"

"As I said," Tonko keeps trying to explain himself, "I forgot to take…"

"You didn't forget anything," Face interrupts him.

Matej covers his ears. "Can I ask you to stop? Something will happen if you don't. Five thousand Lucifers will leap on us out of the dark. They'll devour us. Me last. I'll listen how they crunch your bones in their chops!"

"Did you hear what awaits you, Mr. Tax Inspector?"

"Can I take the bike now, Face?" Gugec asks. "You said…"

"Later. I need help with this fatso now."

"I want to get out, out, out!" Matej yells and starts running back and forth in front of the bench. Then he crouches. "Out of this shit." He grabs his head. "Out of myself. I deserve something better. Every day my grandma tells me: 'Matej, you deserve something better. How am I supposed to tell her I won't even have enough for her funeral?'"

"I'll loan it to you," says Katarina.

"You?" Face glowers at her. "You won't have enough for your own funeral."

"Then give me more!" Katarina hollers. "Give me more!"

"You know what, you whore," Face replies. "You already get too much for what you do."

"Because I might," says Katarina, "jump out the studio window six floors above the sidewalk, and then what will you do?"

"I'll even open the window for you," says Face.

"I know you would!" Katarina responds. "I know you would!" She breaks into tears.

"If you don't mind," says Tonko, "I'll be going now."

Face steps in front of him. "Nowhere without paying."

"There was nothing I should have to pay for," the tax inspector tells him, knowing the laws.

"Sir," says Face, who doesn't know the laws or decided a long time ago not to respect them, "I'm not in the habit of wasting time. I've already lost enough on you."

The tax inspector pulls out his cell phone and with quivering fingers enters a number.

Face rips it out of his hand. "Who are you calling, big shot? The police?"

"I'm a victim of violence," Tonko calmly explains.

Matej walks around anxiously. "Me too... Me too... But... I'm going to take revenge. On the first one who makes me mad. And then the next. And the third. I'll have to slaughter all of them. That's what the night of the world commands!"

"You should be afraid of this one," says Gugec. "He is mad."

"That's not true," Katarina feels a responsibility to stand up for Matej. "Go on, sir. Leave. In the name of the past and in the name of the future, leave."

"Since when do you give clients orders?" Face puts his fingers on her neck. "And what are you talking about?"

"I wouldn't do it with him even for a thousand euros," Katarina shoots back.

"The government doesn't put up with unemployed people who refuse work," Face warns her.

Katarina stares at Tonko pleadingly. "Go, sir. Please. Now."

Tonko is so anxious that he doesn't know what to do.

"If he leaves," says Face, "you'll pay instead of him. You'll give me a hundred euros, period, and I don't give a fuck where you get them. I'll deduct them from the next pay."

"There won't be a next pay," Katarina hurls at him.

"You hear that?" Matej hurls at him. "There won't be!"

"Are you threatening me?" Face replies, calm and collected. "You're threatening me, you common fag, who always bothered me most of all with your small dick?"

Tonko, as awkward as he is, suddenly sets off running.

"Quick, quick!" Katarina yells.

Face runs after the fugitive client, grabs him by the ties, and hauls him back. Terrified, Tonko meekly gives in. Face shoves him on the bench in a sitting position.

"You'll be tried for attempted flight," he says.

"That's right," Gugec puts in. "Where were you when my folks were let go without pay for more than half a year? Did you go onto the square and yell: That can't be allowed to happen?"

"And where were you," Face concludes, "when this slut here had no choice but to start banging guys like you?"

"You owe us," Gugec says.

"That's right," Face agrees. "What would your wife say if she found out that you're picking up whores in the park?"

"I'm not married," Tonko admits with relief.

"And one more thing," Gugec suddenly recalls. "Where were you when they took the supplement payment from my friend's grandma and he had to go out and steal?"

"You're not going to heap all those wrongs on me?" Tonko is sincerely surprised.

"On who then?" Face strengthens his grip.

"On who," Gugec leans aggressively over at Tonko, "if not you, who steals taxes out of poor peoples' pockets."

"We can agree on a compromise," Tonko decides to yield a little.

"Ohh," says Face, "the gentleman is ready to bargain!"

"Seems so," Gugec takes credit for the development.

"What compromise did you have in mind, sir?" Face becomes nicer.

"I really did come without cash," says Tonko, "but I always have a bank card with me." He pulls the card out of an inside pocket.

Face stares sharply at Gugec. "Didn't you?... You cretin!"

"You told me to look for a wallet!" Gugec defends himself. "I looked for a wallet!"

Face rips the card out of Tonko's hand. "Well? What compromise are we going to make with this card, Mr. Tax Inspector?"

"I suggest," says Tonko, "we go together to the nearest ATM, I'll take out thirty euros, and the problem is solved."

"All of us?" Face is surprised.

"Just one can come with me."

"For thirty euros? It's not worth it, sir," Face shakes his head.

"I'll go," Gugec offers.

"You be quiet, because you're a dope," Face turns him down. "How are you going to get money without a pin?" He turns to Tonko. "Tell us the pin, sir."

Tonko pleads: "I can't do that. I'll get the money out."

"No," Face shakes his head.

"It can be fifty," Tonko decides to be generous. "I can't do more."

"We'll get the money out, sir," Face tells him. "And we'll decide how much."

"Then it's off," Tonko gets stubborn.

"Do you know who you said that to?" Face asks him. "Do you actually know who's standing here in front of you?"

"Do you actually know who were are?" Gugec joins the attack.

"The pin, sir," Face demands.

Tonko looks over at the others. "I hope you're aware this is robbery?"

"I can't do anything," Katarina blubbers. "Please, run."

"One more word," Face threatens her, "and I'll cut off your ear. "As for the creature that fell out of your ass, I'll cut off his nose!"

"Let him leave," Katarina folds her hands in front of his face. "Please. It won't end well."

"When did anything end well with you?"

"Let him leave. I'm asking you on my knees."

"You're pleading for a whore-aholic who thinks you're so ugly he can screw you for small change?"

Katarina covers her face and sobs.

"Big fucking deal," says Gugec, "the people don't have bread, and he doesn't want to give more than fifty euros? What do you get for that? Toilet paper?"

"The pin, sir, the pin," Face keeps on demanding.

"Everyone's the same," Gugec goes on. "Parasites. All that crowd should be robbed. Shaken down, real good, fleeced, eradicated, and skinned. Sweep them in a pile and burn them."

Matej, standing with his back to them, suddenly yells at the top of his voice: "I'm on edge! On edge! On edge!"

"Sir, do you ever read crime reports in your daily paper?" Face asks Tonko. "Would you like to read tomorrow how unknown persons cut a tax inspector's thumbs off in the park? *And* index finger? So he won't be able to count money anymore, which he takes out of poor people's pockets in the name of the government?"

"This is a nightmare," Tonko shakes his head.

"The pin, sir," Face insists.

"Unfortunately I have only a hundred and fifty euros on my account," Tonko tries to explain.

"We'll se," says Face. "The pin."

"3264."

"You swear on your mother's grave?"

"That's the right number," Tonko affirms.

"If not, we'll burn your house down."

"And everything else you stole," Gugec agrees.

"That's the right number," Tonko repeats stubbornly.

Face hands Matej the bank card. "Take the bike and go to an ATM."

"Why me?" Matej is surprised.

"Because of all of us you're the dumbest and so the most honest."

"Go yourself," Matej turns his back. "I won't steal for you."

"If I go myself, there won't be a soul here when I get back," says Face.

"It doesn't matter," Matej replies. "You'll have the money."

"If the pin is right."

"It is," Tonko asserts, "and I want the card back."

"Sir," Face grabs him by the collar again, "why are you butting into a discussion that doesn't concern you?"

"Give it to me," says Gugec. "I'll be back in five minutes."

"I believe it. But you'll hide half the money somewhere."

"Come on," says Gugec. "You've known me for…"

"That's why."

"There's an ATM there across the street. I'll hop on the bike and be back one, two, three."

Face shifts anxiously. He doesn't know what to do. "The gentleman will get a bank receipt, right? And I'll ask him how much you took out. He'll tell me. Because from now on we'll be friends. Right, sir?" He looks around at Tonko.

"I'll bring you the last cent," Gugec assures him.

Face hands him the card. "If you're not back in five minutes, I'll come looking for you. With a bazooka."

"How many times do I have to say…"

"Get going."

Gugec shoves the card in his chest pocket.

"Take out five hundred if it works," says Face.

"It won't," insists Tonko, "because, like I said, I have only a hundred and fifty euros. For safety. All the rest I sock away."

Face looks at Gugec. "You back already?"

"Five minutes," Gugec promises, gets on the bike, and rides off.

Face pulls out a thin cigar. "I really deserve a small treat now." He lights the cigar and blows smoke at Tonko. "Want a puff?"

"I don't smoke," Tonko shakes his head.

"You like young girls more. Although this one isn't young anymore. She's pretty worn out. Too many clients and too little love for her work. She should take care of herself. You hear, Katarina? The gentleman says you should take better care of yourself."

"I didn't say that," Tonko objects, who, despite everything, wants to defend Katarina.

Face looks at the time. "I knew this morning that nothing would go right. And you are to blame for everything!" he barks in Katarina's face.

"Me?"

"If you would have been here alone, all would have gone as usual."

"You said we'd meet here, by this bench. This one, you said. Under the street lamp. It's not my fault that Matej and Gugec were already here."

"You should have chased them away."

"Why didn't you, since you're an expert at such things?"

"I don't know, I don't know... I don't know..." Matej is talking to himself. "I have to do something... I have to do something... I can't go on like this!"

"He'll soon be back inside," Face says to Tonko.

"Matej..." Katarina puts out a hand to him.

"I deserve something better," Matej goes on. "My grandma told me a hundred and more times. We all do. We all deserve something better."

"I agree." Tonko nods, as if wanting to give the impression of having reconciled himself to his fate.

"Ohh!" Face is surprised. "The gentleman agrees. But with what?"

"That we're all victims," Tonko explains.

"Don't shit me, are we?"

"Each in his own way."

"The gentleman is going to give a lecture?" Face asks him. "Well, go on… Because it's a little boring waiting for money like this… Entertain us."

"I'm also trying to understand what's going on in our society," says Tonko frankly, sincerely, although no doubt hoping for an ounce of understanding in his desperate situation.

"It's true these are hard times," says Face.

"How did we come to this?" Tonko asks rhetorically.

"You tell us," says Face, "since you're at least partly responsible for what we've come to."

"The only thing I can say is that I sympathize with you. And in my own way I'm grateful for the experience. Most people read about bad things and shrug. That's all they do."

"Sir," says Face, "we were relatively fine, but now you've spoiled everything."

"I don't understand," Tonko says with fear.

"You're making fun of us."

"That's not true," Tonko disagrees.

"You leave me no choice but to hit you on the head with a boot."

He takes off a boot and strikes Tonko hard on the head. Tonko rolls forward and lies on the path.

"Are you crazy," Katarina jumps to her feet, "you killed him!"

"Not yet," says Face, "but it could happen." He puts on his boot.

"Jesus!" Katarina covers her face with her palms.

"Yeah, he'll for sure take care of everything when he comes back to earth," says Face. "Why didn't you tell me you are religious? I could have got you some priest. Don't you read the papers? Even that happens nowadays. Though they like children more."

Tonko painfully sits up. He shakes his head.

"Thank God," Katarina crosses herself and collapses on the bench.

Matej comes up and says: "You don't know how to, you don't know at all... It works differently with the likes of him."

"You're shitting me," says Face. "Then show me."

"Like this," says Matej. "Punch after punch." He starts hitting Face.

"Are you crazy? What are you doing?"

Matej pulls the knife out of his pocket. "I'll show you how it works with the likes of him."

"Give me the knife back. Katarina, tell him to give me the knife!"

Matej raises his hands in the air, waves the knife, and sings: "When blood flows, my oh my, a red bird flies into the sky!"

"Tonko," Katarina whispers to her friend from the past, "run, I'm asking you, run!"

"I'm dizzy," says Tonko, still sitting on the ground.

"I'll count to three," says Matej and extends his hand with the knife. "One..."

"Two," says Face, hoping that Matej's just joking.

Matej violently grabs Face by the collar and sticks the tip of the knife under his chin. "Three!"

"What do you think you're doing?"

"Why are you threatening the child?" Matej sprays saliva in his face from up close.

"Child?" Face can't believe it. "What child?"

"My child!" Matej yells at him. "Why are you threatening him?"

"Yours?!"

"Mine!" Matej repeats.

"Katarina," Face turns his eyes towards her, "what lie did you tell him?"

"I told him the truth, Brane, the truth!"

"It can't be his!" Face is surprised. "Matej is a fag!"

"You're aware," Matej asks him, "that Katarina and I lived together in London for five years as husband and wife?"

"You didn't tell me that!" Face turns his eyes towards Katarina.

The knife tip sinks ever deeper into his neck.

"Should I have?" Katarina replies.

"If you don't swear you won't touch a hair on the child's head," Matej threatens Face, "and that you won't come closer than a kilometer to him, there will be blood. And when blood flows, my oh my, a red bird flies into the sky!"

"Matej, think…" Face tries to talk him out of it.

"Not me," says Matej. "You."

"Matej, we were always friends. Did you forget? Even before you rented a room from this whore…"

Matej slaps him with his free hand. "You forced her into prostitution. Swear you'll leave the child alone. I'll count to three. One…"

"You'll regret all of this," says Face.

"Two…" Matej continues.

"The child is safe with her aunt," says Face.

"That's not true!" Katarina shouts. "The child isn't with my aunt. He took him and carried him off somewhere. He says to one of his relatives, but he won't say where."

"Why didn't you tell me?" Matej looks at her accusingly.

"I didn't dare. I was afraid you'd go crazy."

"You stole my child?" Matej sticks the knife tip a little deeper into Face's neck, but without drawing blood.

"Look…" Face tries to explain something, although it's obvious he has no idea what.

"What kind of person are you?" Matej asks him completely calmly. "I liked you at one time. Now I look at you and see a piece of vermin!"

"It can be fixed…" Face tries to calm him.

"It's too late!" Matej says calmly. "It's too late, Brane! It's too late, friend. It's too late, thief who lied to me that I'm gay. Do you see now that I'm not?"

He stabs him forcefully in the stomach.

"Jesus, no!" Katarina screams. She starts to shake and cry.

"The child isn't his!" Tonko suddenly yells. "The child is Damjan's!"

"It can't be," Matej says coldly.

But Face doesn't hear him. He clutches his stomach and tumbles forward. When he's on the ground, Matej stabs him again, in the back.

Face doesn't flinch.

"Why did you do that?" Katarina screams.

Matej looks at the bloody knife in his hand. "Because the night of the world is coming. I warned you. I warned everyone."

"How am I going to find my child now?" Katarina rips at her hair. The tears violently shake her.

"Why didn't you tell me?" Matej asks her cold-bloodedly.

"Because… because I was afraid it would turn out the way it did!"

"I wanted to protect the child. You don't get it? I wanted to protect him from this devil's claws."

He kicks Face on the ground.

"That you did," Katarina says with deep bitterness. "You protected him so well I'll never find him!"

"Are you aware," Matej says calmly, "that most bad things in the world happen because women claim the right not to confide truth to men?"

Gugec rides up on the bike. He has a leather woman's purse over his shoulder. He doesn't see Face lying behind the bench right away.

"Mr. Tax Inspector," he says, "it looks bad for you." He throws the bike down. "You gave us a pin that doesn't work."

"That's not true!" Tonko protests, having almost lost the gift of speech after the events of the last several minutes. "I gave you the right one!"

"Then why couldn't I get money out?" Gugec asks him.

"That's impossible," Tonko disagrees stubbornly.

Gugec suddenly sees Face on the ground.

"What' wrong with him? Did he fall asleep? Wait a minute... Is that blood?"

"Nothing's wrong," Matej calms him with no visible emotion. "He tripped and fell on the knife."

He sees the woman's purse on the handlebars. It's black, old-fashioned, and slightly worn.

"Nice purse," he says, "where did you get it?"

"You know," says Gugec, "I was so mad after I didn't get any money out of the ATM, I was so mad, that I said to myself: son of a bitch, this is no good. Because an old lady got three hundred euros out before me without any trouble. And I said to myself..."

"An old lady?" Matej interrupts him.

"Yeah," Gugec goes on, "an old granny who should have been two meters under a long time ago. And I said to myself, that's no good. We're hungry, we have to eat something. And I said to myself, son of a bitch, she'll get by without the three hundred euros."

"And you knocked her on the ground," says Matej.

"No, she fell down herself. I just pulled on the purse, but she didn't want to let go. When she saw I wanted the purse, she could have let go! She should have!"

"But she wouldn't?"

"No. She wouldn't, the stupid woman."

"And where is she now?" Matej asks.

"I have no idea," Gugec shrugs. "I made off as fast as I could. Someone will help her. I mean, we have to eat, too. Right? We have to have something to eat, too!"

"And where are those euros?" Matej asks him.

Gugec starts opening the purse. "We can divide it up. Everybody gets a hundred."

Matej takes a step towards him. "I have a better idea."

"What..." says Gugec.

Matej forcefully stabs him in the belly. Gugec wobbles, clutches his belly, and falls to his knees. Matej grabs him by the hair, bends over him, and stabs him in the back. Gugec tumbles to the path and lies motionless.

Katarina reaches her arms out to Tonko and faints. Tonko catches her and sits down with her in his arms.

Matej picks up the purse, which had fallen to the ground, and yells at the top of his voice, "Grandma!"

He gets on the bike and races off in the direction Gugec had come from, yelling the whole time, "Grandma...! Grandma...! Grandma...!"

He gradually gets farther away, but it takes almost a minute for his cries to become faint.

Tonko strokes Katarina's head. "Katarina... Wake up!"

He remains sitting with her head in his arms. He feels uncomfortable and doesn't know what to do. He looks at his watch. He shakes Katarina again, this time harder.

Katarina opens her eyes. She slowly rises and sits up. She looks at Tonko and stares at Gugec's body in front of her.

"What... what..." she mumbles.

Tonko gets up.

"I'm sorry but I have a meeting in half an hour. I don't want to be late."

"What about me?" Katarina yells after him.

"People usually call the police in situations like this," Tonko says and goes off.

Katarina stares senselessly ahead. She reaches into her purse and finds her phone. She dials 112 and puts the phone to her ear.

"Police," a male voice is heard on the other end. "Hello...? Can you hear me?"

Katarina ends the call and sits there with the phone in her hand. Then she shoves it in her purse. She sits and stares into the void for a moment. Then she gets up and goes down the path to the park exit.

It's dark, night has come.

www.ingramcontent.com/pod-product-compliance
Lightning Source LLC
Chambersburg PA
CBHW021954010726
47494CB00003B/734